PEANUTS®

by SCHULZ

Where Beagles Dare!

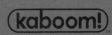

PEANUTS: WHERE BEAGLES DARE, September 2015. Published by KaBOOM!, a division of Boom Entertainment, Inc. Peanuts is ™ & © 2015 Peanuts Worldwide, LLC. All rights reserved. KaBOOM!™ and the KaBOOM! logo are trademarks of Boom Entertainment, Inc., registered in various countries and categories. All characters, events, and institutions depicted herein are fictional. Any similarity between any of the names, characters, persons, events, and/or institutions in this publication to actual names, characters, and persons, whether living or dead, events, and/or institutions is unintended and purely coincidental. KaBOOM! does not read or accept unsolicited submissions of ideas, stories, or artwork.

A catalog record of this book is available from OCLC and from the KaBOOM! website, www.kaboom-studios.com, on the Librarians Page.

BOOM! Studios, 5670 Wilshire Boulevard, Suite 450, Los Angeles, CA 90036-5679. Printed in USA. First Printing.

ISBN: 978-1-60886-711-0, eISBN: 978-1-61398-382-9

Designer
Scott Newman

Assistant Editor
Alex Galer

Editor
Shannon Watters

For Charles M. Schulz Creative Associates

Creative Director
Paige Braddock

Managing Editor
Alexis E. Fajardo

Special thanks to the Schulz family, everyone at Charles M. Schulz Creative Associates, and Charles M. Schulz for his singular achievement in shaping these beloved characters.

Based on the comic strip, *Peanuts*, by
Charles M. Schulz

Story by
Jason Cooper

Pencils by
Vicki Scott

Inks by
Paige Braddock

Colors by
Whitney Cogar

Letters & Post Production by
Donna Almendrala
& Denis St. John

Cover
Pencils by
Vicki Scott

Inks by
Paige Braddock

Colors by
Nina Kester

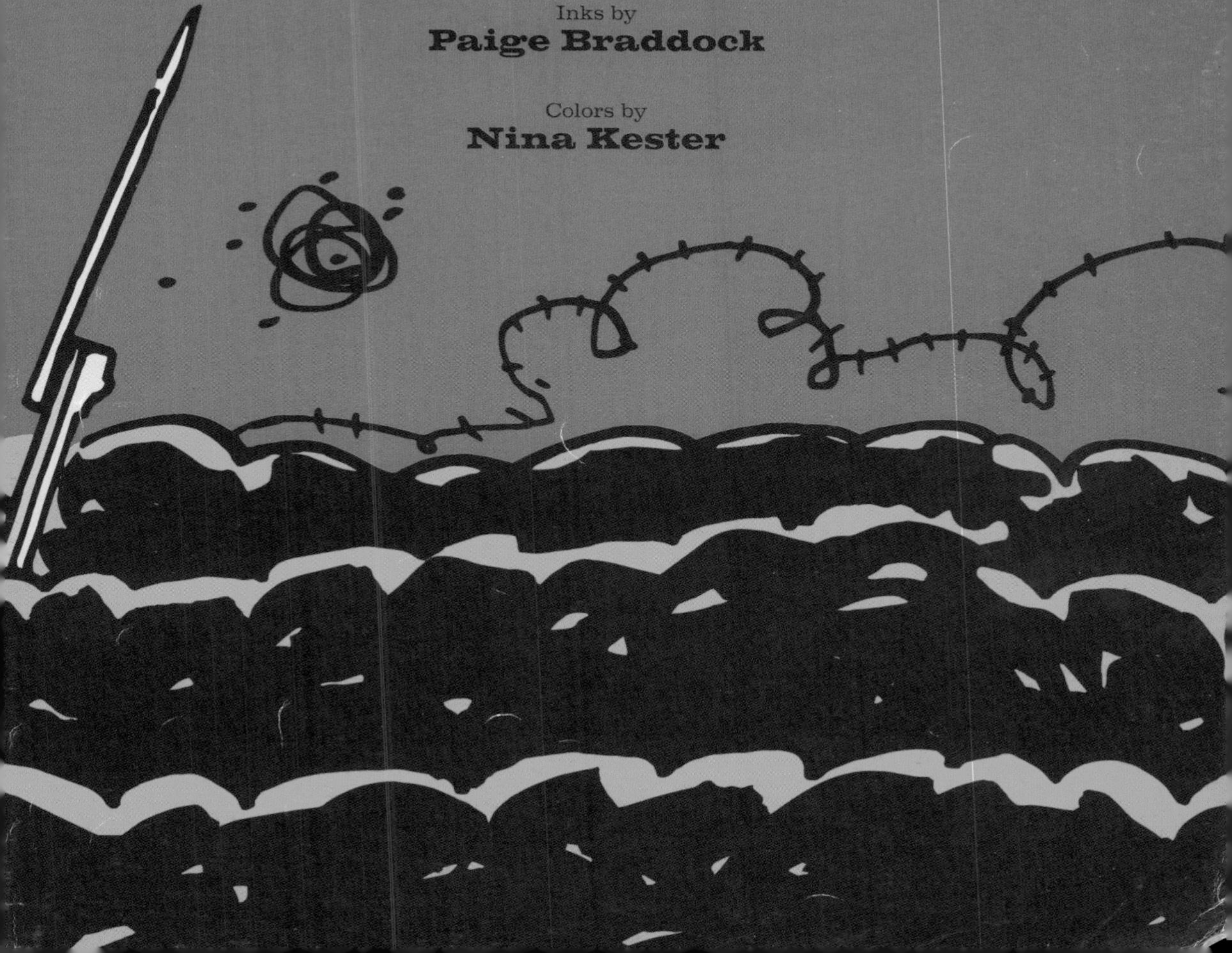

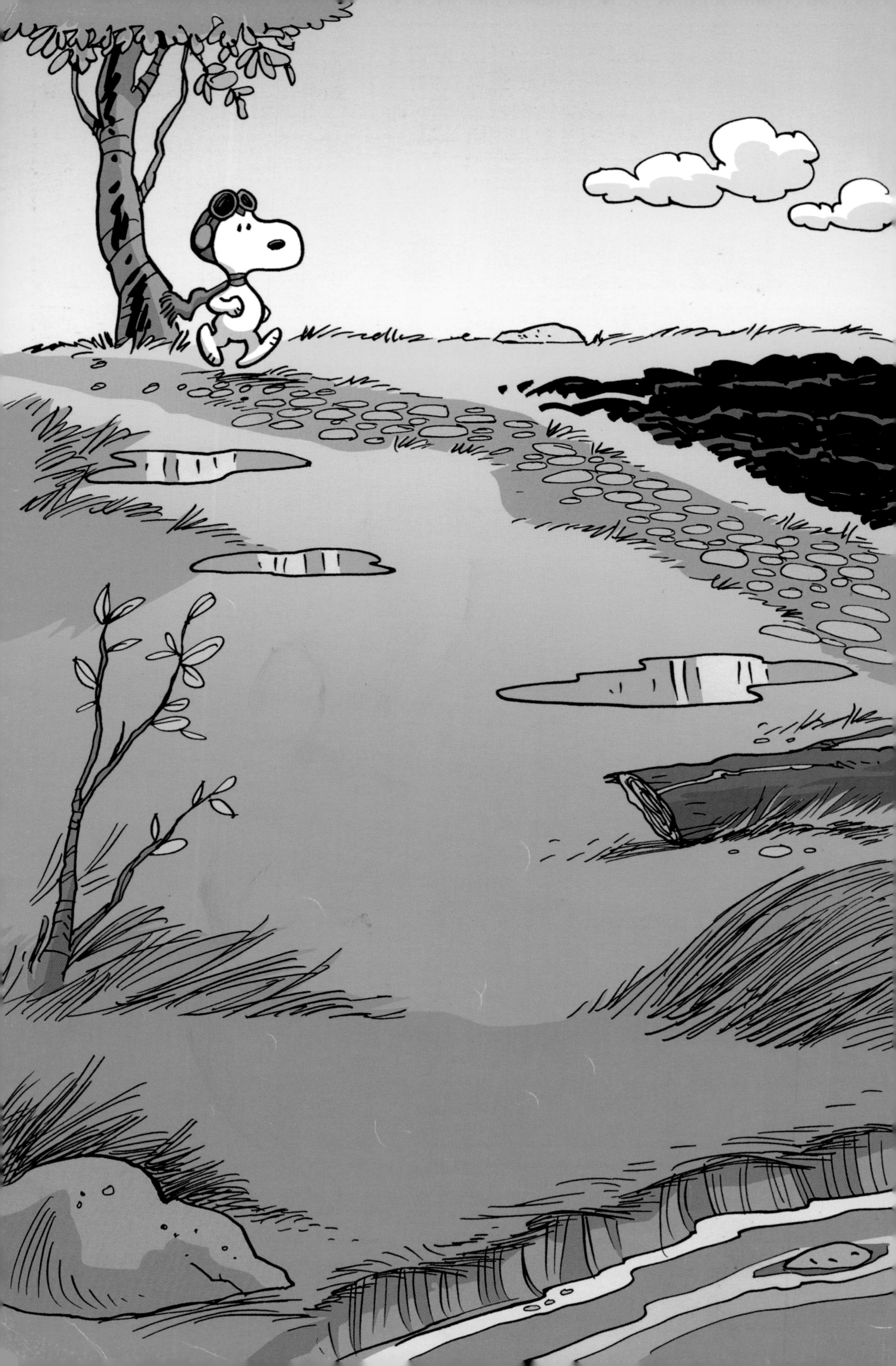

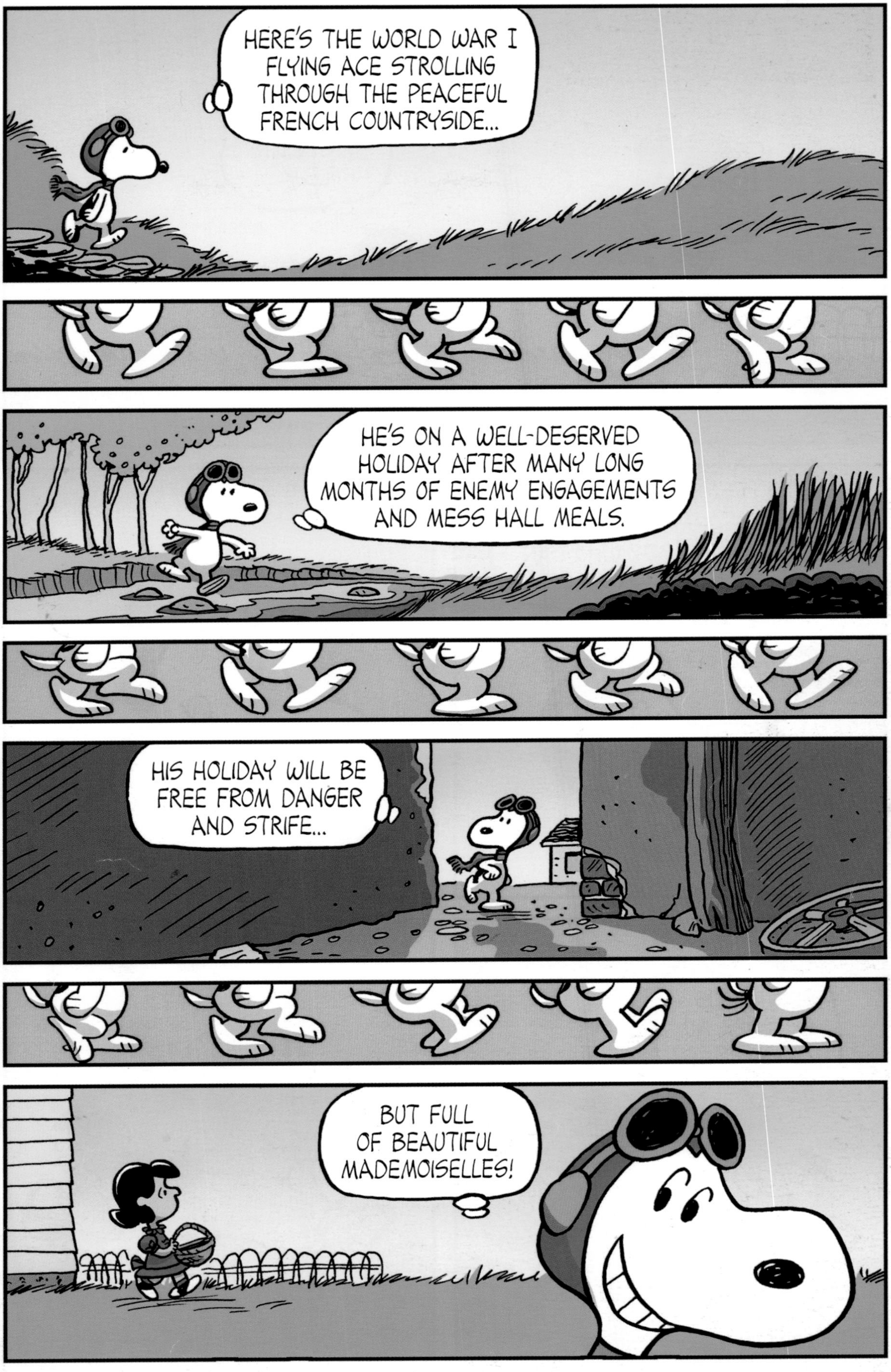
HERE'S THE WORLD WAR I FLYING ACE STROLLING THROUGH THE PEACEFUL FRENCH COUNTRYSIDE...
HE'S ON A WELL-DESERVED HOLIDAY AFTER MANY LONG MONTHS OF ENEMY ENGAGEMENTS AND MESS HALL MEALS.
HIS HOLIDAY WILL BE FREE FROM DANGER AND STRIFE...
BUT FULL OF BEAUTIFUL MADEMOISELLES!

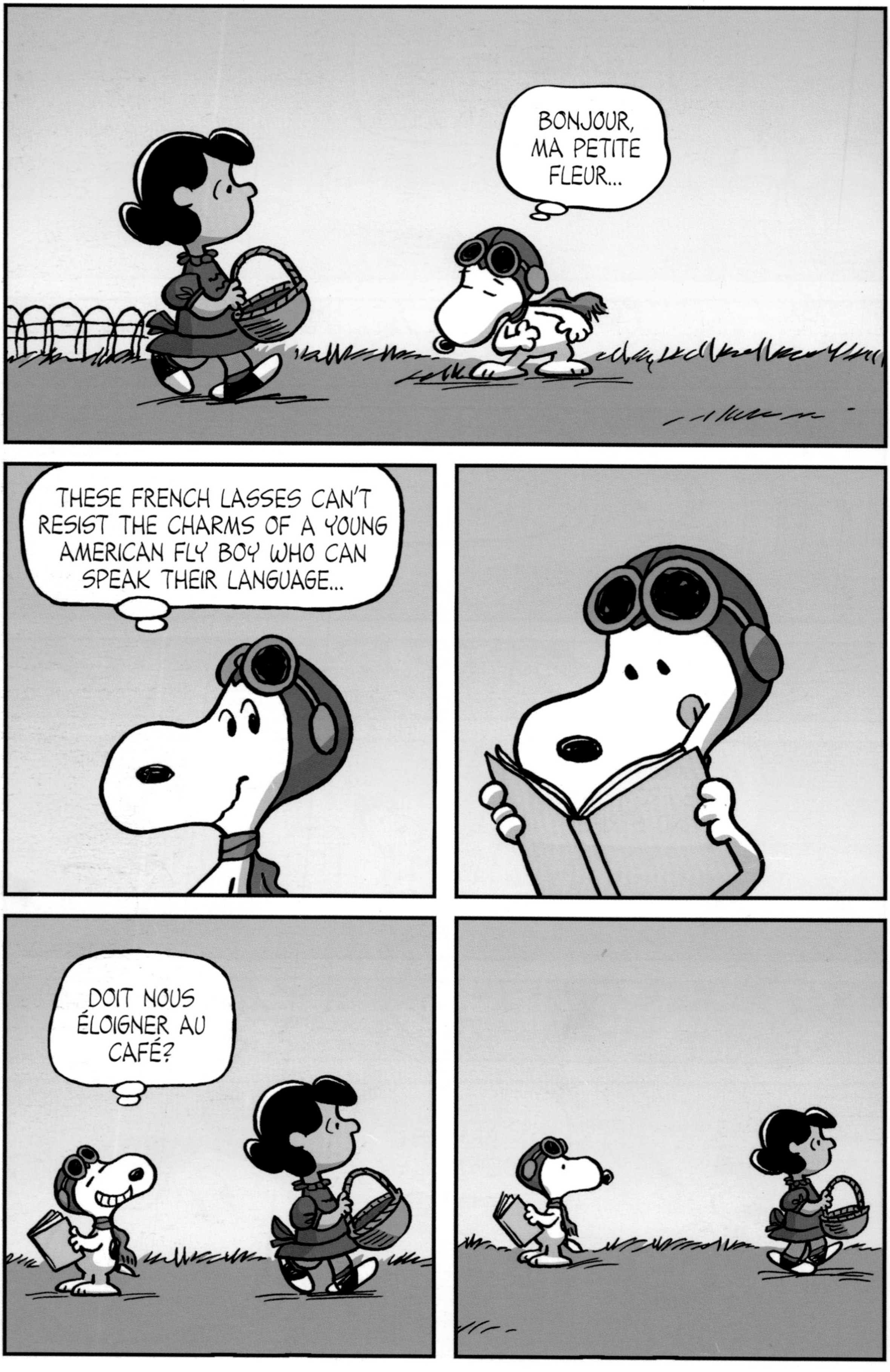
BONJOUR, MA PETITE FLEUR...
THESE FRENCH LASSES CAN'T RESIST THE CHARMS OF A YOUNG AMERICAN FLY BOY WHO CAN SPEAK THEIR LANGUAGE...
DOIT NOUS ÉLOIGNER AU CAFÉ?

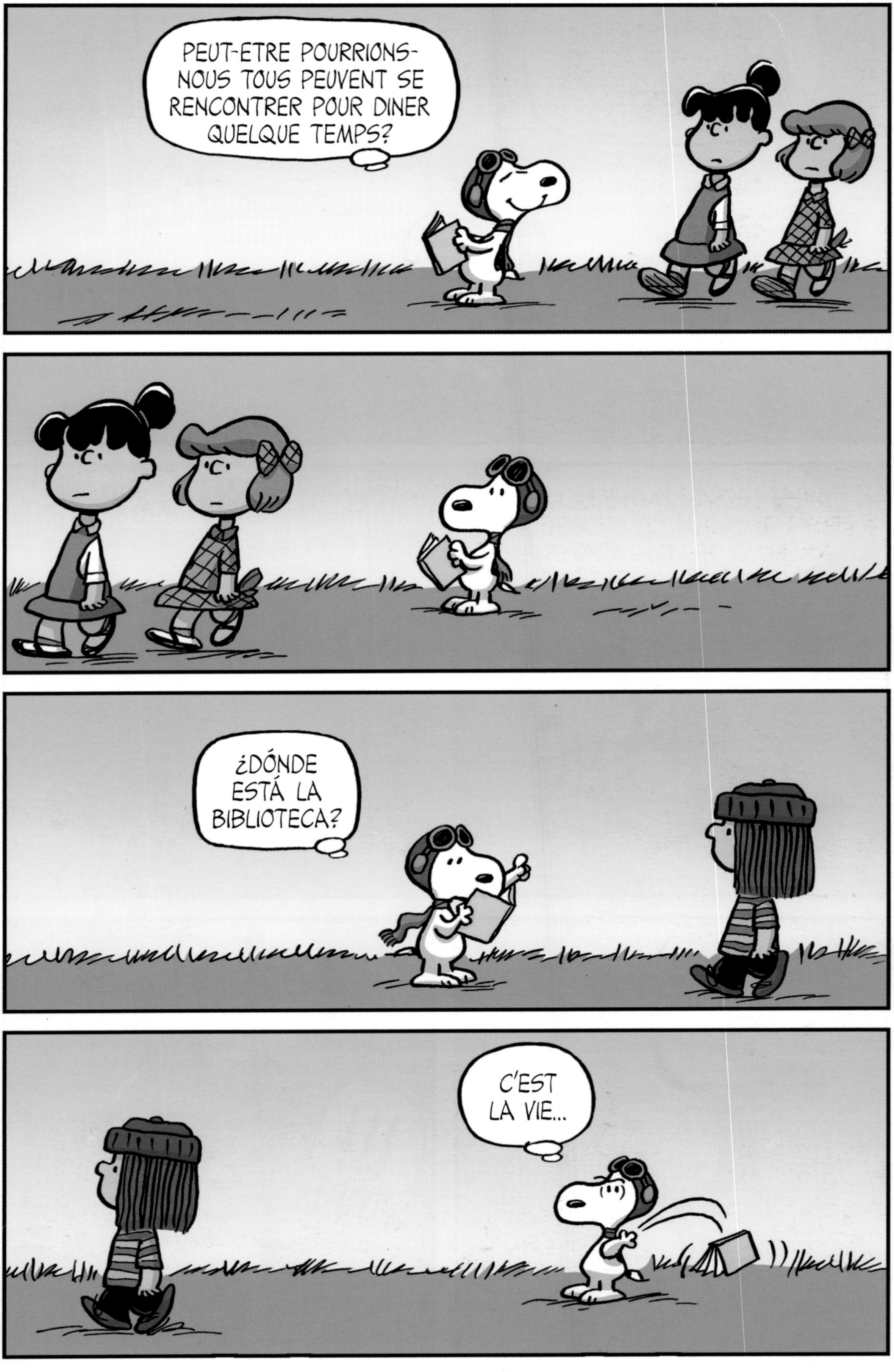
PEUT-ETRE POURRIONS-NOUS TOUS PEUVENT SE RENCONTRER POUR DINER QUELQUE TEMPS?
¿DÓNDE ESTÁ LA BIBLIOTECA?
C'EST LA VIE...

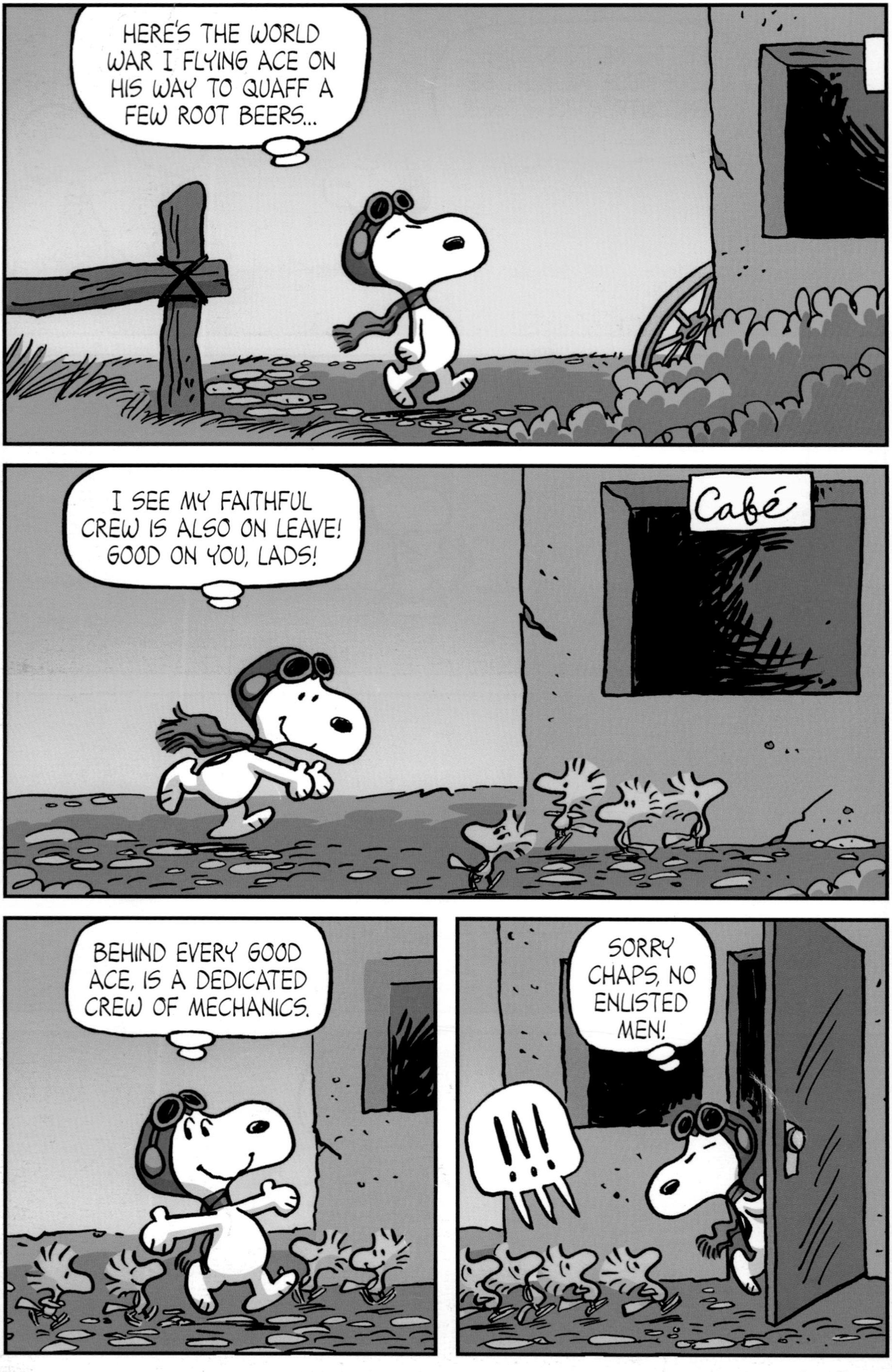
HERE'S THE WORLD WAR I FLYING ACE ON HIS WAY TO QUAFF A FEW ROOT BEERS...
I SEE MY FAITHFUL CREW IS ALSO ON LEAVE! GOOD ON YOU, LADS!
Café
BEHIND EVERY GOOD ACE, IS A DEDICATED CREW OF MECHANICS.
SORRY CHAPS, NO ENLISTED MEN!
!!!!

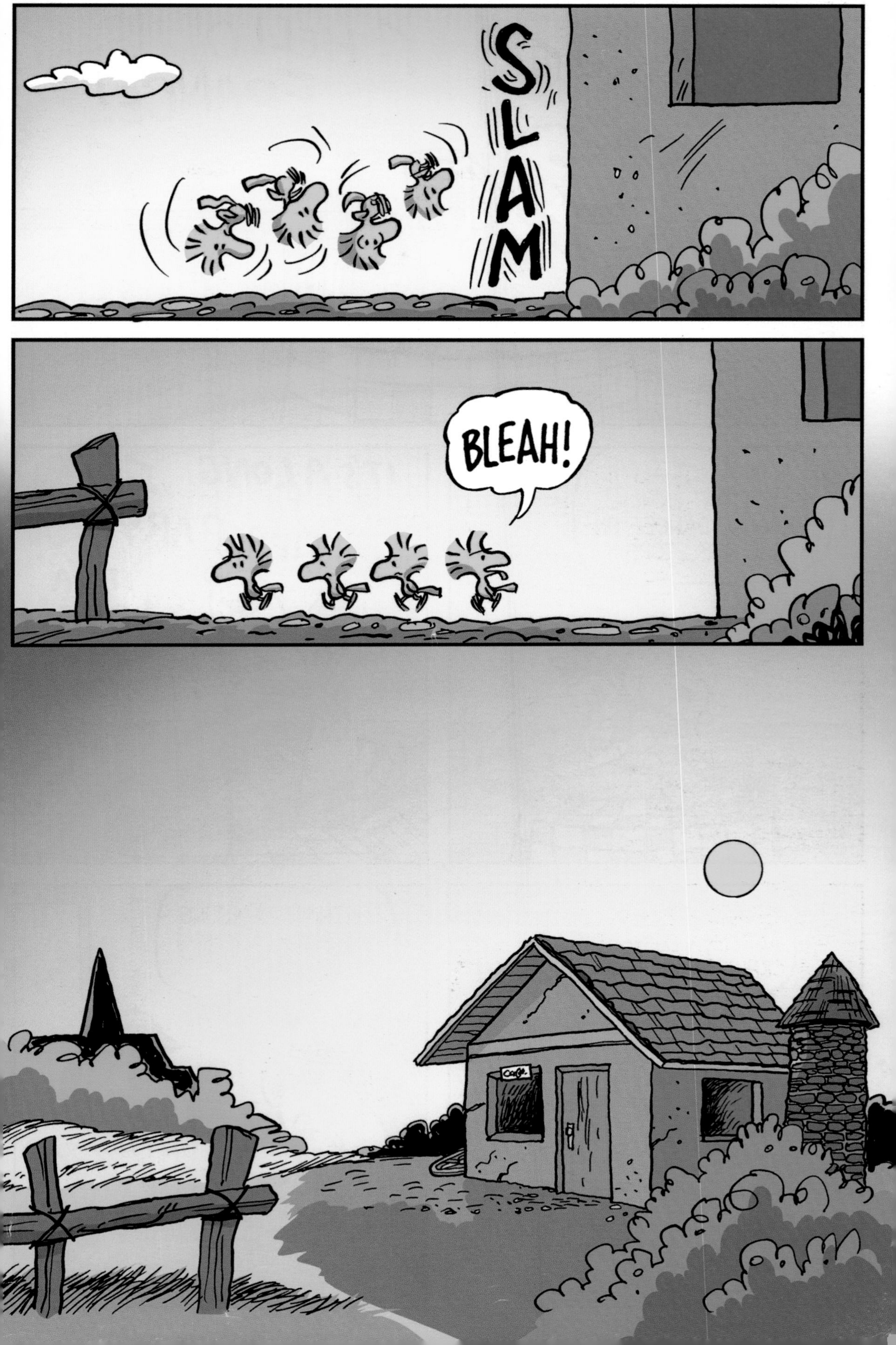
SLAM
BLEAH!

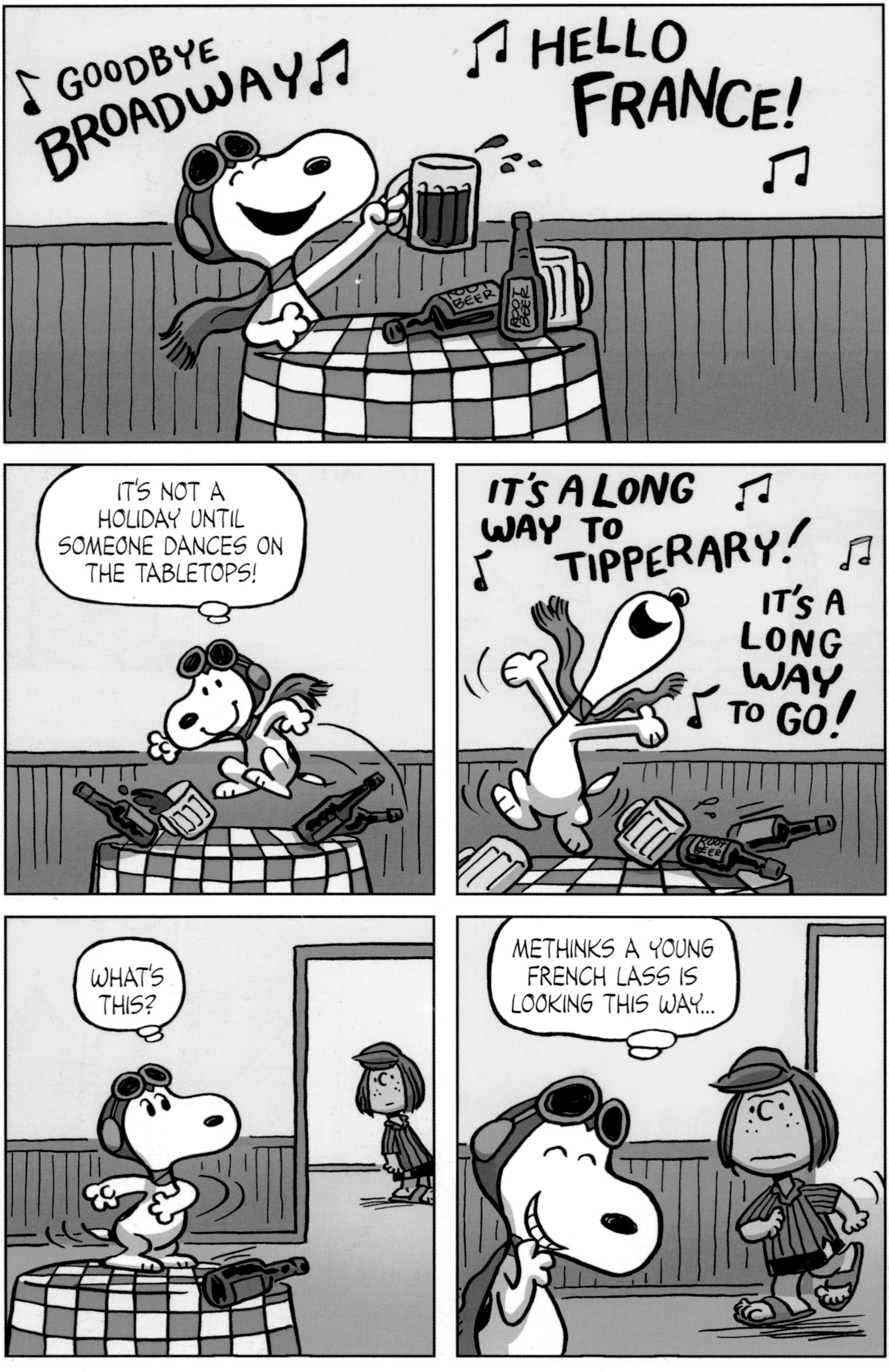

GOODBYE BROADWAY
HELLO FRANCE!
ROOT BEER
ROOT BEER
IT'S NOT A HOLIDAY UNTIL SOMEONE DANCES ON THE TABLETOPS!
IT'S A LONG WAY TO TIPPERARY!
IT'S A LONG WAY TO GO!
ROOT BEER
WHAT'S THIS?
METHINKS A YOUNG FRENCH LASS IS LOOKING THIS WAY...

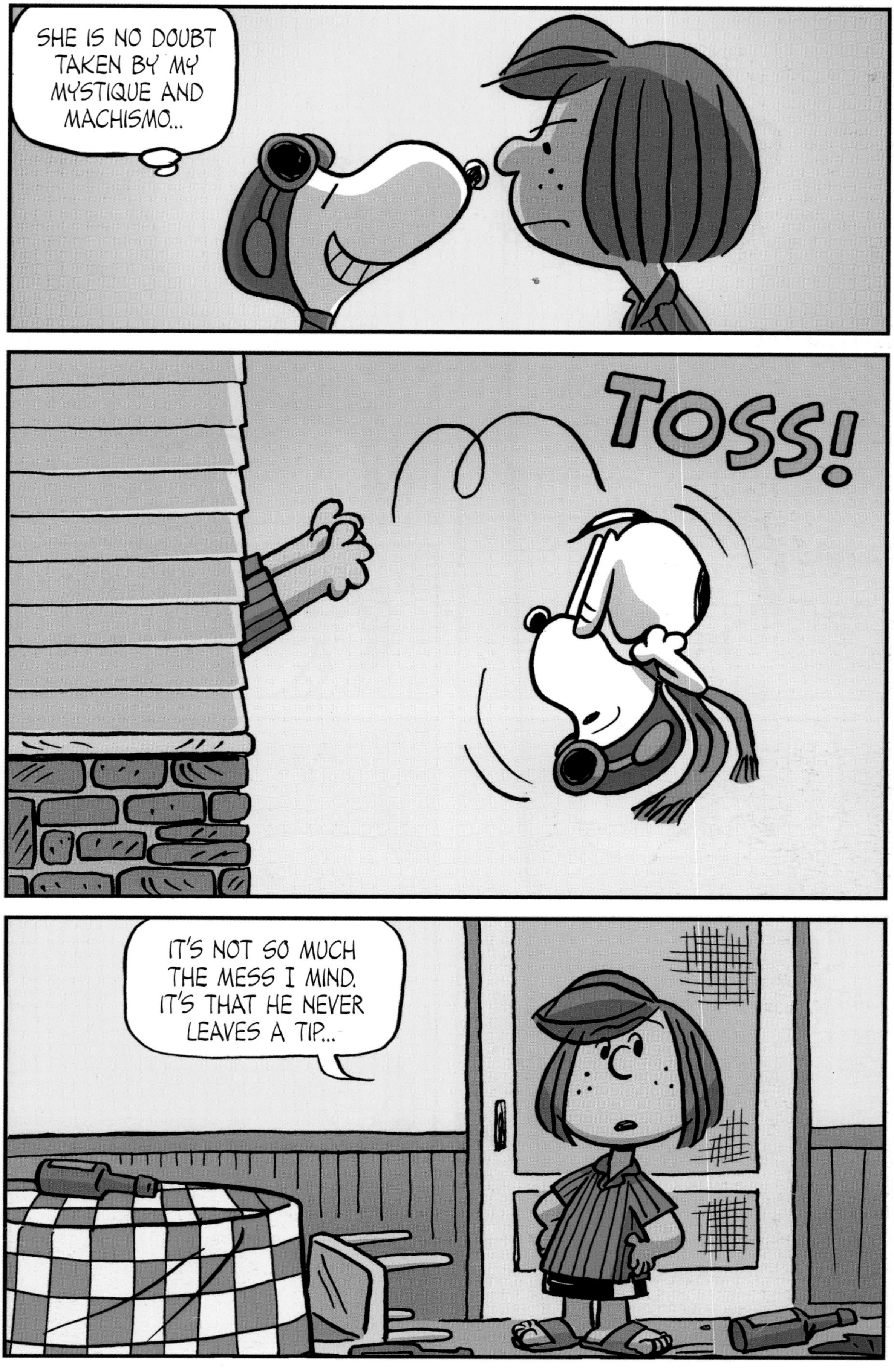
SHE IS NO DOUBT TAKEN BY MY MYSTIQUE AND MACHISMO...
TOSS!
IT'S NOT SO MUCH THE MESS I MIND. IT'S THAT HE NEVER LEAVES A TIP...

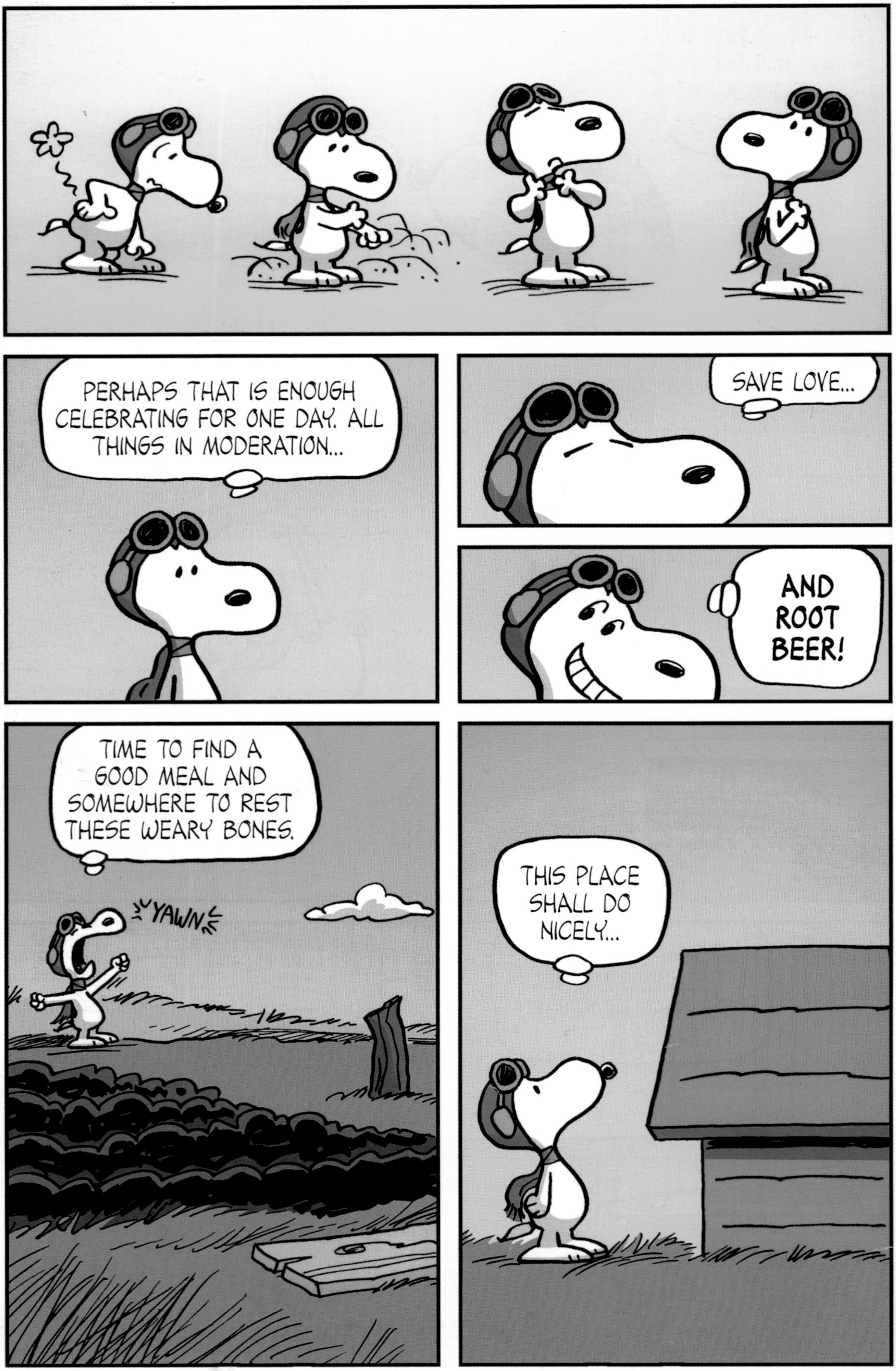
PERHAPS THAT IS ENOUGH CELEBRATING FOR ONE DAY. ALL THINGS IN MODERATION...
SAVE LOVE...
AND ROOT BEER!
TIME TO FIND A GOOD MEAL AND SOMEWHERE TO REST THESE WEARY BONES.
YAWN
THIS PLACE SHALL DO NICELY...

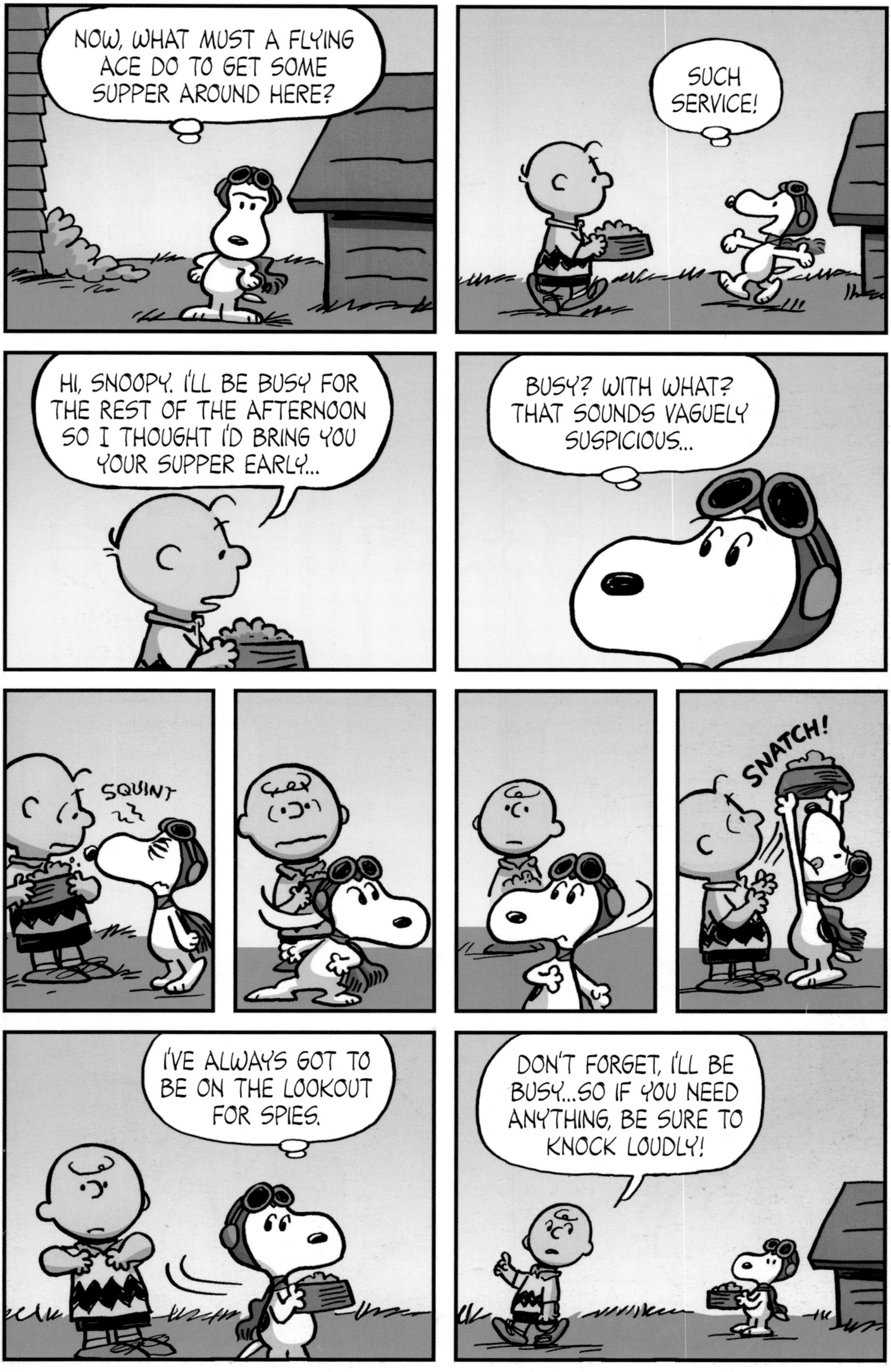
NOW, WHAT MUST A FLYING ACE DO TO GET SOME SUPPER AROUND HERE?
SUCH SERVICE!
HI, SNOOPY. I'LL BE BUSY FOR THE REST OF THE AFTERNOON SO I THOUGHT I'D BRING YOU YOUR SUPPER EARLY...
BUSY? WITH WHAT? THAT SOUNDS VAGUELY SUSPICIOUS...
SQUINT
SNATCH!
I'VE ALWAYS GOT TO BE ON THE LOOKOUT FOR SPIES.
DON'T FORGET, I'LL BE BUSY...SO IF YOU NEED ANYTHING, BE SURE TO KNOCK LOUDLY!

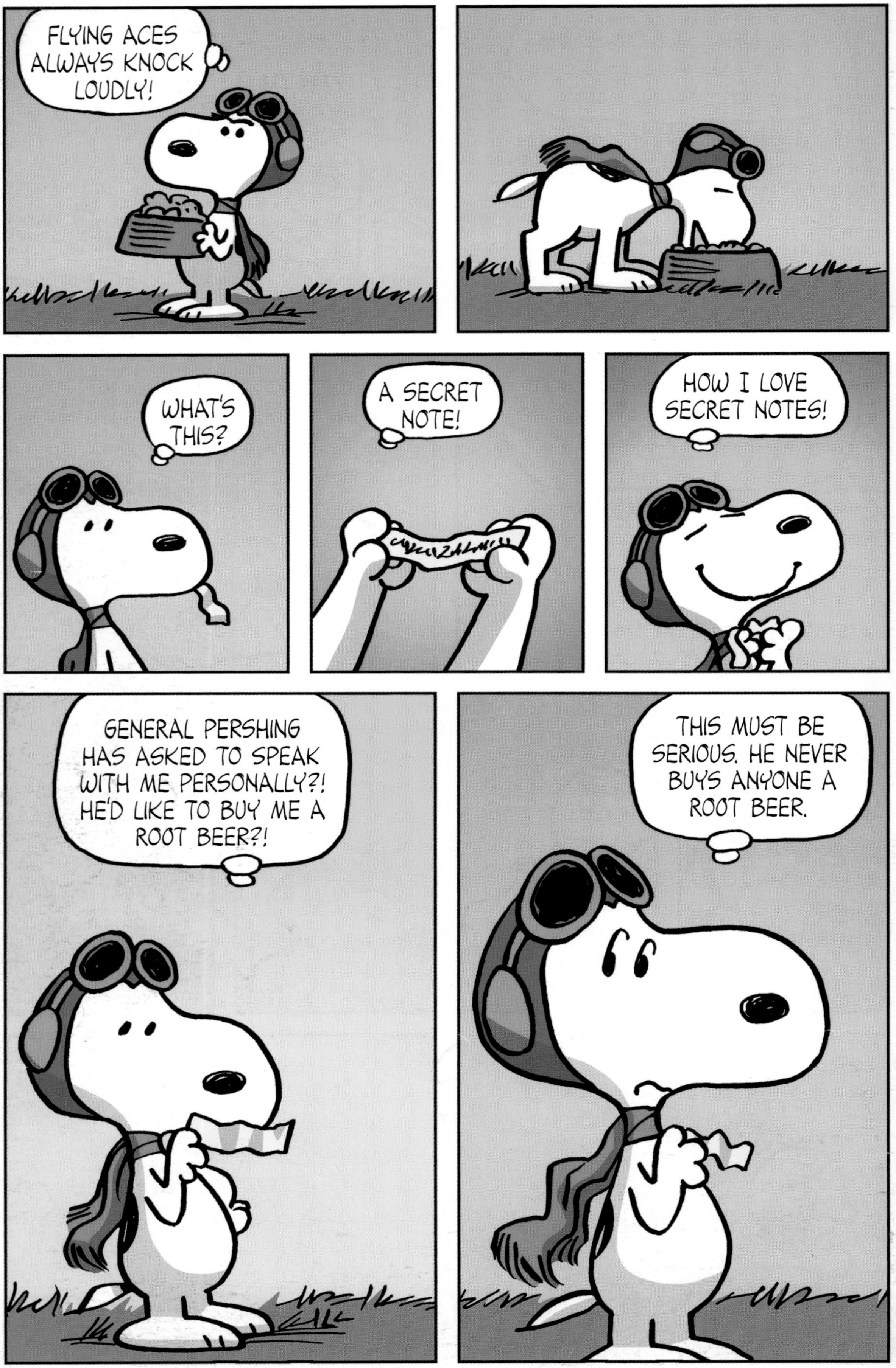
FLYING ACES ALWAYS KNOCK LOUDLY!
WHAT'S THIS?
A SECRET NOTE!
HOW I LOVE SECRET NOTES!
GENERAL PERSHING HAS ASKED TO SPEAK WITH ME PERSONALLY?! HE'D LIKE TO BUY ME A ROOT BEER?!
THIS MUST BE SERIOUS. HE NEVER BUYS ANYONE A ROOT BEER.

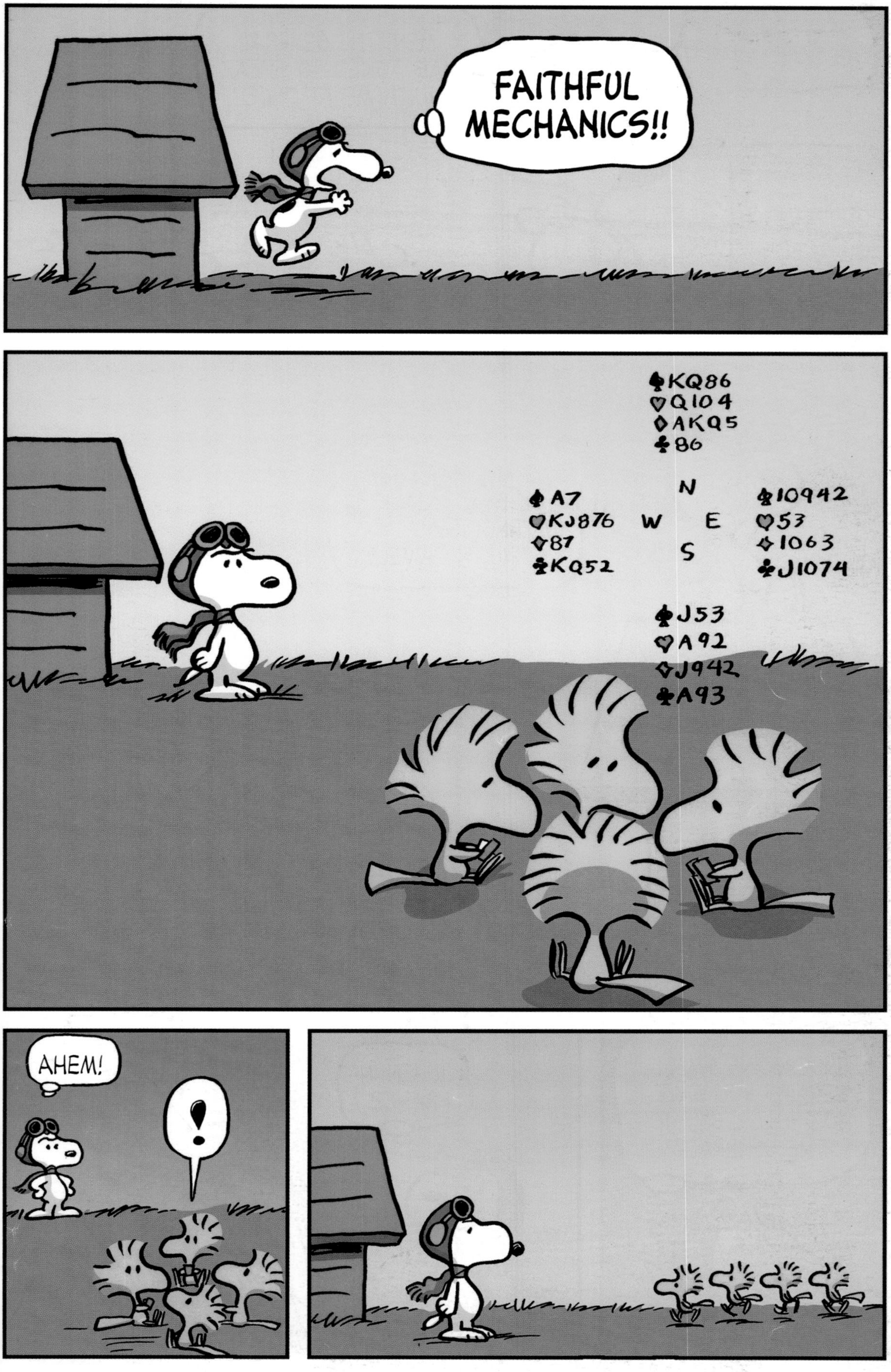
FAITHFUL MECHANICS!!
♠KQ86
♡Q104
♢AKQ5
♣86
N
W
E
S
♠A7
♡KJ876
♢87
♣KQ52
♠10942
♡53
♢1063
♣J1074
♠J53
♡A92
♢J942
♣A93
AHEM!
!

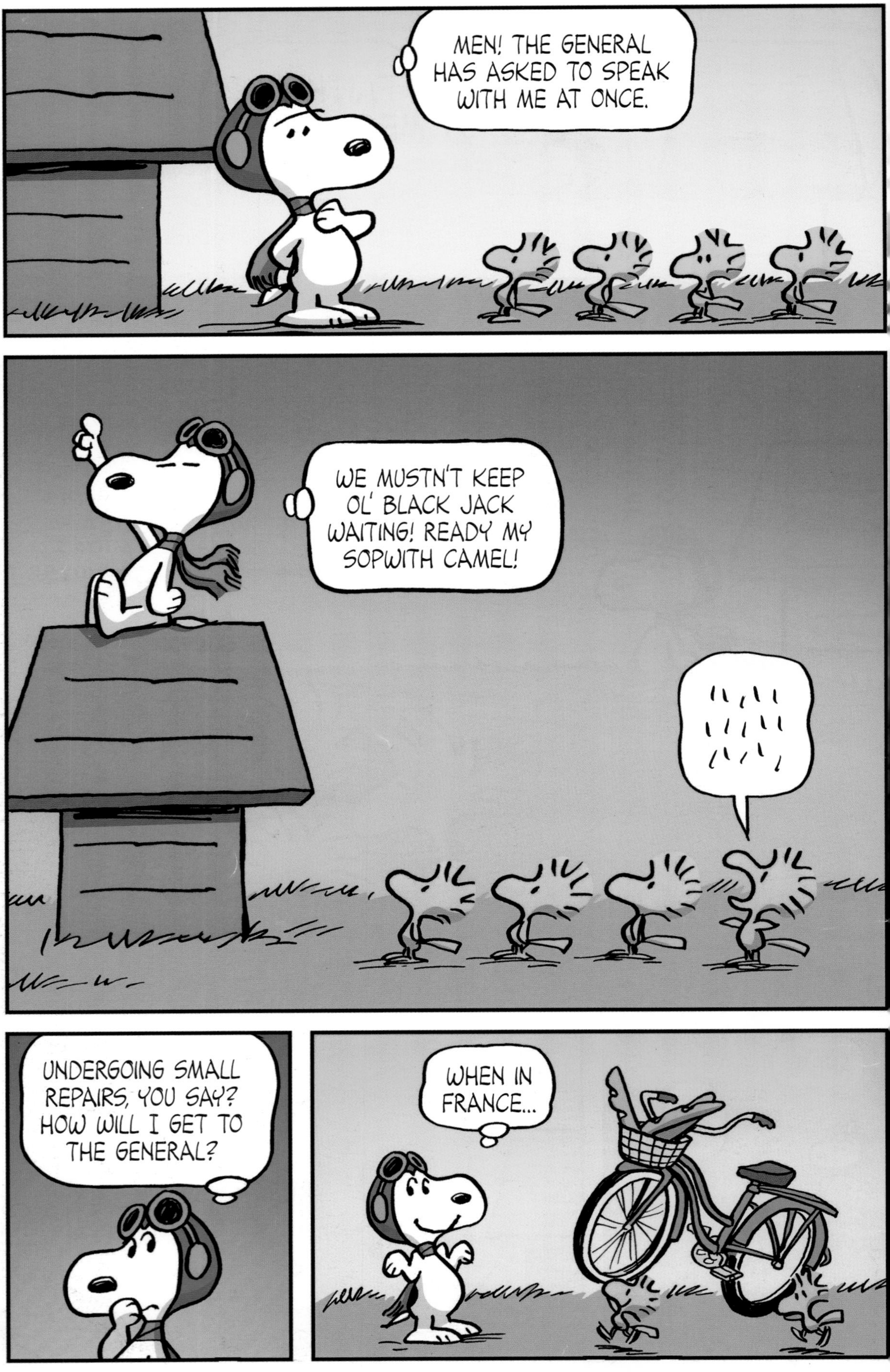
MEN! THE GENERAL HAS ASKED TO SPEAK WITH ME AT ONCE.
WE MUSTN'T KEEP OL' BLACK JACK WAITING! READY MY SOPWITH CAMEL!
UNDERGOING SMALL REPAIRS, YOU SAY? HOW WILL I GET TO THE GENERAL?
WHEN IN FRANCE...

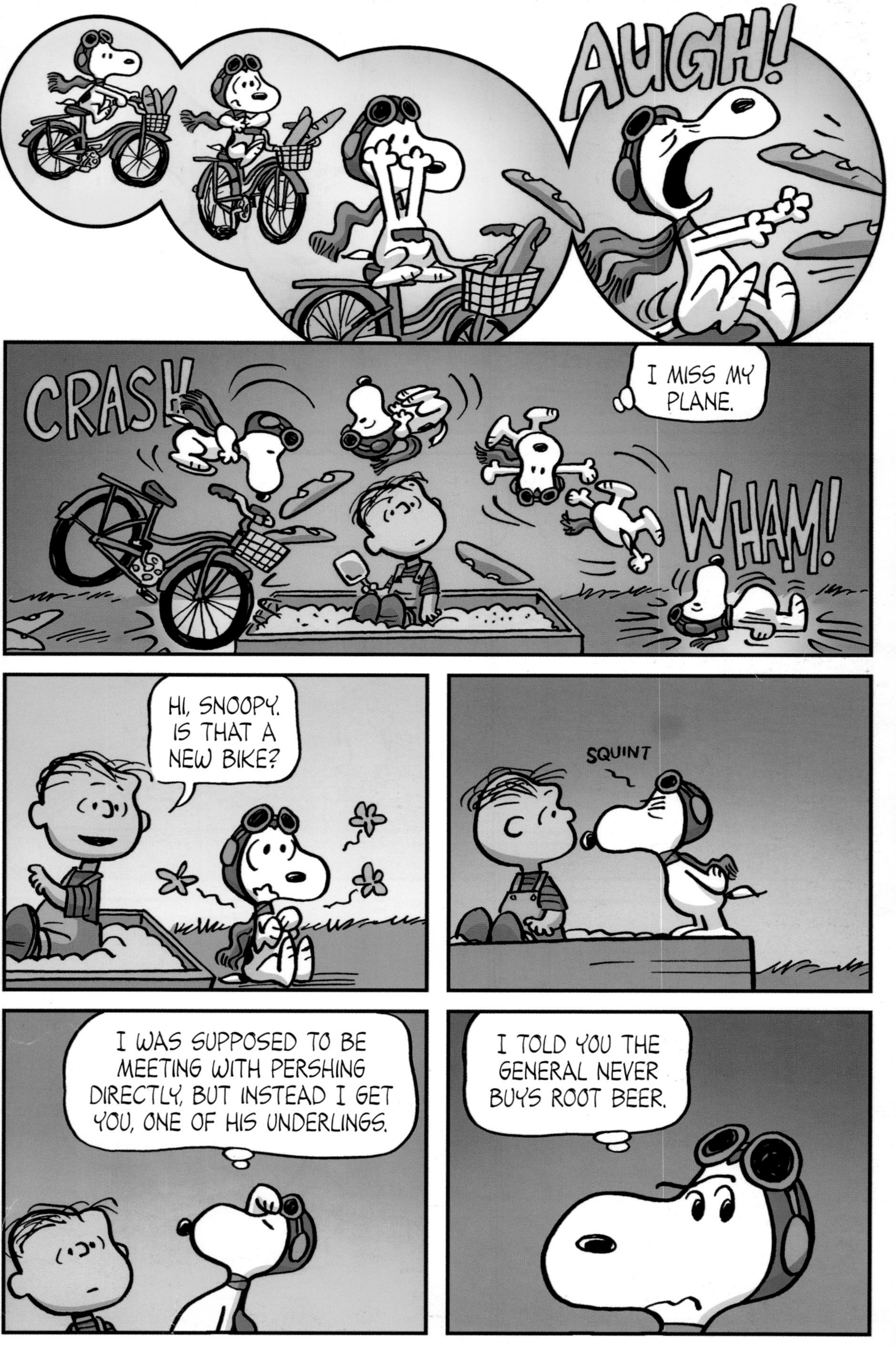
AUGH!
CRASH!
I MISS MY PLANE.
WHAM!
HI, SNOOPY. IS THAT A NEW BIKE?
SQUINT
I WAS SUPPOSED TO BE MEETING WITH PERSHING DIRECTLY, BUT INSTEAD I GET YOU, ONE OF HIS UNDERLINGS.
I TOLD YOU THE GENERAL NEVER BUYS ROOT BEER.

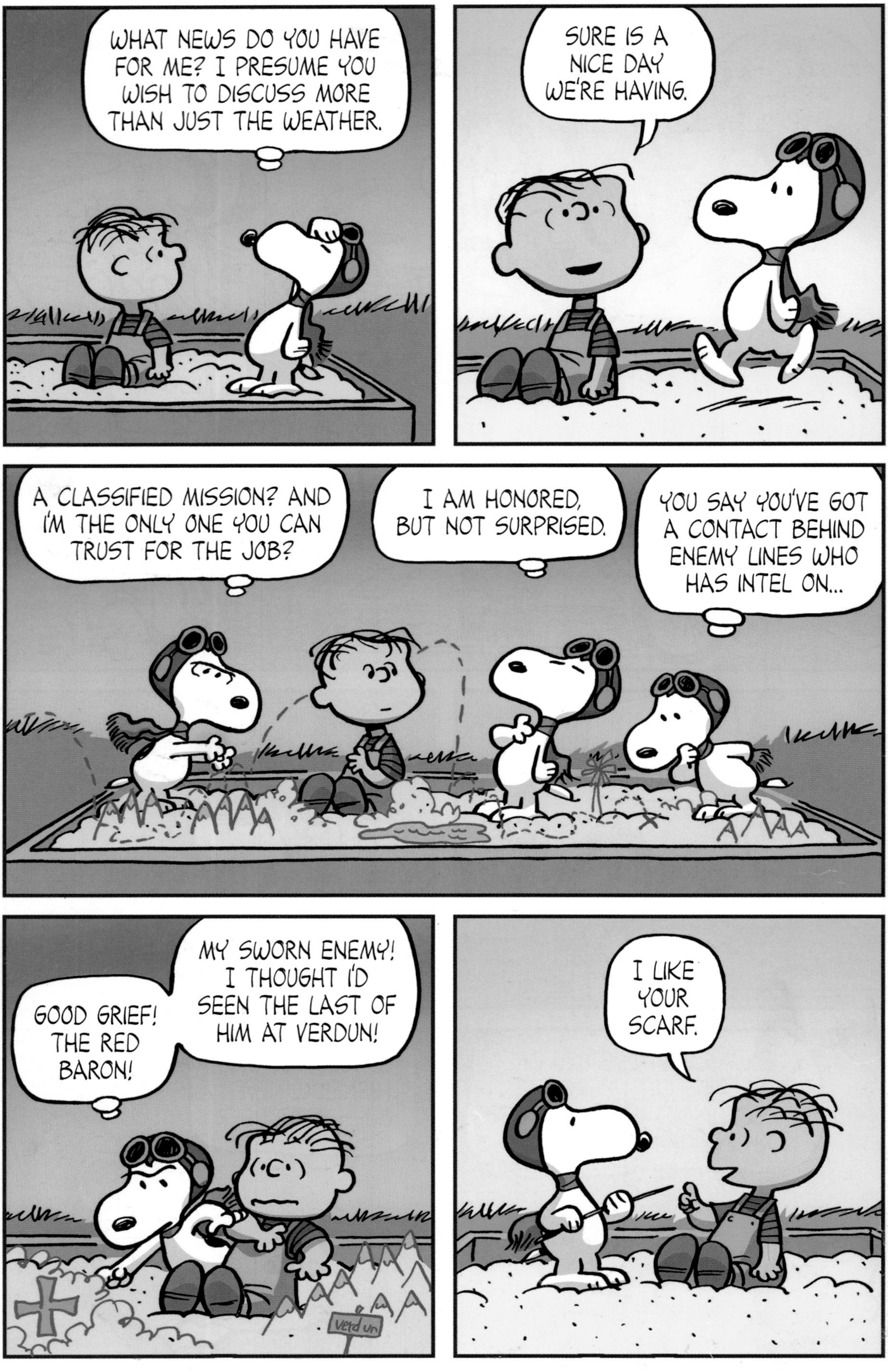
WHAT NEWS DO YOU HAVE FOR ME? I PRESUME YOU WISH TO DISCUSS MORE THAN JUST THE WEATHER.
SURE IS A NICE DAY WE'RE HAVING.
A CLASSIFIED MISSION? AND I'M THE ONLY ONE YOU CAN TRUST FOR THE JOB?
I AM HONORED, BUT NOT SURPRISED.
YOU SAY YOU'VE GOT A CONTACT BEHIND ENEMY LINES WHO HAS INTEL ON...
GOOD GRIEF! THE RED BARON!
MY SWORN ENEMY! I THOUGHT I'D SEEN THE LAST OF HIM AT VERDUN!
verdun
I LIKE YOUR SCARF.

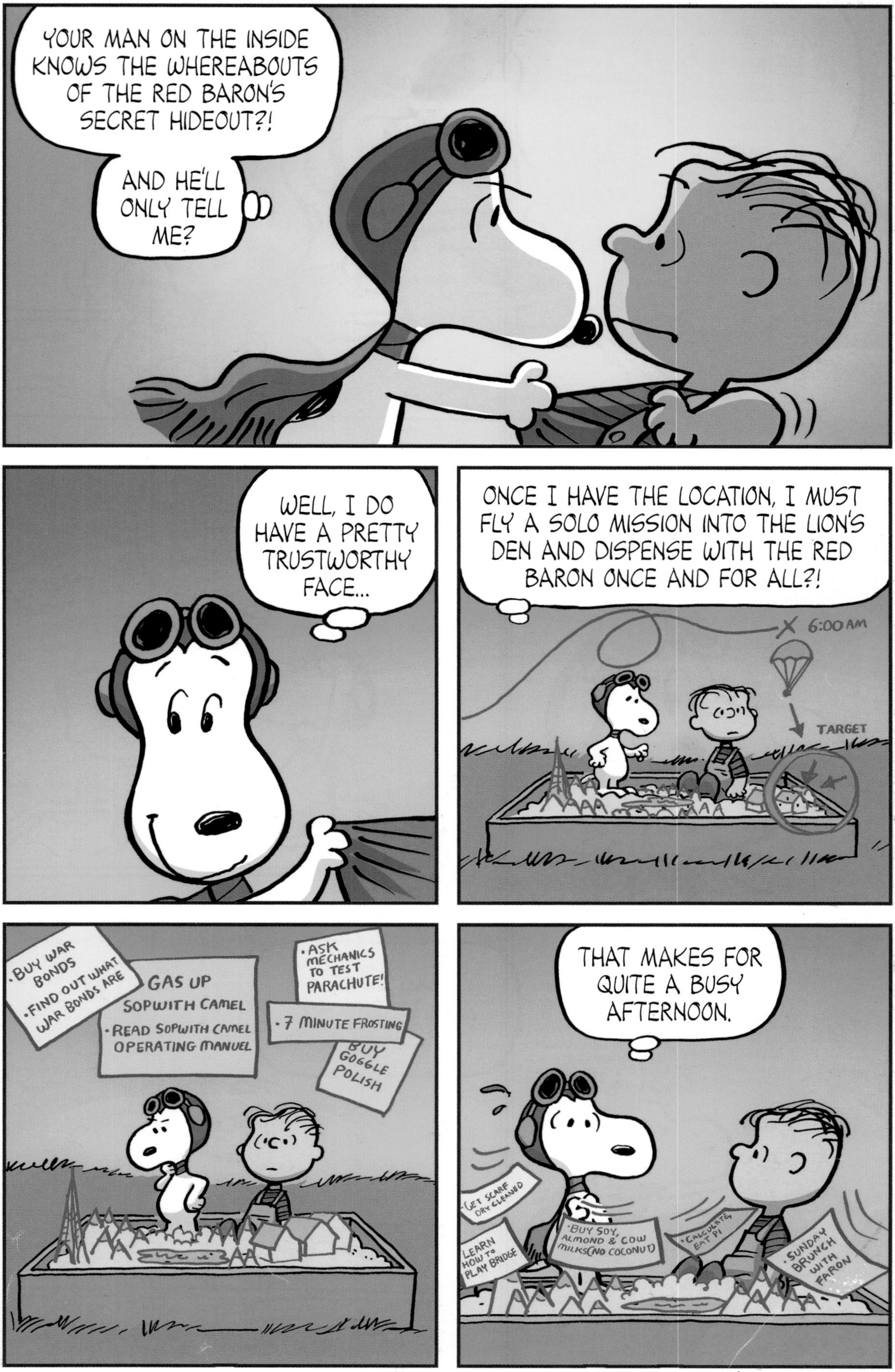
YOUR MAN ON THE INSIDE KNOWS THE WHEREABOUTS OF THE RED BARON'S SECRET HIDEOUT?!
AND HE'LL ONLY TELL ME?
WELL, I DO HAVE A PRETTY TRUSTWORTHY FACE...
ONCE I HAVE THE LOCATION, I MUST FLY A SOLO MISSION INTO THE LION'S DEN AND DISPENSE WITH THE RED BARON ONCE AND FOR ALL?!
6:00 AM
TARGET
· BUY WAR BONDS
· FIND OUT WHAT WAR BONDS ARE
GAS UP SOPWITH CAMEL
· READ SOPWITH CAMEL OPERATING MANUEL
· ASK MECHANICS TO TEST PARACHUTE!
· 7 MINUTE FROSTING
BUY GOGGLE POLISH
THAT MAKES FOR QUITE A BUSY AFTERNOON.
· GET SCARF DRY CLEANED
LEARN HOW TO PLAY BRIDGE
· BUY SOY, ALMOND & COW MILKS (NO COCONUT)
· CALCULATE, EAT PI
· SUNDAY BRUNCH WITH FARON

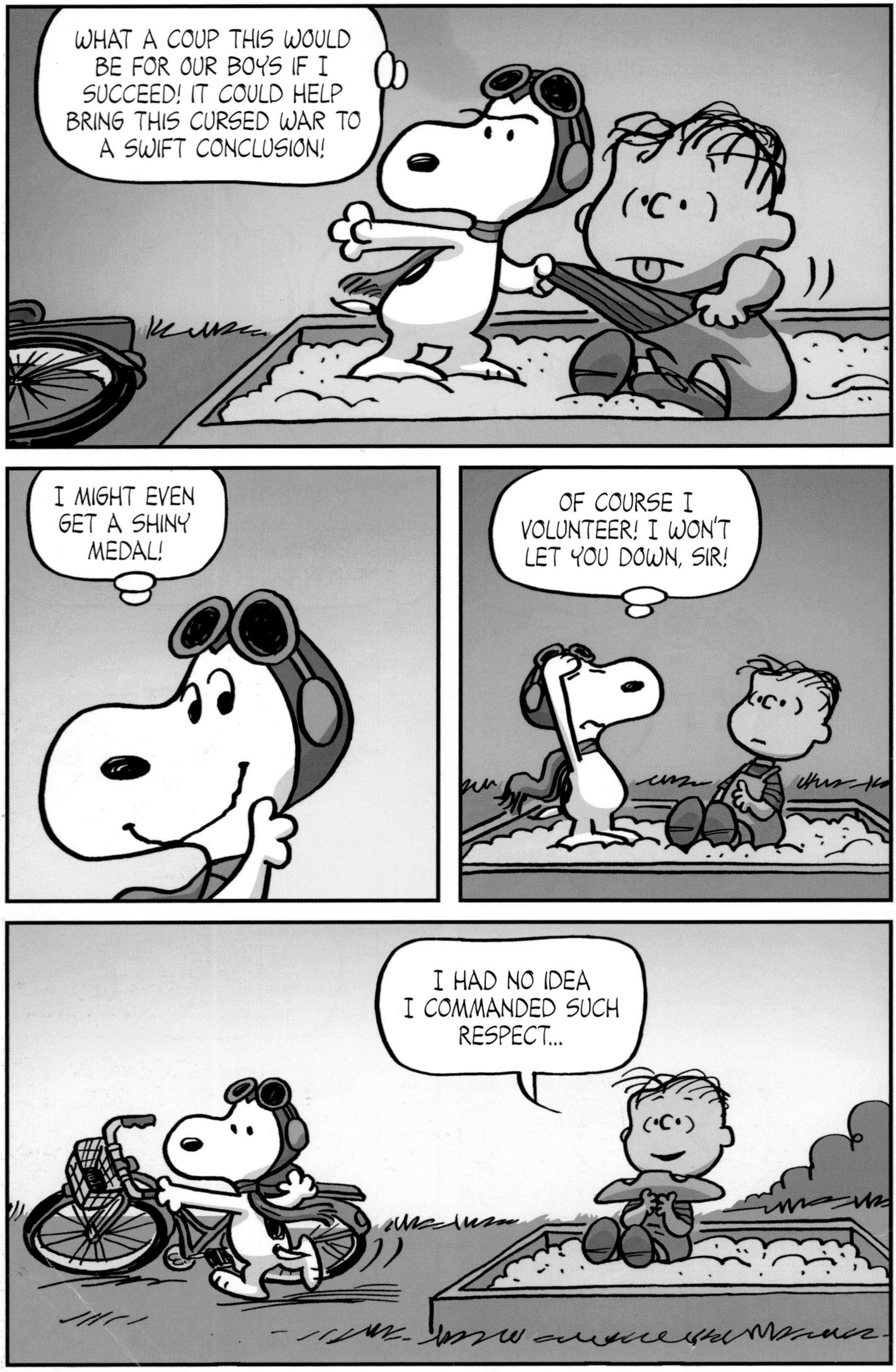
WHAT A COUP THIS WOULD BE FOR OUR BOYS IF I SUCCEED! IT COULD HELP BRING THIS CURSED WAR TO A SWIFT CONCLUSION!
I MIGHT EVEN GET A SHINY MEDAL!
OF COURSE I VOLUNTEER! I WON'T LET YOU DOWN, SIR!
I HAD NO IDEA I COMMANDED SUCH RESPECT...

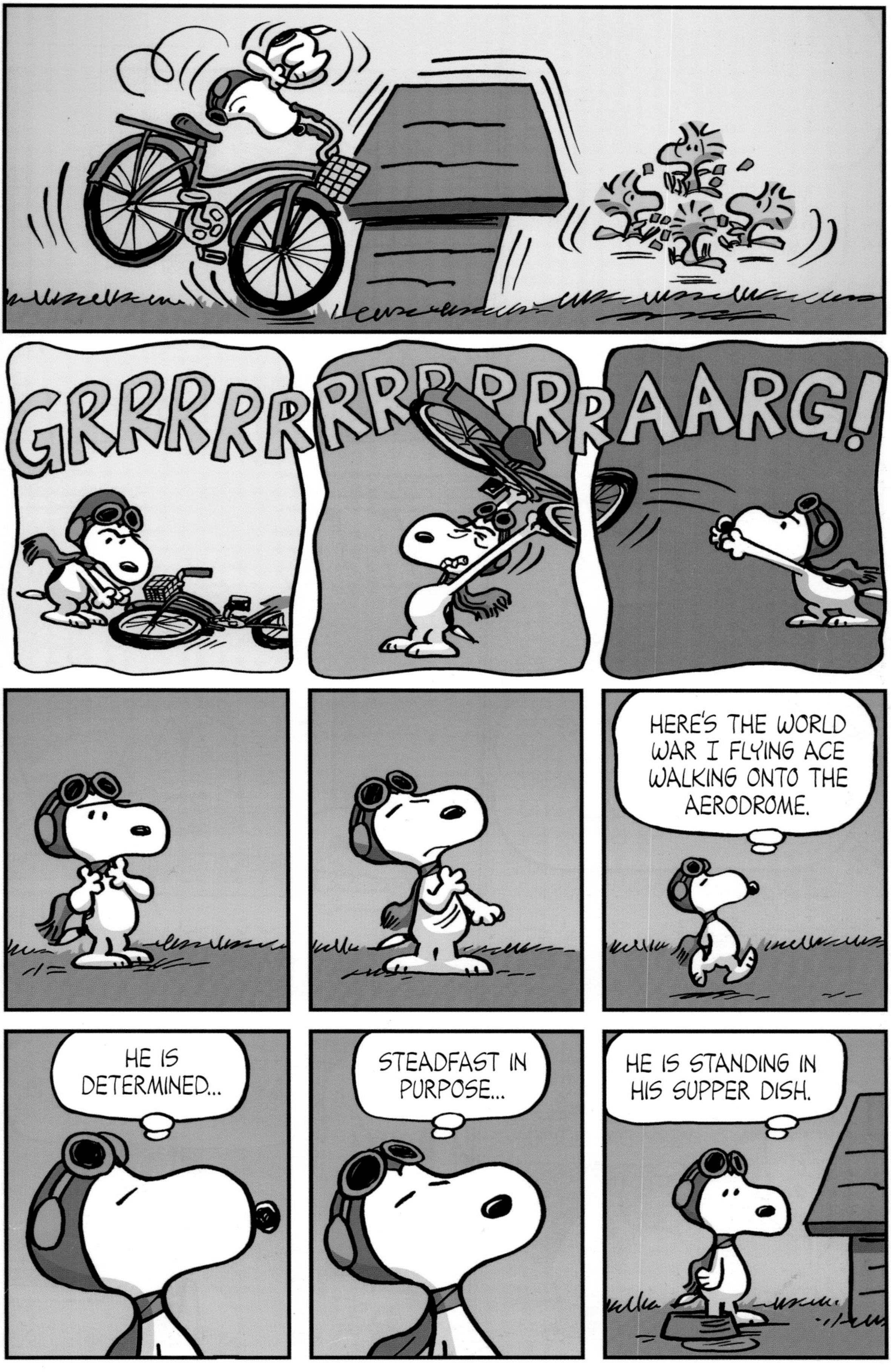
GRRRRRRRRRRRRRAARG!
HERE'S THE WORLD WAR I FLYING ACE WALKING ONTO THE AERODROME.
HE IS DETERMINED...
STEADFAST IN PURPOSE...
HE IS STANDING IN HIS SUPPER DISH.

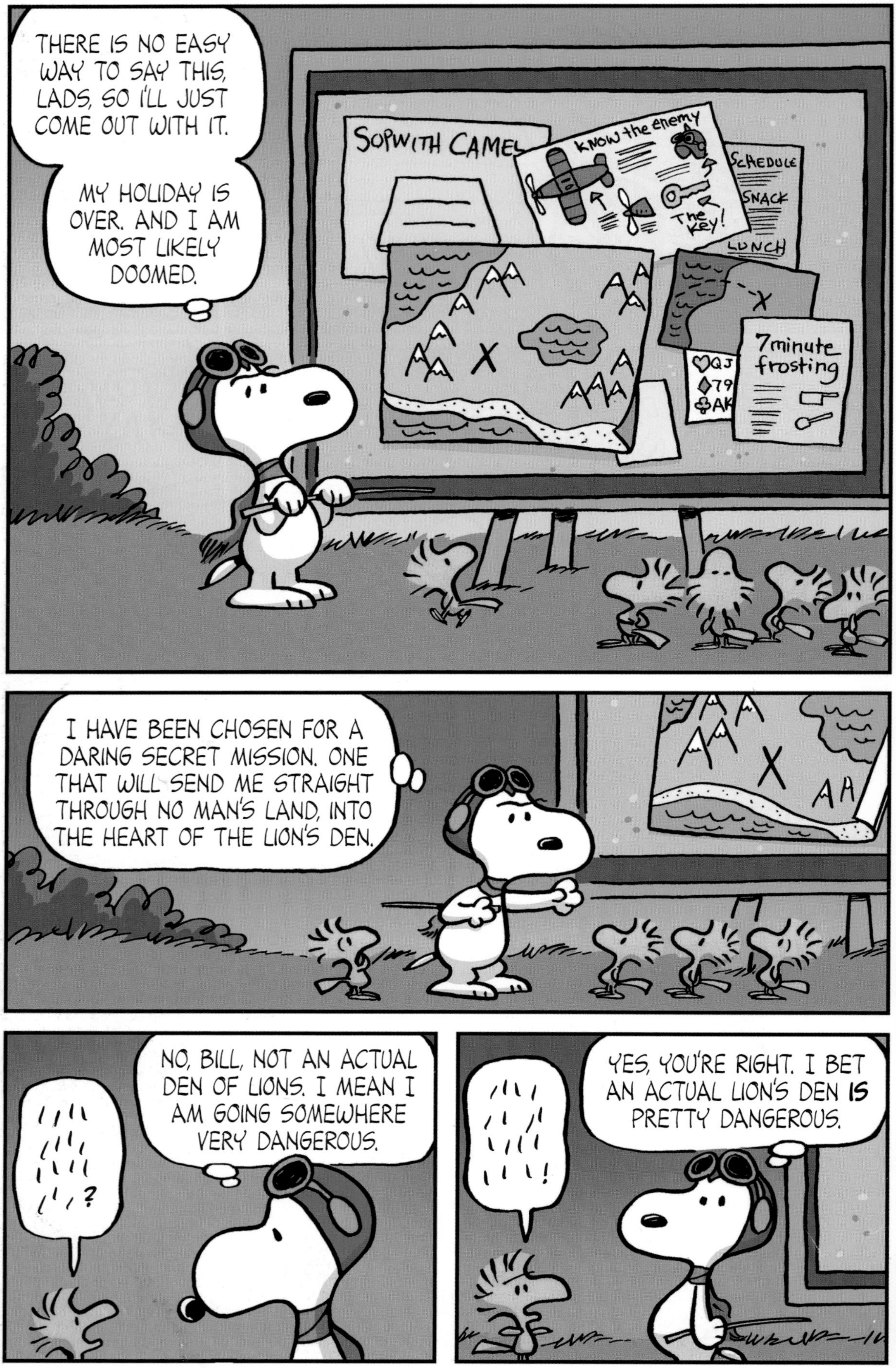
THERE IS NO EASY WAY TO SAY THIS, LADS, SO I'LL JUST COME OUT WITH IT.
MY HOLIDAY IS OVER. AND I AM MOST LIKELY DOOMED.
SOPWITH CAME
Know the enemy
The Key!
SCHEDULE
SNACK
LUNCH
7minute frosting
I HAVE BEEN CHOSEN FOR A DARING SECRET MISSION. ONE THAT WILL SEND ME STRAIGHT THROUGH NO MAN'S LAND, INTO THE HEART OF THE LION'S DEN.
NO, BILL, NOT AN ACTUAL DEN OF LIONS. I MEAN I AM GOING SOMEWHERE VERY DANGEROUS.
YES, YOU'RE RIGHT. I BET AN ACTUAL LION'S DEN **IS** PRETTY DANGEROUS.

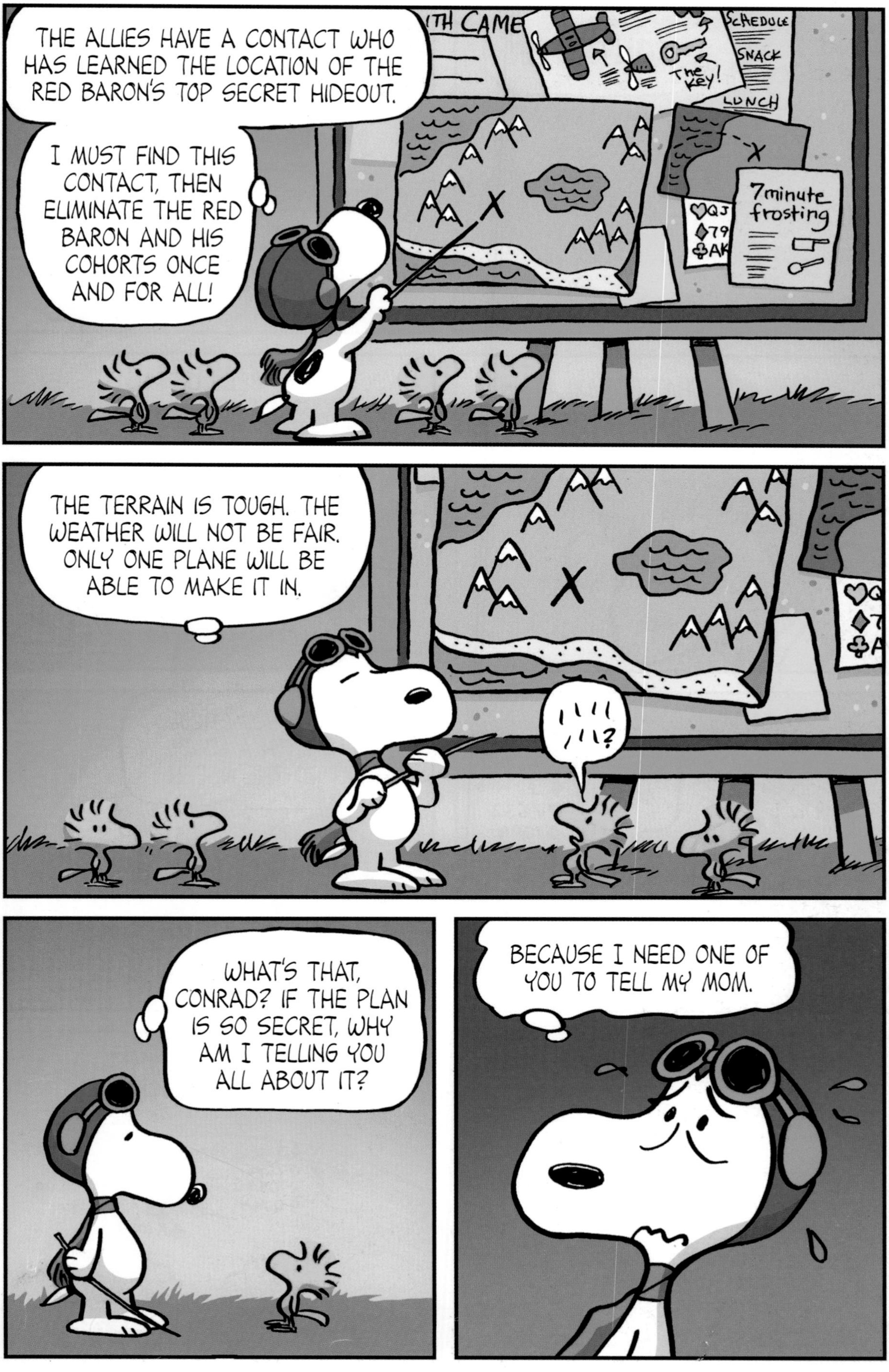

THE ALLIES HAVE A CONTACT WHO HAS LEARNED THE LOCATION OF THE RED BARON'S TOP SECRET HIDEOUT.
I MUST FIND THIS CONTACT, THEN ELIMINATE THE RED BARON AND HIS COHORTS ONCE AND FOR ALL!
SCHEDULE
SNACK
LUNCH
The key!
7minute frosting
THE TERRAIN IS TOUGH. THE WEATHER WILL NOT BE FAIR. ONLY ONE PLANE WILL BE ABLE TO MAKE IT IN.
WHAT'S THAT, CONRAD? IF THE PLAN IS SO SECRET, WHY AM I TELLING YOU ALL ABOUT IT?
BECAUSE I NEED ONE OF YOU TO TELL MY MOM.

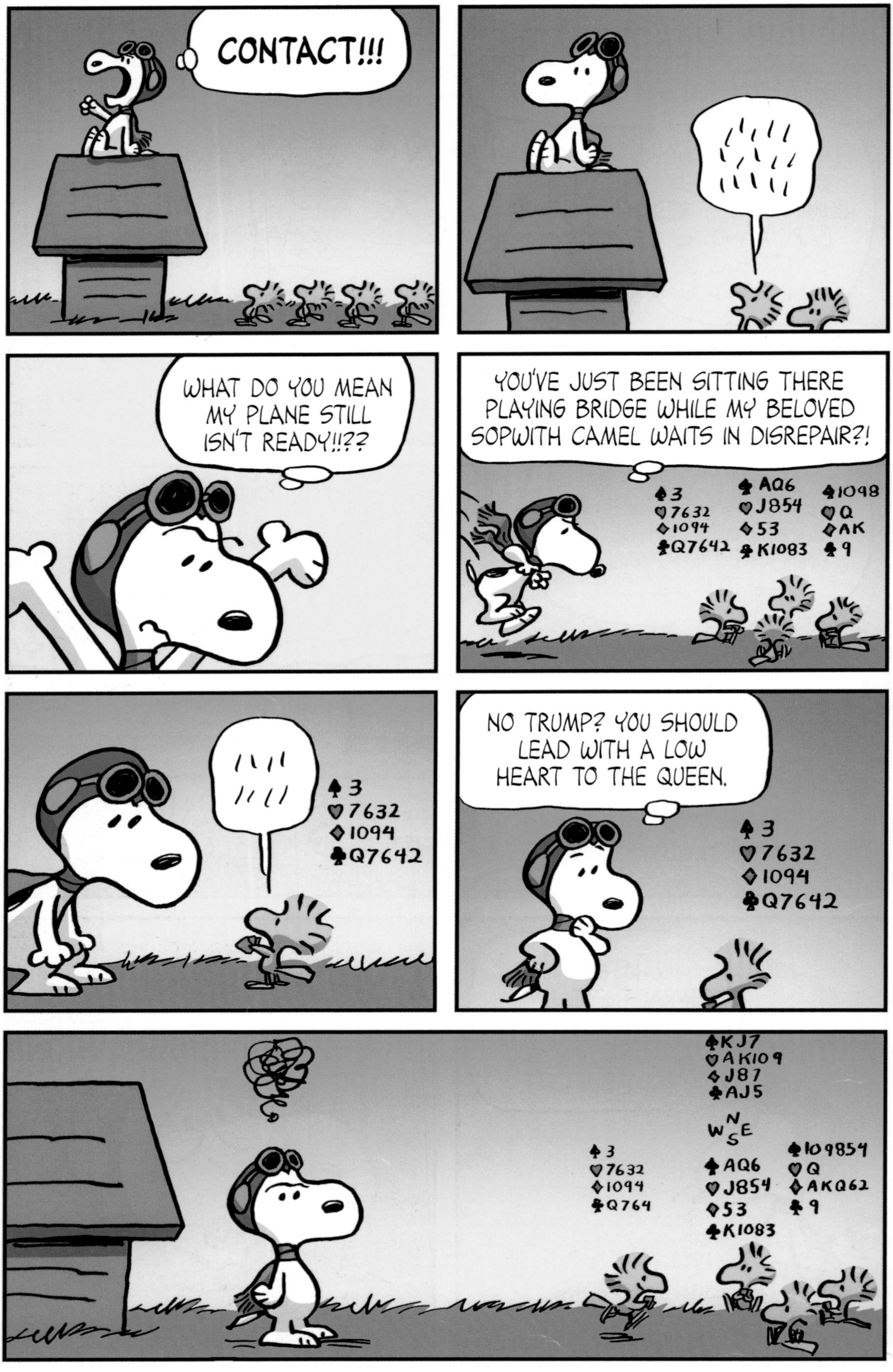

CONTACT!!!
WHAT DO YOU MEAN MY PLANE STILL ISN'T READY!!??
YOU'VE JUST BEEN SITTING THERE PLAYING BRIDGE WHILE MY BELOVED SOPWITH CAMEL WAITS IN DISREPAIR?!
♠3 ♡7632 ◇1094 ♣Q7642
♠AQ6 ♡J854 ◇53 ♣K1083
♠1098 ♡Q ◇AK ♣9
♠3 ♡7632 ◇1094 ♣Q7642
NO TRUMP? YOU SHOULD LEAD WITH A LOW HEART TO THE QUEEN.
♠3 ♡7632 ◇1094 ♣Q7642
♠KJ7 ♡AK109 ◇J87 ♣AJ5
N W E S
♠3 ♡7632 ◇1094 ♣Q764
♠AQ6 ♡J854 ◇53 ♣K1083
♠109854 ♡Q ◇AKQ62 ♣9

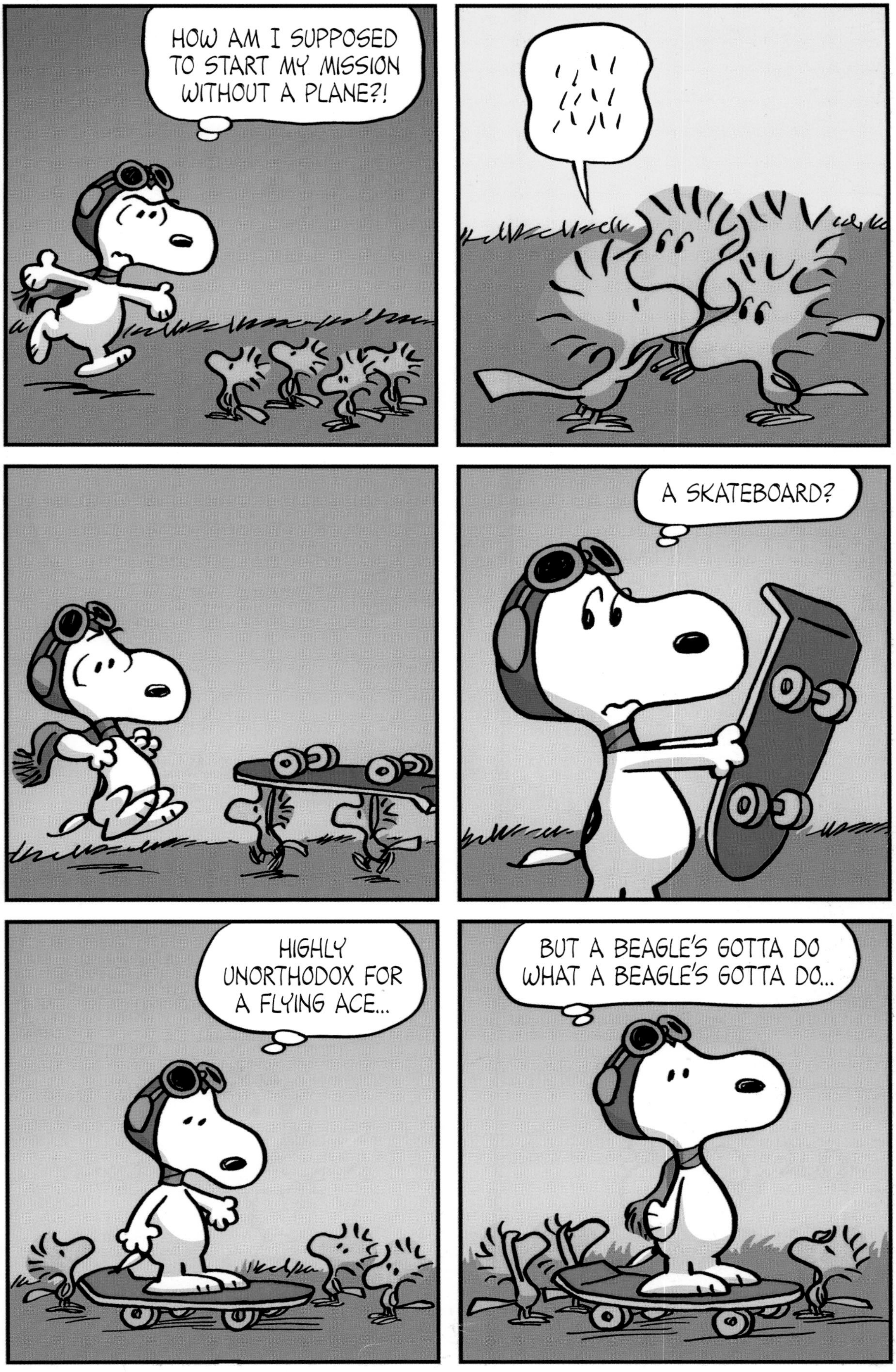
HOW AM I SUPPOSED TO START MY MISSION WITHOUT A PLANE?!
A SKATEBOARD?
HIGHLY UNORTHODOX FOR A FLYING ACE...
BUT A BEAGLE'S GOTTA DO WHAT A BEAGLE'S GOTTA DO...

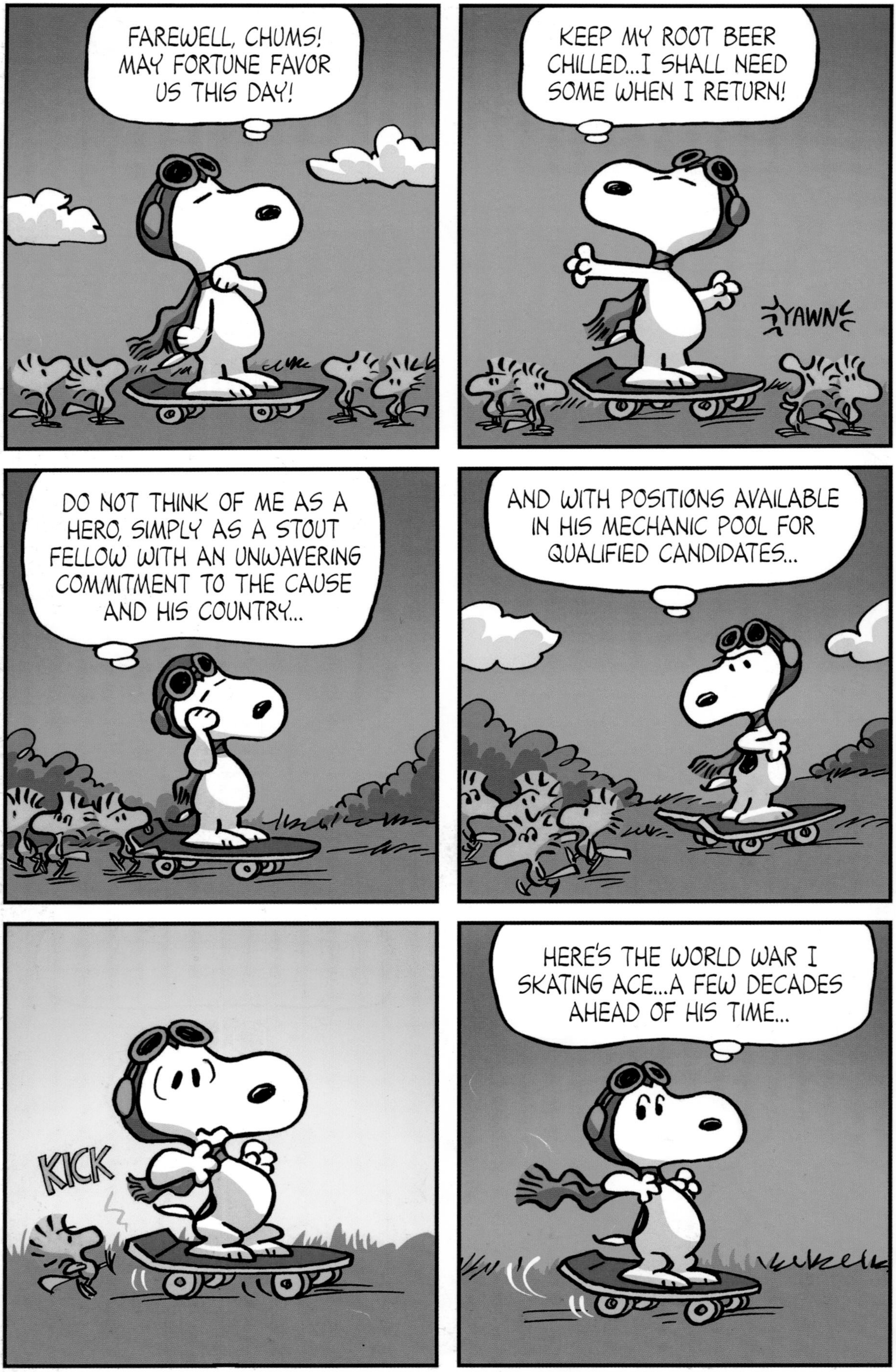
FAREWELL, CHUMS! MAY FORTUNE FAVOR US THIS DAY!
KEEP MY ROOT BEER CHILLED...I SHALL NEED SOME WHEN I RETURN!
YAWN
DO NOT THINK OF ME AS A HERO, SIMPLY AS A STOUT FELLOW WITH AN UNWAVERING COMMITMENT TO THE CAUSE AND HIS COUNTRY...
AND WITH POSITIONS AVAILABLE IN HIS MECHANIC POOL FOR QUALIFIED CANDIDATES...
KICK
HERE'S THE WORLD WAR I SKATING ACE...A FEW DECADES AHEAD OF HIS TIME...

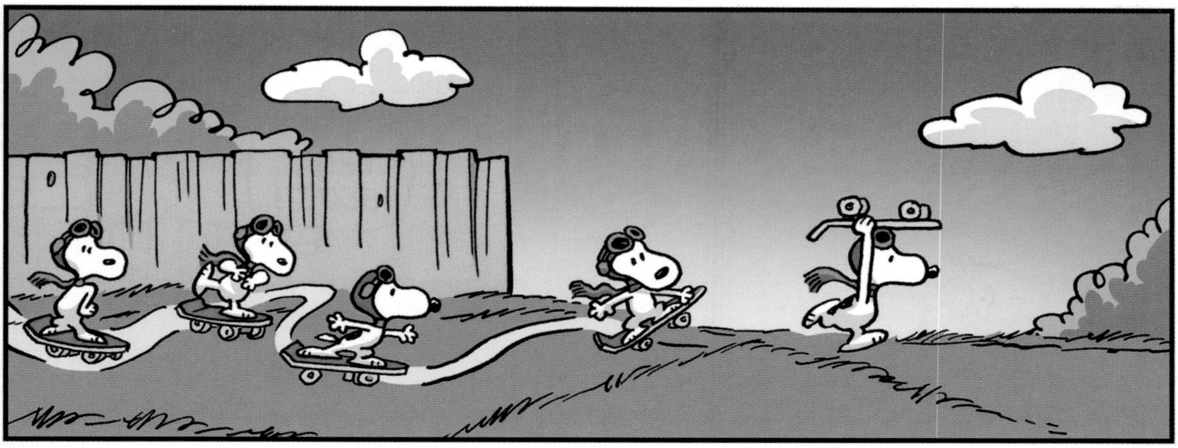

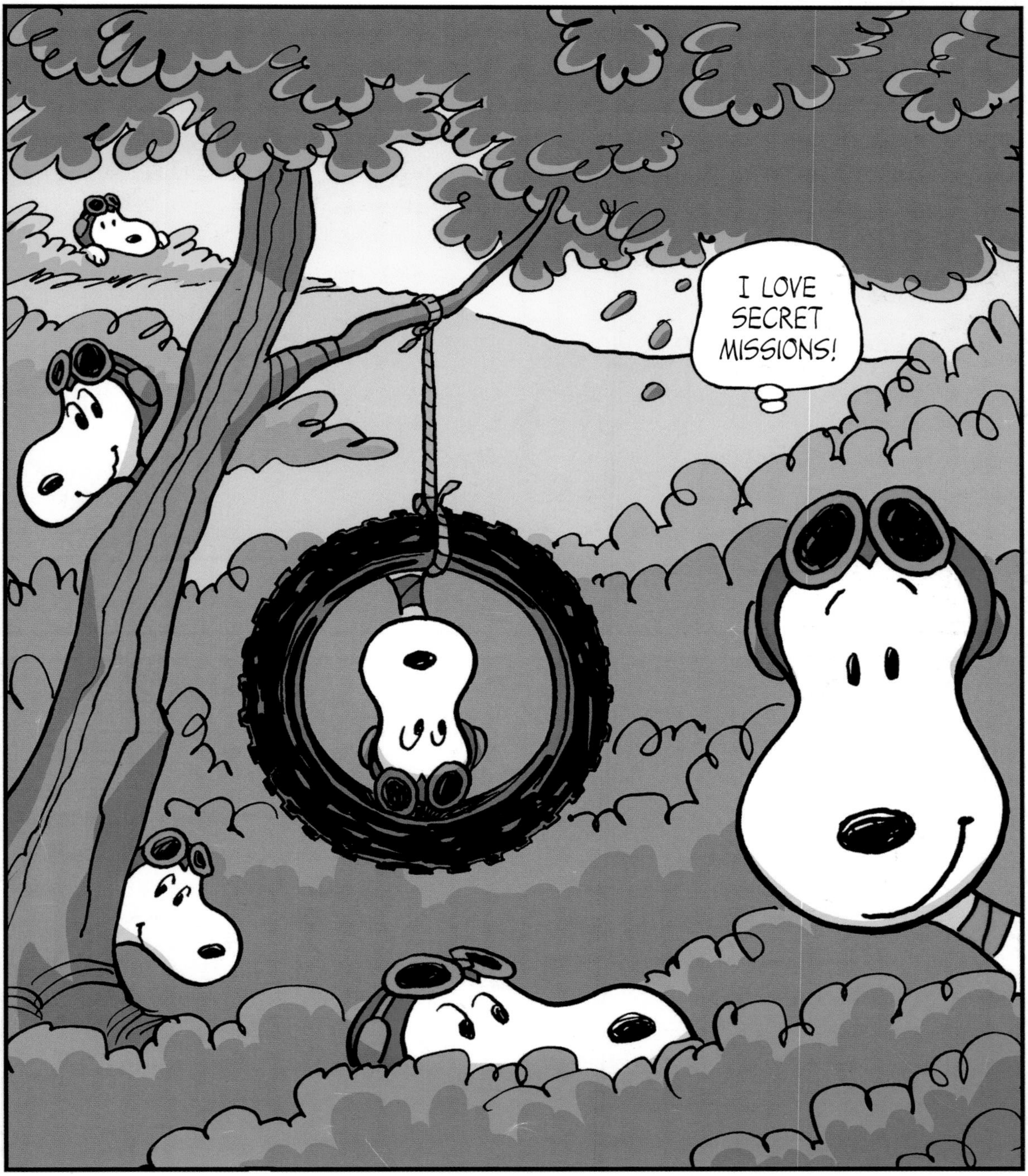
I LOVE SECRET MISSIONS!

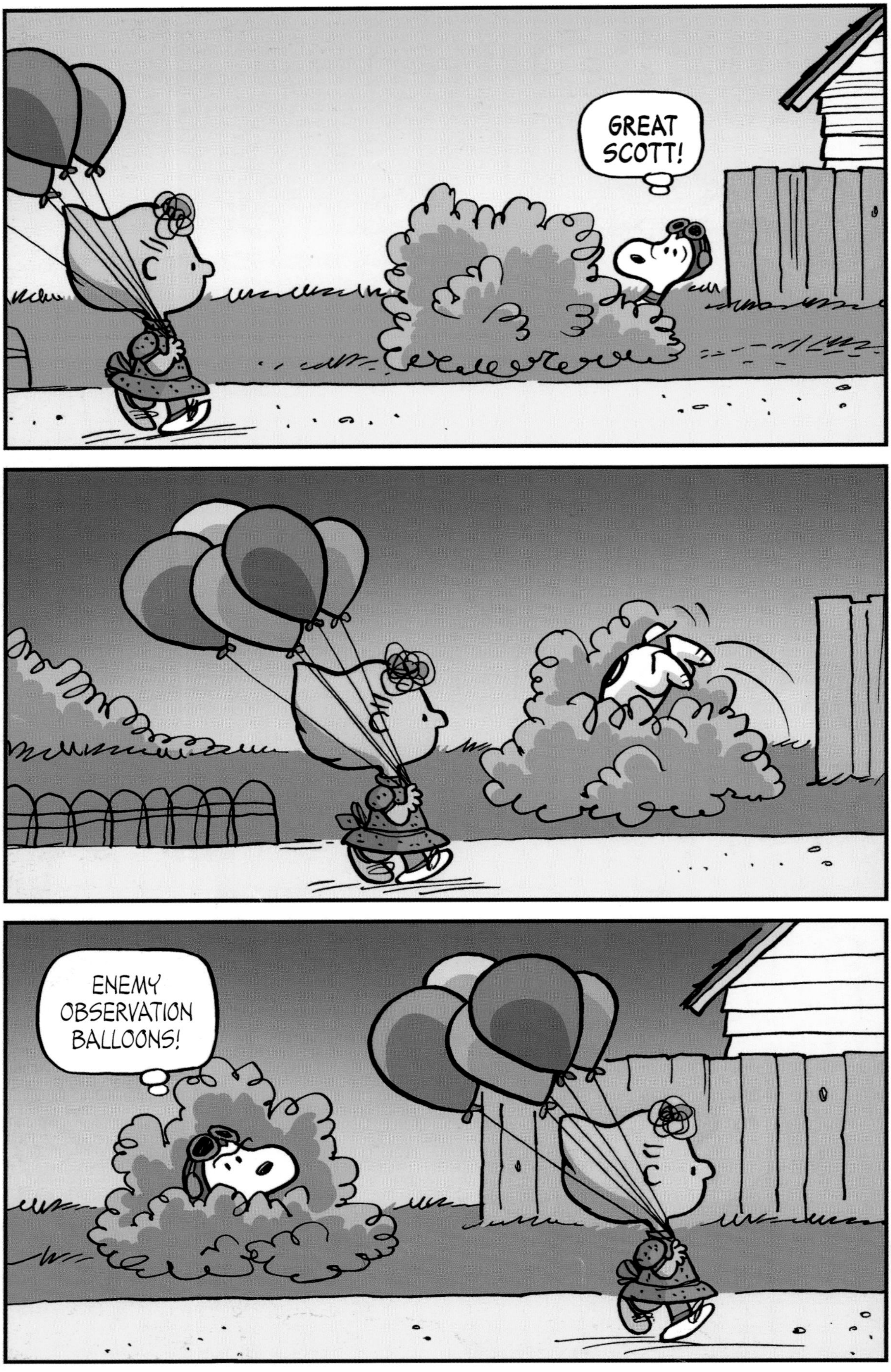
GREAT SCOTT!
ENEMY OBSERVATION BALLOONS!

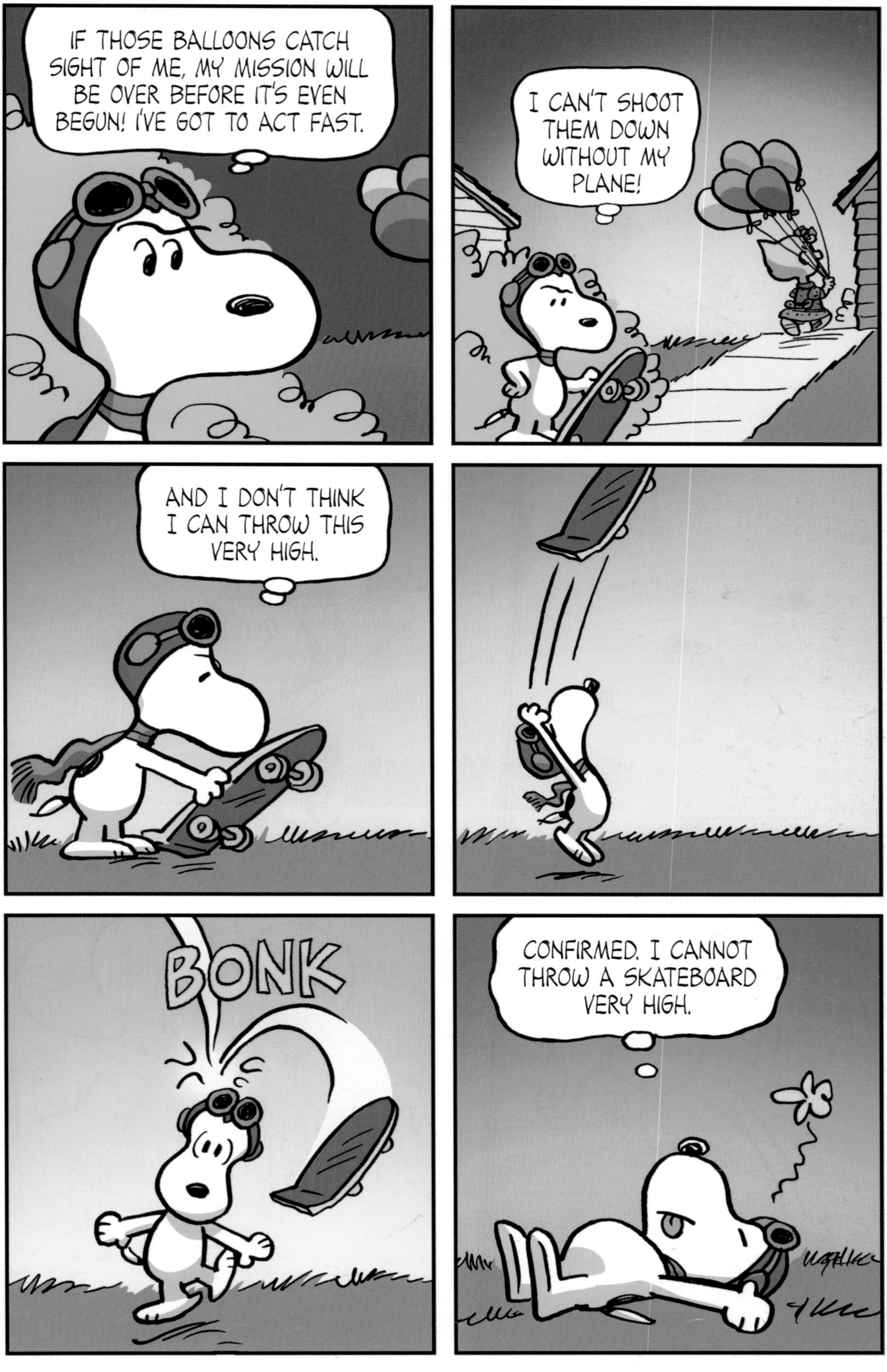
IF THOSE BALLOONS CATCH SIGHT OF ME, MY MISSION WILL BE OVER BEFORE IT'S EVEN BEGUN! I'VE GOT TO ACT FAST.
I CAN'T SHOOT THEM DOWN WITHOUT MY PLANE!
AND I DON'T THINK I CAN THROW THIS VERY HIGH.
BONK
CONFIRMED. I CANNOT THROW A SKATEBOARD VERY HIGH.

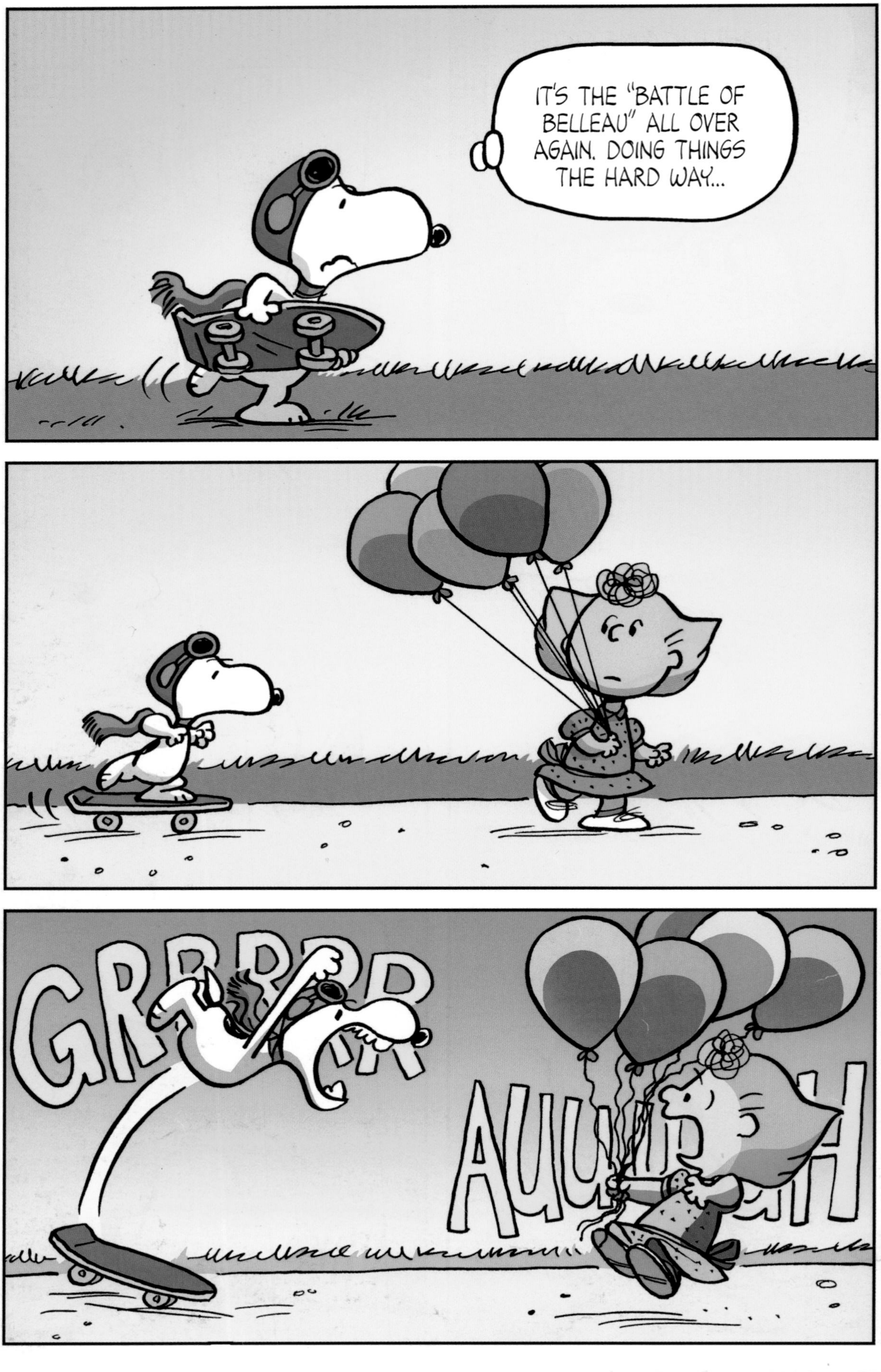
IT'S THE "BATTLE OF BELLEAU" ALL OVER AGAIN. DOING THINGS THE HARD WAY...
GRRRRR
AUUUGH

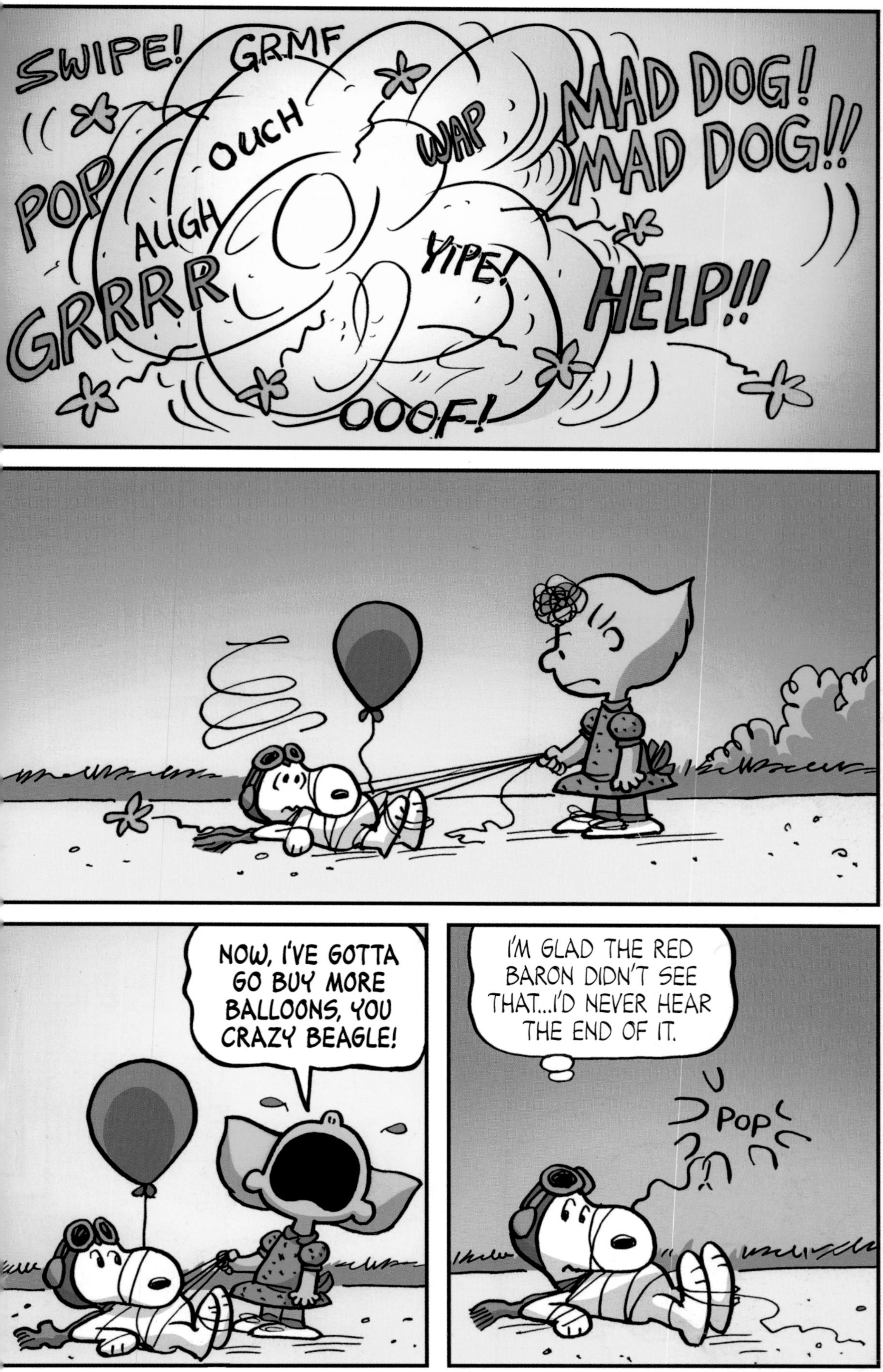
SWIPE!
GRMF
MAD DOG! MAD DOG!!
POP
OUCH
WAP
ALIGH
GRRRR
YIPE!
HELP!!
OOOF!
NOW, I'VE GOTTA GO BUY MORE BALLOONS, YOU CRAZY BEAGLE!
I'M GLAD THE RED BARON DIDN'T SEE THAT...I'D NEVER HEAR THE END OF IT.
POP

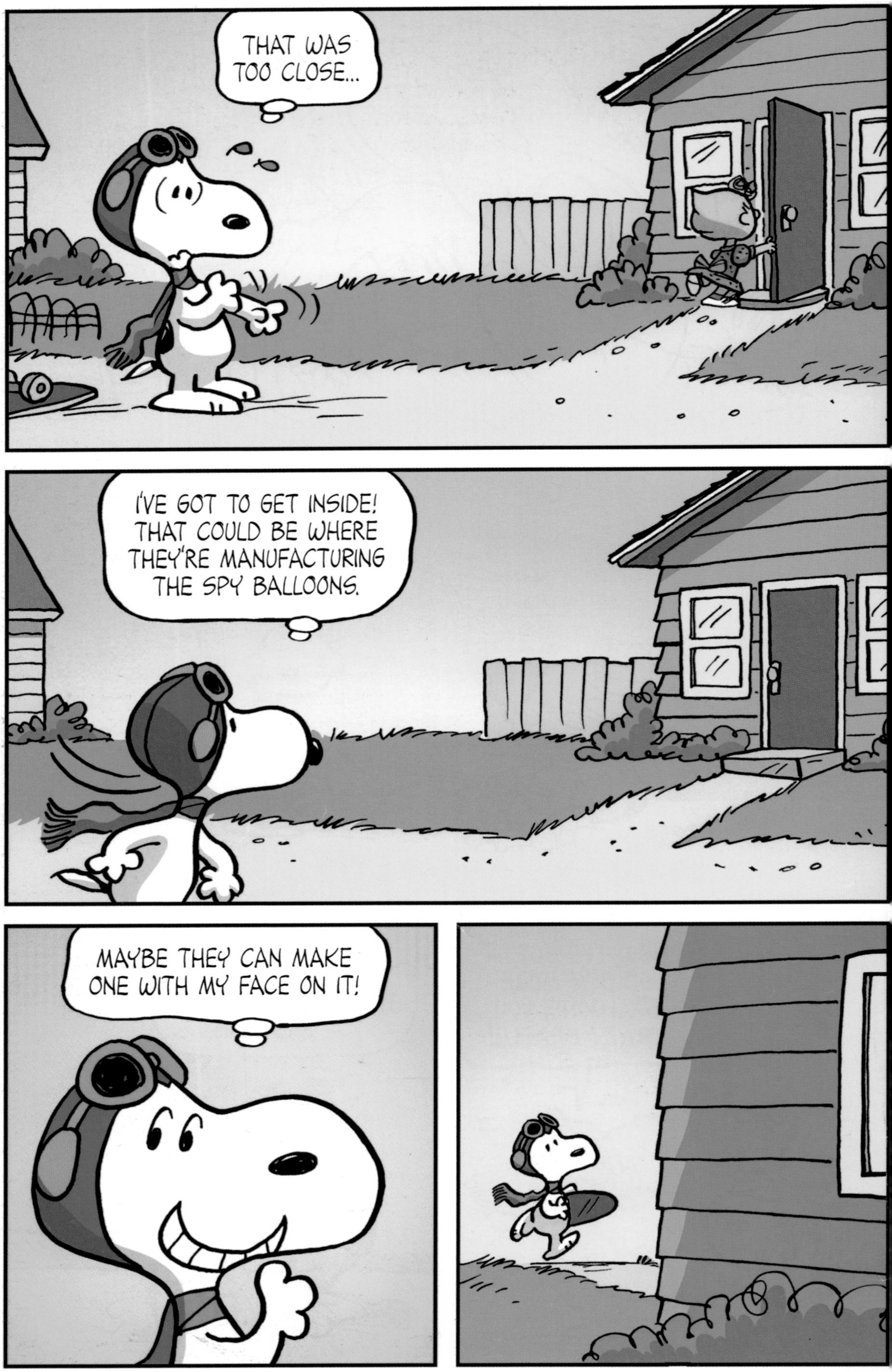
THAT WAS TOO CLOSE...
I'VE GOT TO GET INSIDE! THAT COULD BE WHERE THEY'RE MANUFACTURING THE SPY BALLOONS.
MAYBE THEY CAN MAKE ONE WITH MY FACE ON IT!

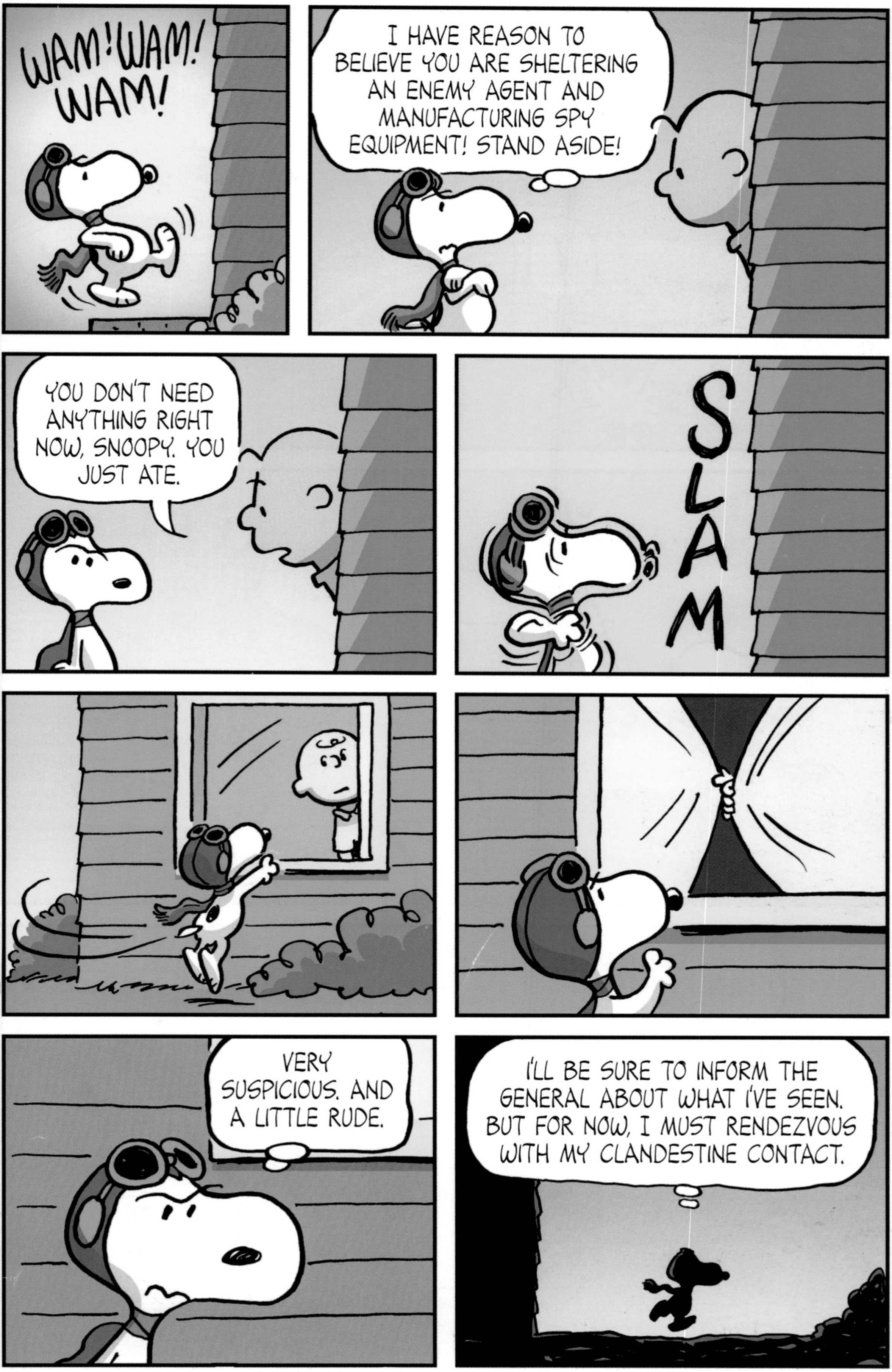
WAM! WAM! WAM!
I HAVE REASON TO BELIEVE YOU ARE SHELTERING AN ENEMY AGENT AND MANUFACTURING SPY EQUIPMENT! STAND ASIDE!
YOU DON'T NEED ANYTHING RIGHT NOW, SNOOPY. YOU JUST ATE.
SLAM
VERY SUSPICIOUS. AND A LITTLE RUDE.
I'LL BE SURE TO INFORM THE GENERAL ABOUT WHAT I'VE SEEN. BUT FOR NOW, I MUST RENDEZVOUS WITH MY CLANDESTINE CONTACT.

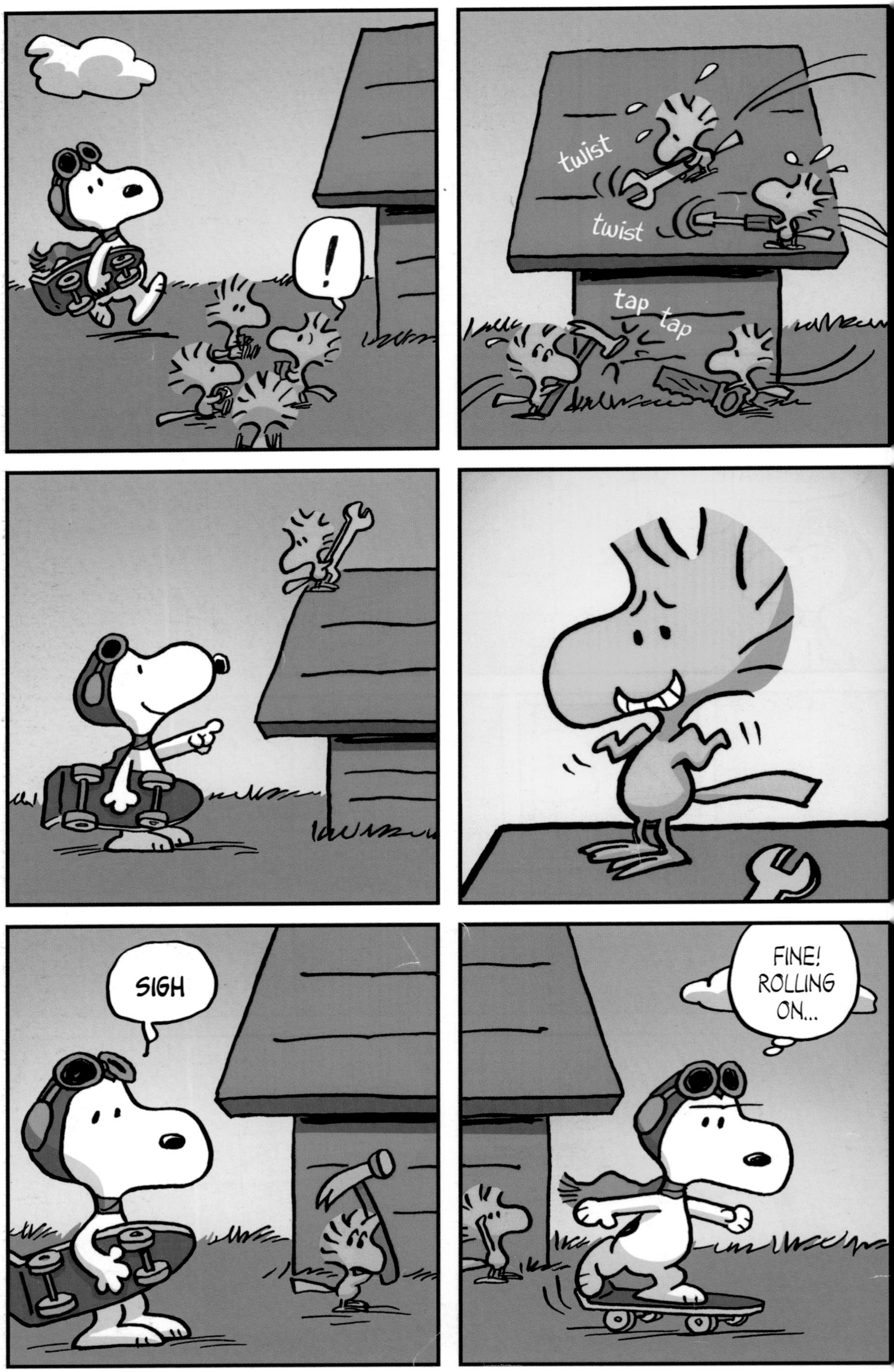
!
twist
twist
tap
tap
SIGH
FINE! ROLLING ON...

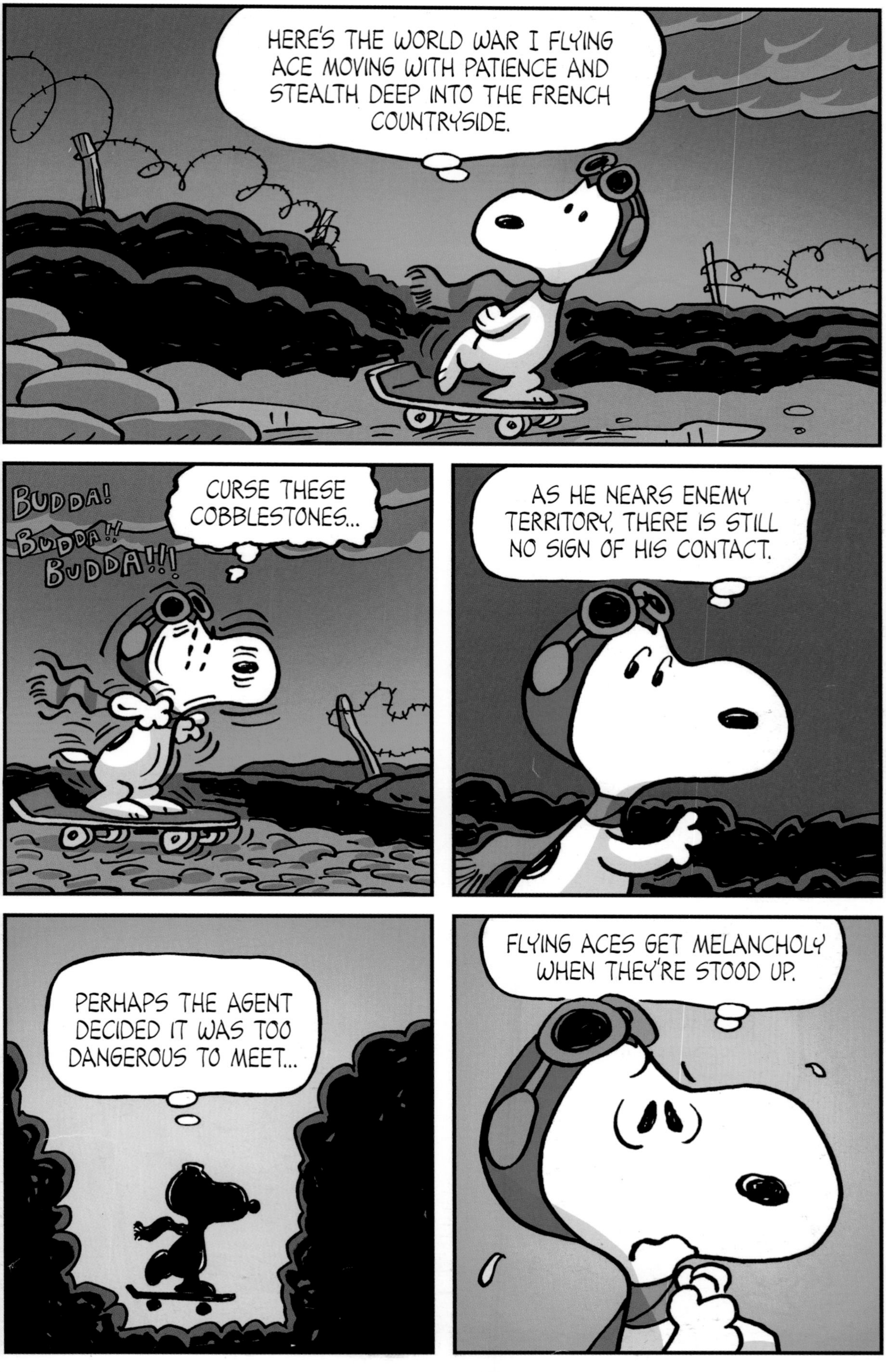
HERE'S THE WORLD WAR I FLYING ACE MOVING WITH PATIENCE AND STEALTH DEEP INTO THE FRENCH COUNTRYSIDE.
BUDDA! BUDDA!! BUDDA!!!
CURSE THESE COBBLESTONES...
AS HE NEARS ENEMY TERRITORY, THERE IS STILL NO SIGN OF HIS CONTACT.
PERHAPS THE AGENT DECIDED IT WAS TOO DANGEROUS TO MEET...
FLYING ACES GET MELANCHOLY WHEN THEY'RE STOOD UP.

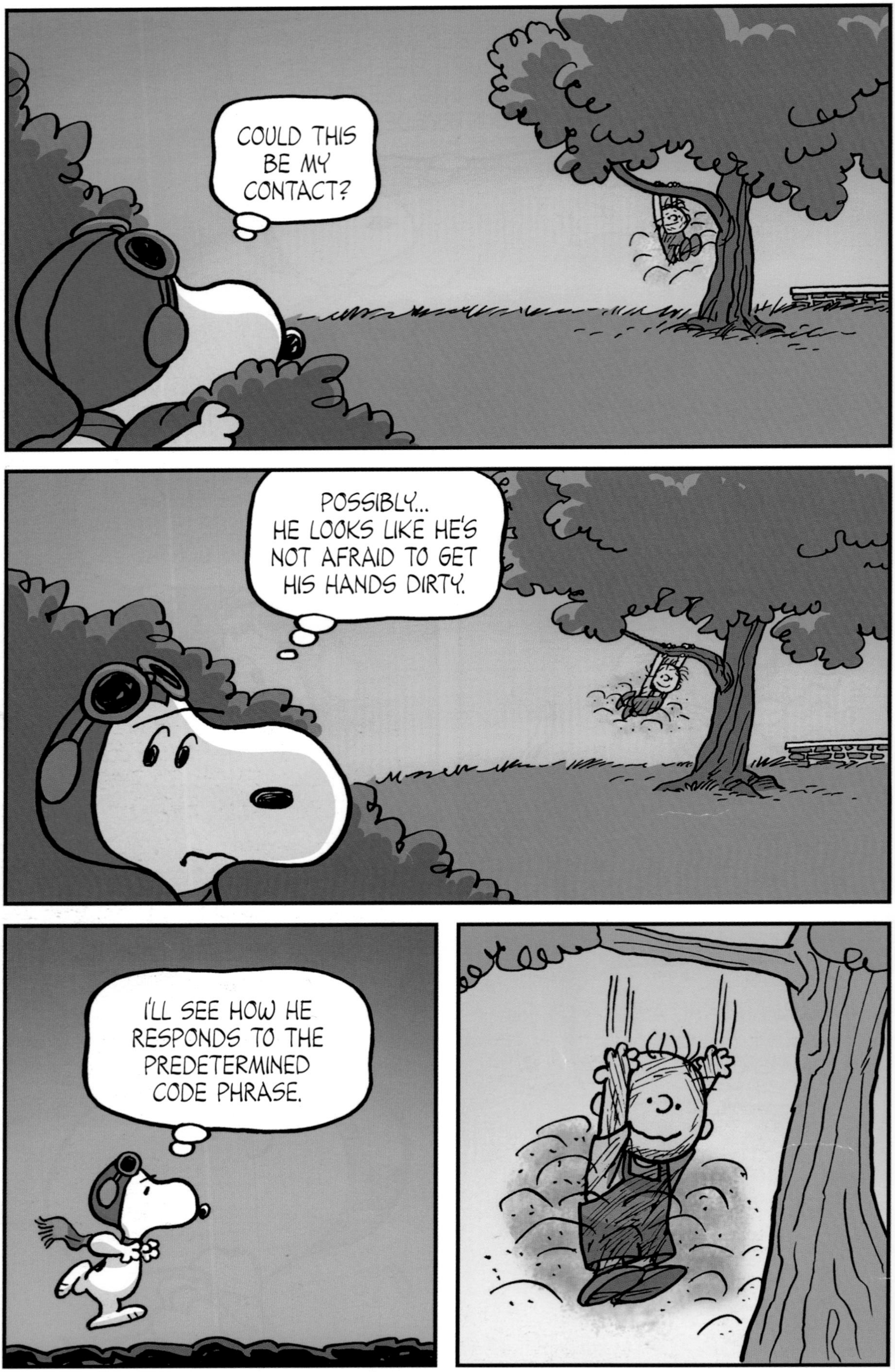
COULD THIS BE MY CONTACT?
POSSIBLY... HE LOOKS LIKE HE'S NOT AFRAID TO GET HIS HANDS DIRTY.
I'LL SEE HOW HE RESPONDS TO THE PREDETERMINED CODE PHRASE.

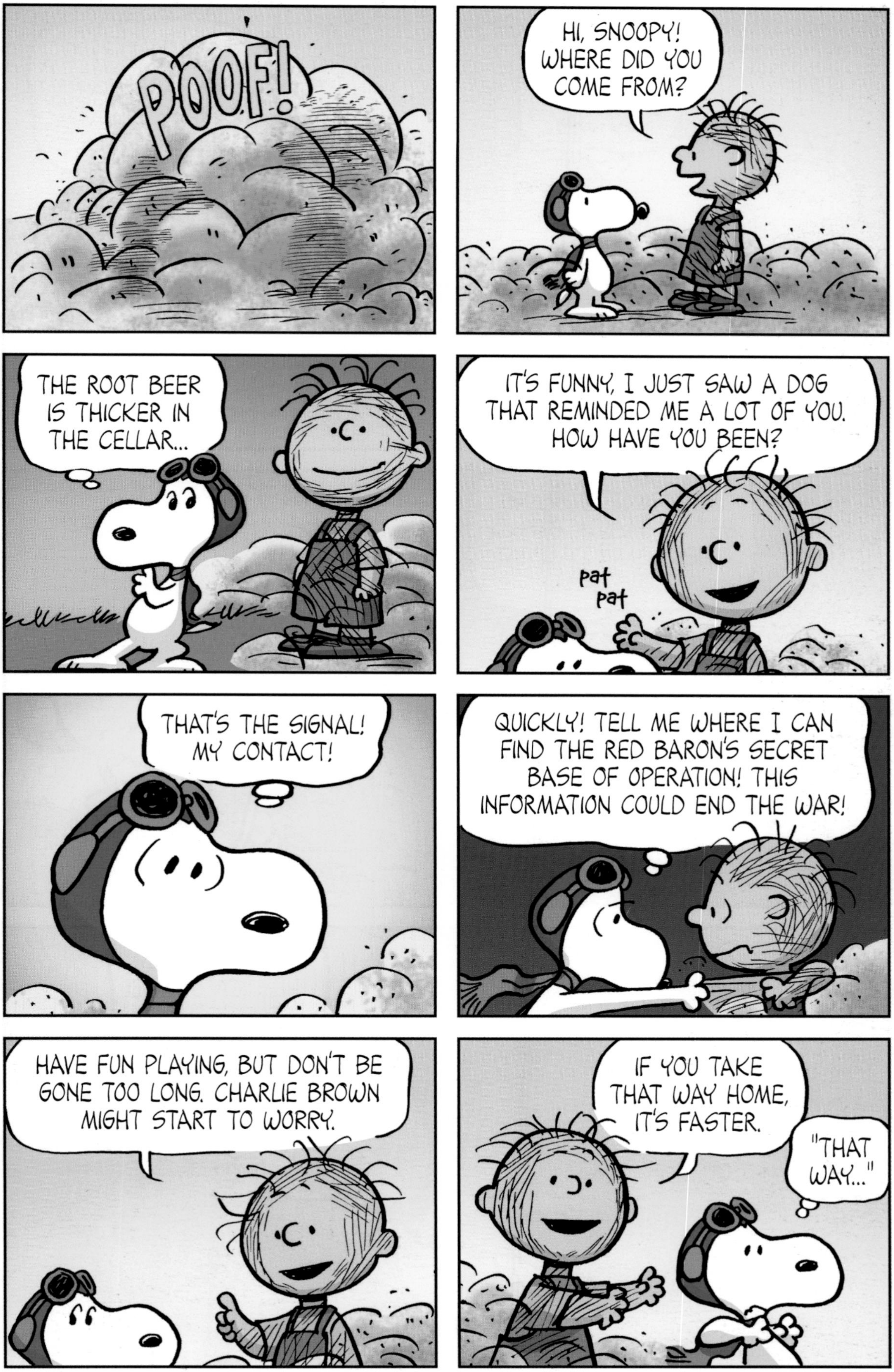
POOF!
HI, SNOOPY! WHERE DID YOU COME FROM?
THE ROOT BEER IS THICKER IN THE CELLAR...
IT'S FUNNY, I JUST SAW A DOG THAT REMINDED ME A LOT OF YOU. HOW HAVE YOU BEEN?
pat pat
THAT'S THE SIGNAL! MY CONTACT!
QUICKLY! TELL ME WHERE I CAN FIND THE RED BARON'S SECRET BASE OF OPERATION! THIS INFORMATION COULD END THE WAR!
HAVE FUN PLAYING, BUT DON'T BE GONE TOO LONG. CHARLIE BROWN MIGHT START TO WORRY.
IF YOU TAKE THAT WAY HOME, IT'S FASTER.
"THAT WAY..."

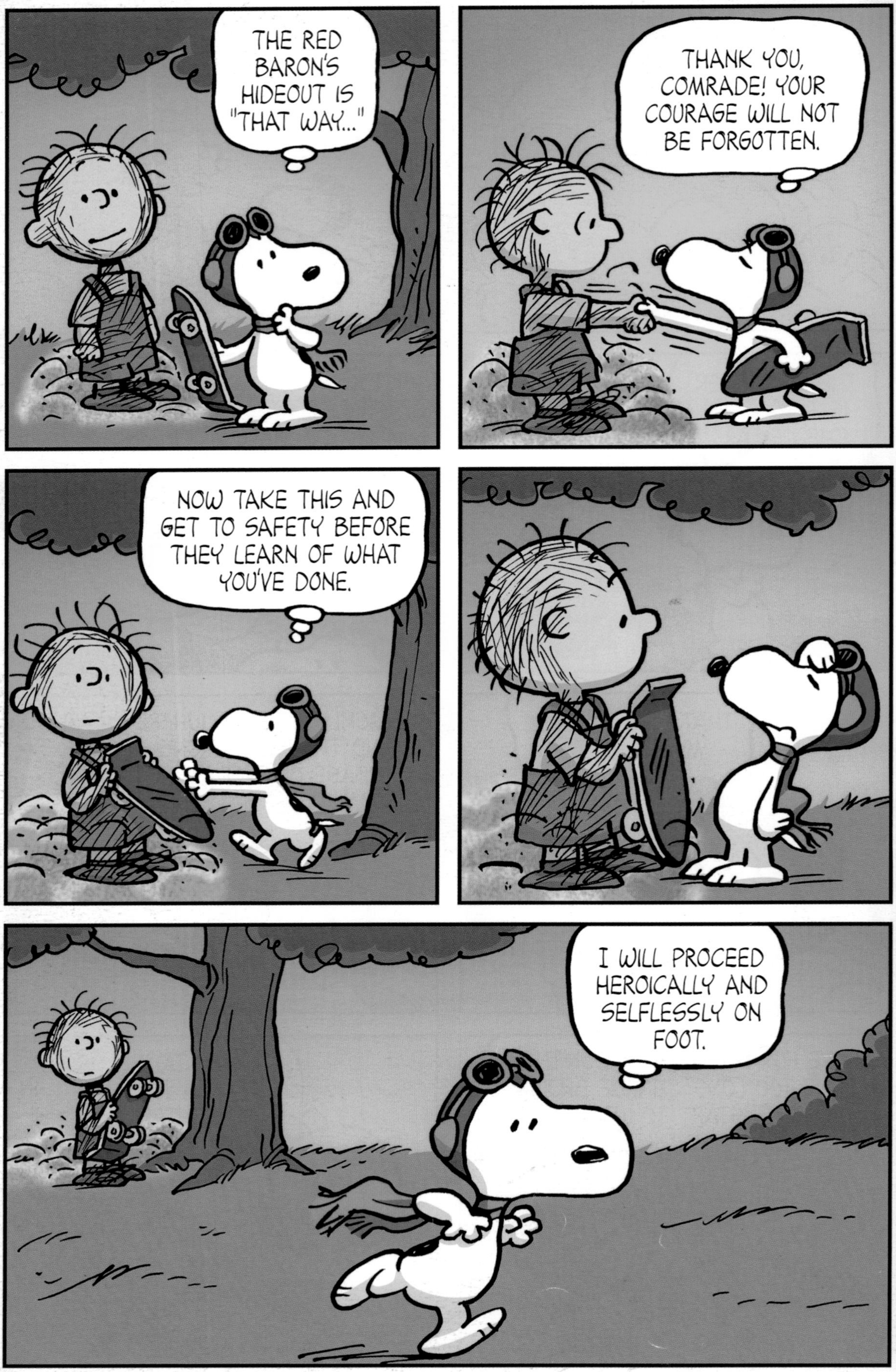
THE RED BARON'S HIDEOUT IS "THAT WAY..."
THANK YOU, COMRADE! YOUR COURAGE WILL NOT BE FORGOTTEN.
NOW TAKE THIS AND GET TO SAFETY BEFORE THEY LEARN OF WHAT YOU'VE DONE.
I WILL PROCEED HEROICALLY AND SELFLESSLY ON FOOT.

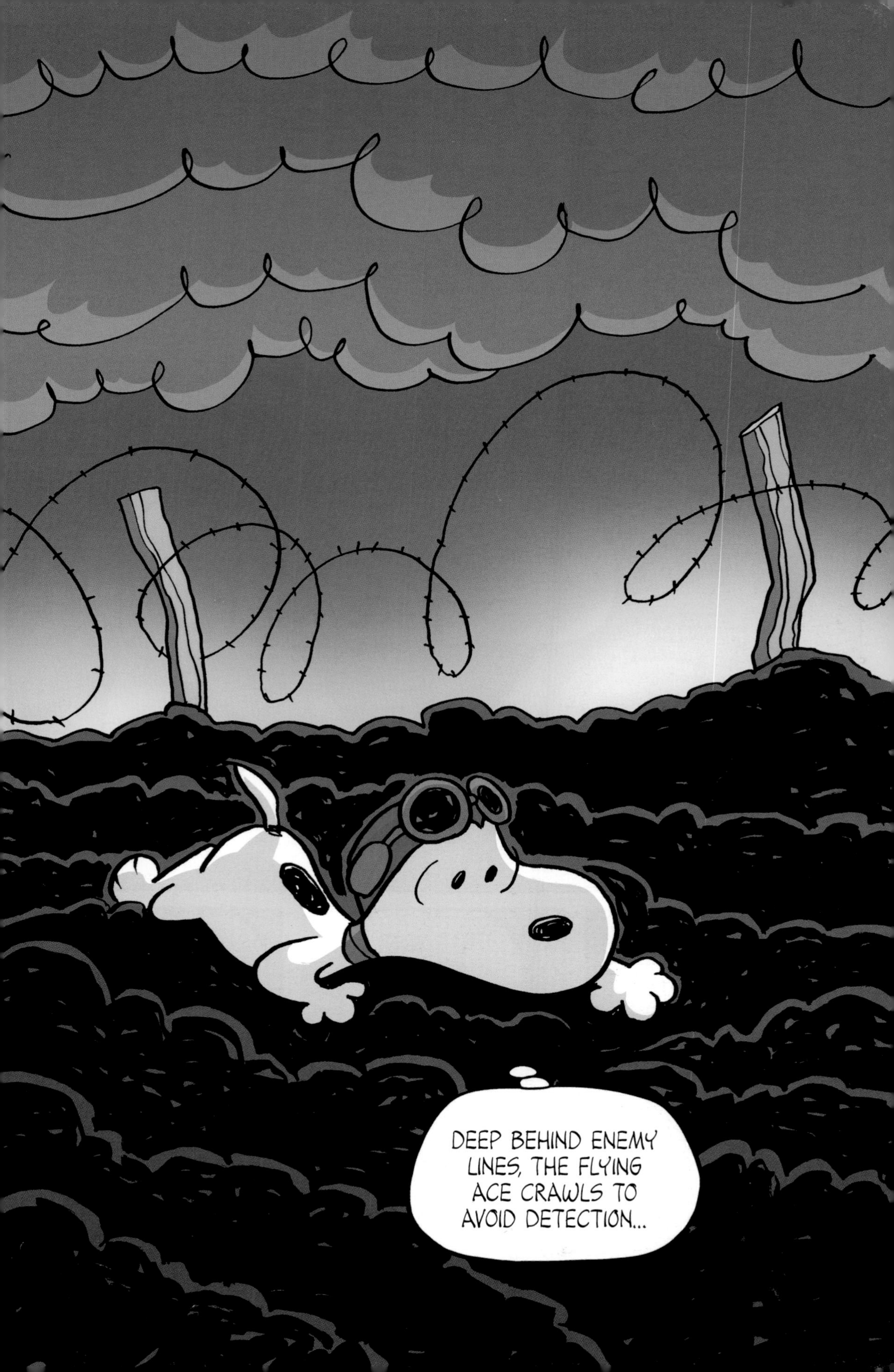
DEEP BEHIND ENEMY LINES, THE FLYING ACE CRAWLS TO AVOID DETECTION...

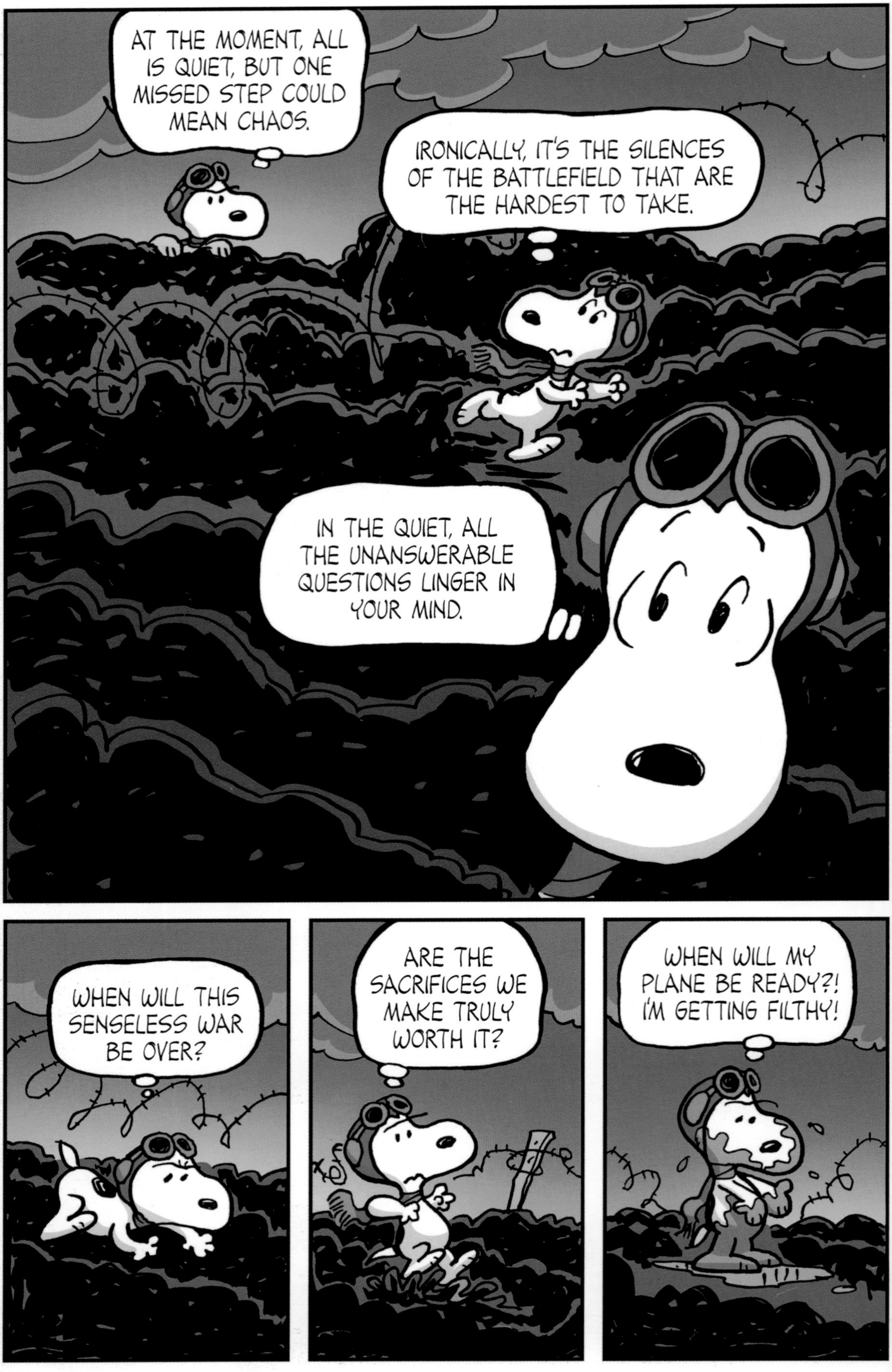
AT THE MOMENT, ALL IS QUIET, BUT ONE MISSED STEP COULD MEAN CHAOS.
IRONICALLY, IT'S THE SILENCES OF THE BATTLEFIELD THAT ARE THE HARDEST TO TAKE.
IN THE QUIET, ALL THE UNANSWERABLE QUESTIONS LINGER IN YOUR MIND.
WHEN WILL THIS SENSELESS WAR BE OVER?
ARE THE SACRIFICES WE MAKE TRULY WORTH IT?
WHEN WILL MY PLANE BE READY?! I'M GETTING FILTHY!

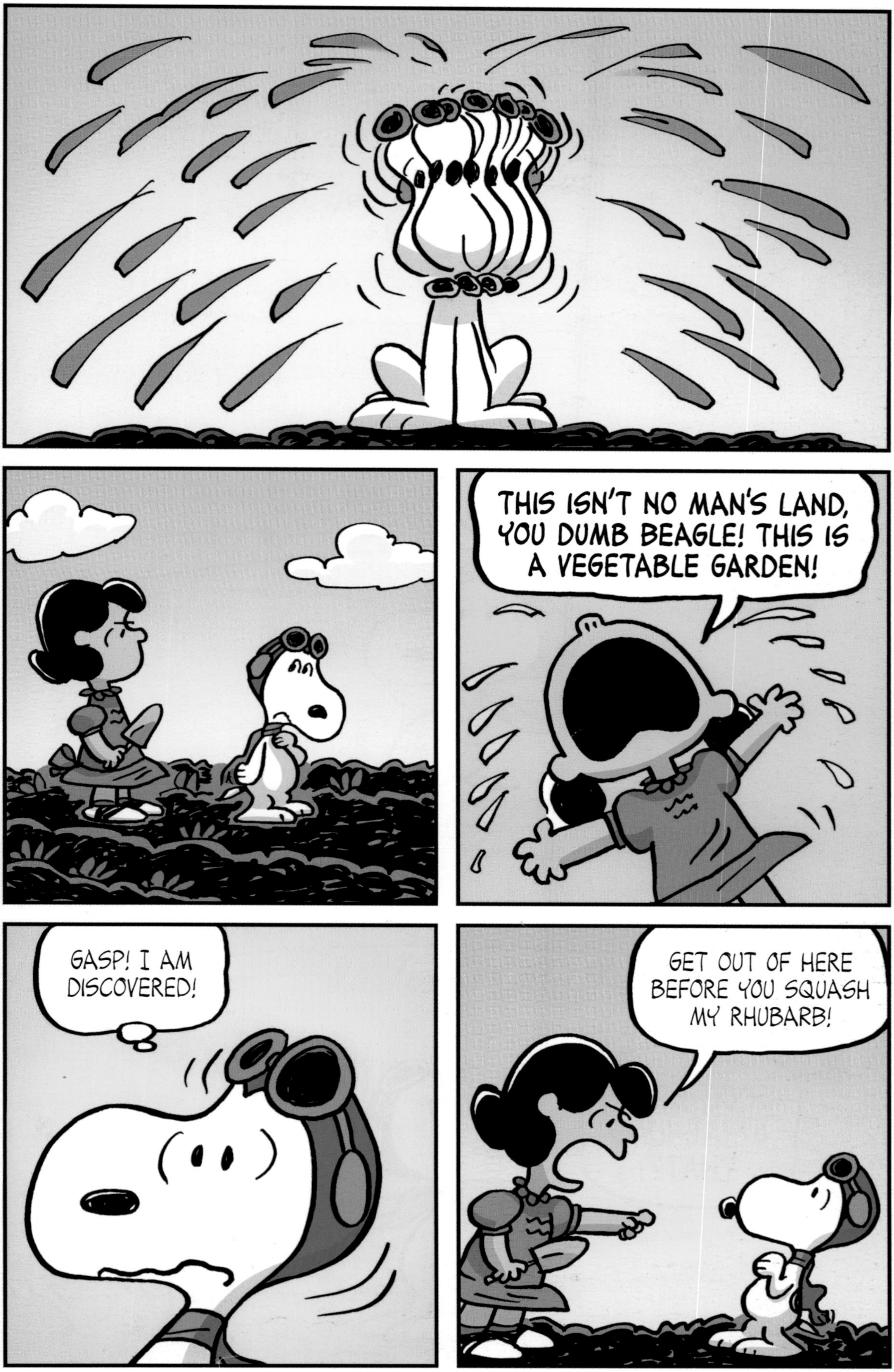
THIS ISN'T NO MAN'S LAND, YOU DUMB BEAGLE! THIS IS A VEGETABLE GARDEN!
GASP! I AM DISCOVERED!
GET OUT OF HERE BEFORE YOU SQUASH MY RHUBARB!

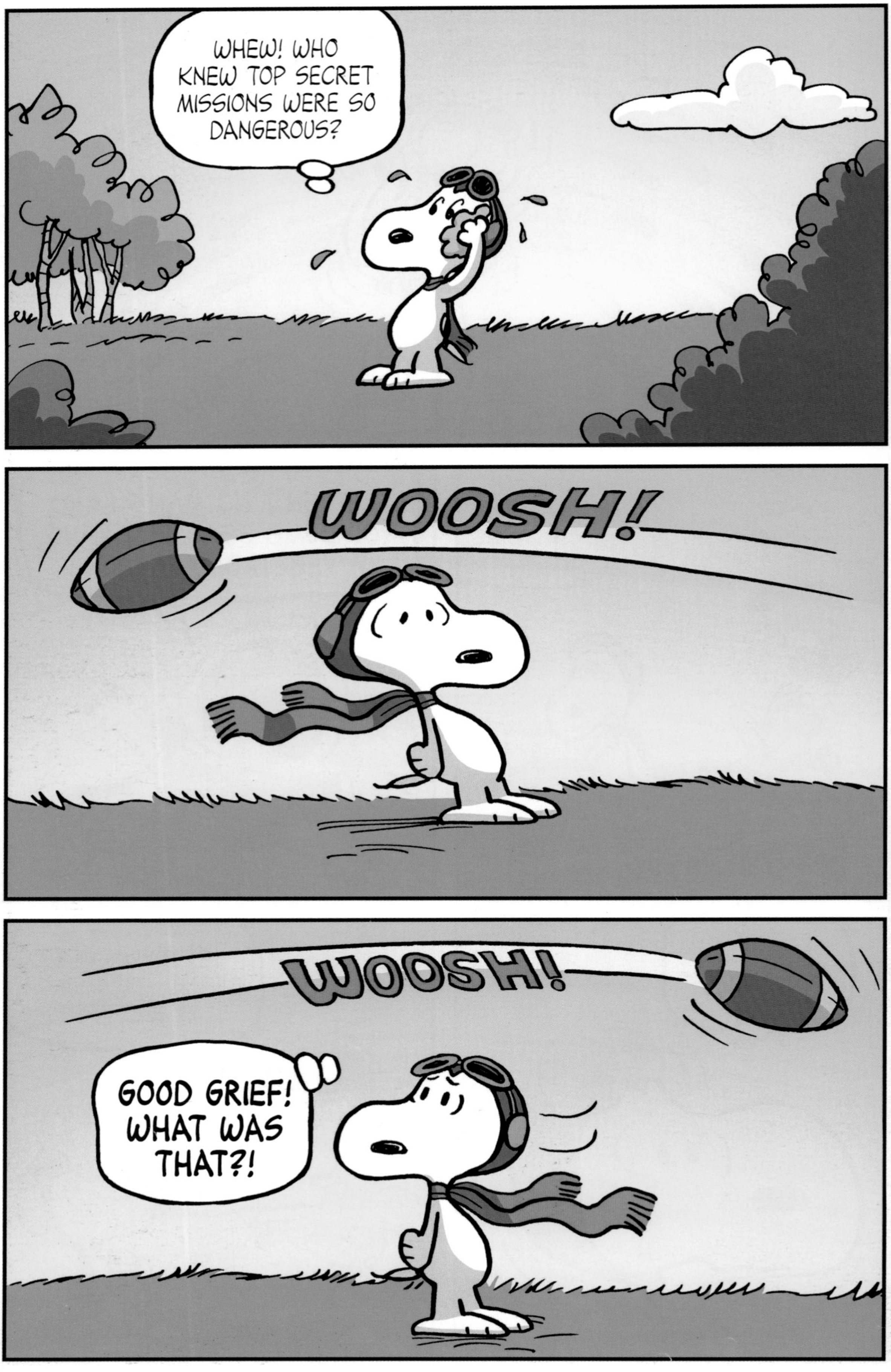
WHEW! WHO KNEW TOP SECRET MISSIONS WERE SO DANGEROUS?
WOOSH!
WOOSH!
GOOD GRIEF! WHAT WAS THAT?!

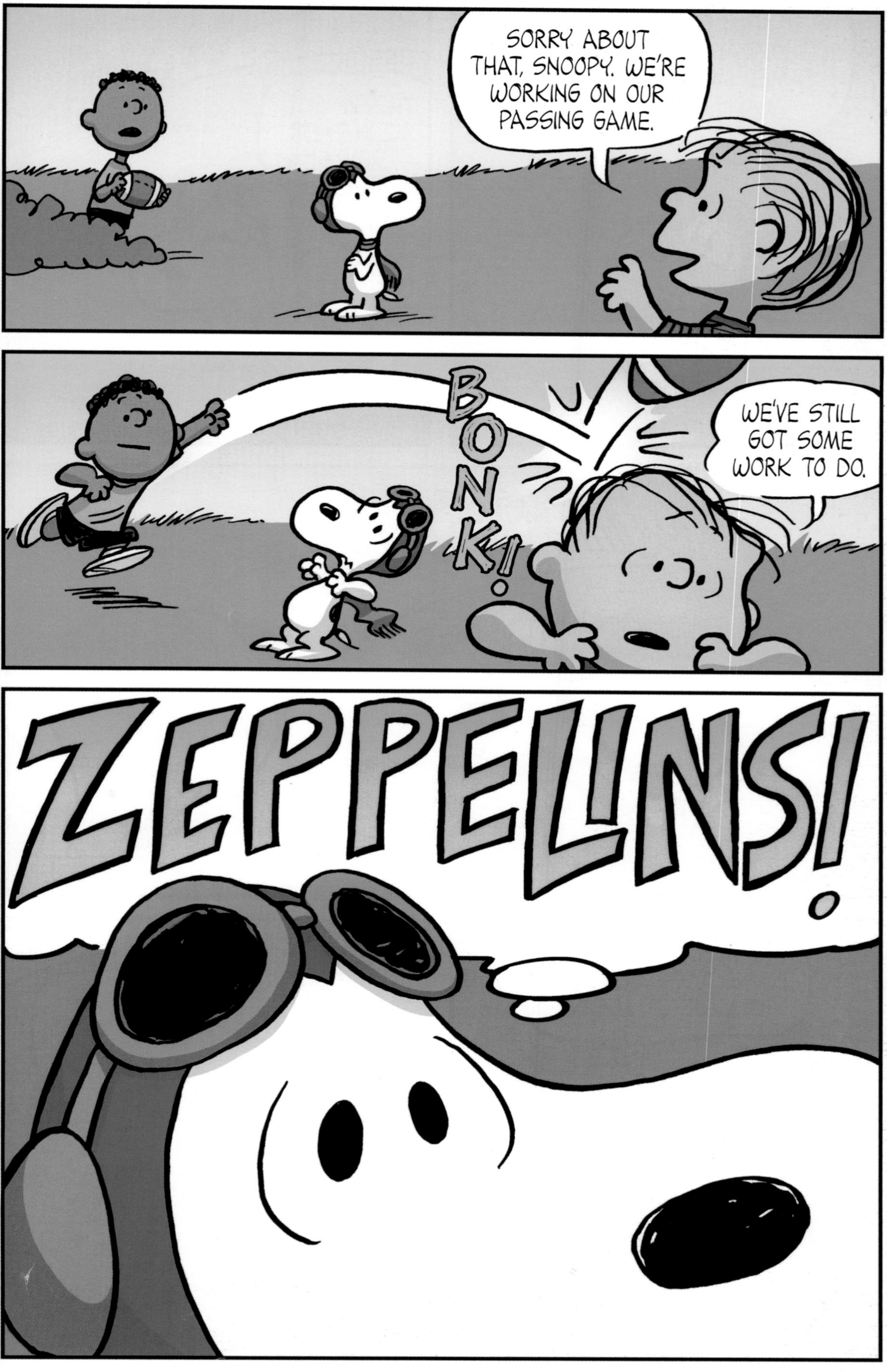
SORRY ABOUT THAT, SNOOPY. WE'RE WORKING ON OUR PASSING GAME.
BONK!
WE'VE STILL GOT SOME WORK TO DO.
ZEPPELINS!

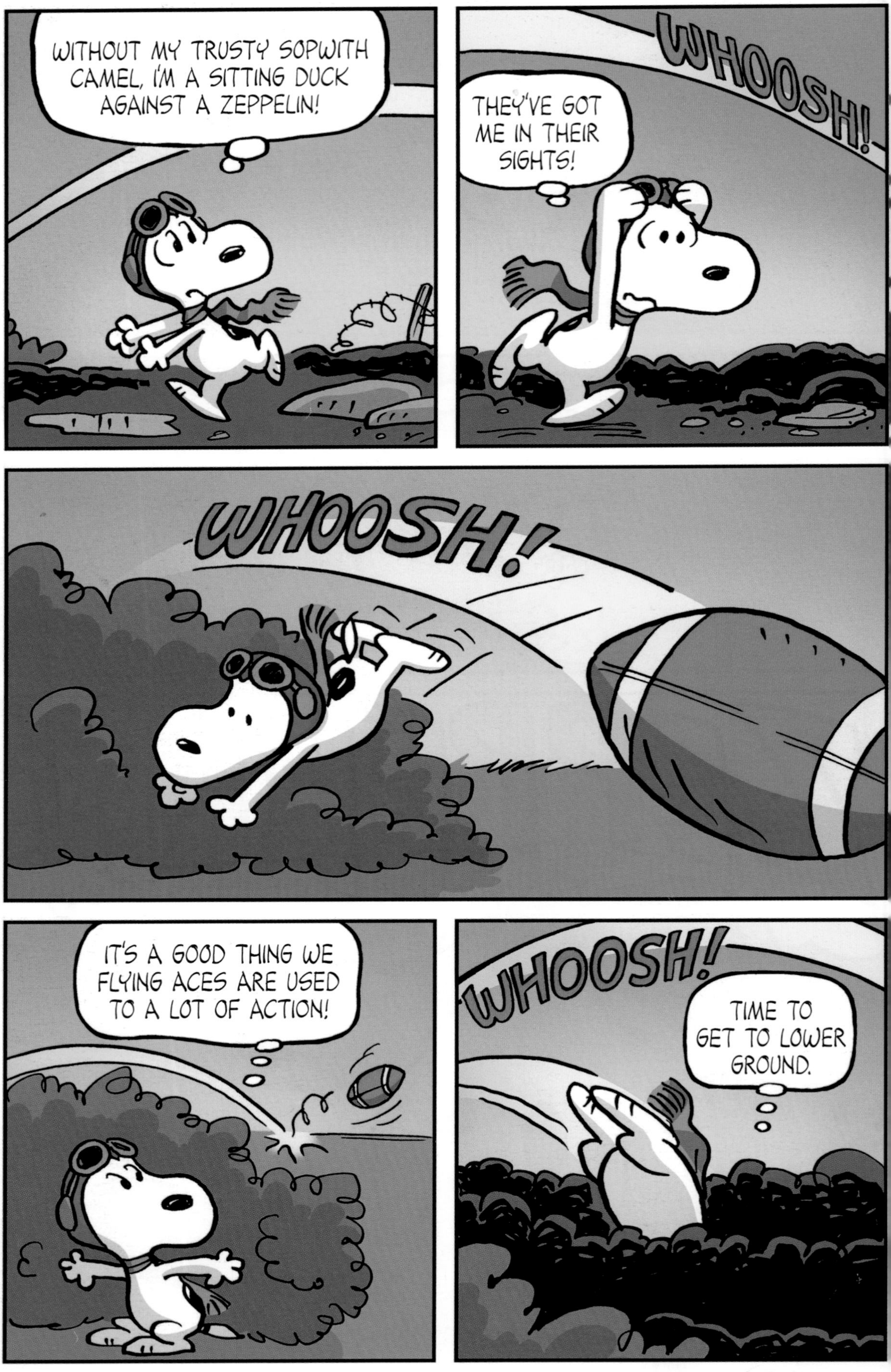
WITHOUT MY TRUSTY SOPWITH CAMEL, I'M A SITTING DUCK AGAINST A ZEPPELIN!
WHOOSH!
THEY'VE GOT ME IN THEIR SIGHTS!
WHOOSH!
IT'S A GOOD THING WE FLYING ACES ARE USED TO A LOT OF ACTION!
WHOOSH!
TIME TO GET TO LOWER GROUND.

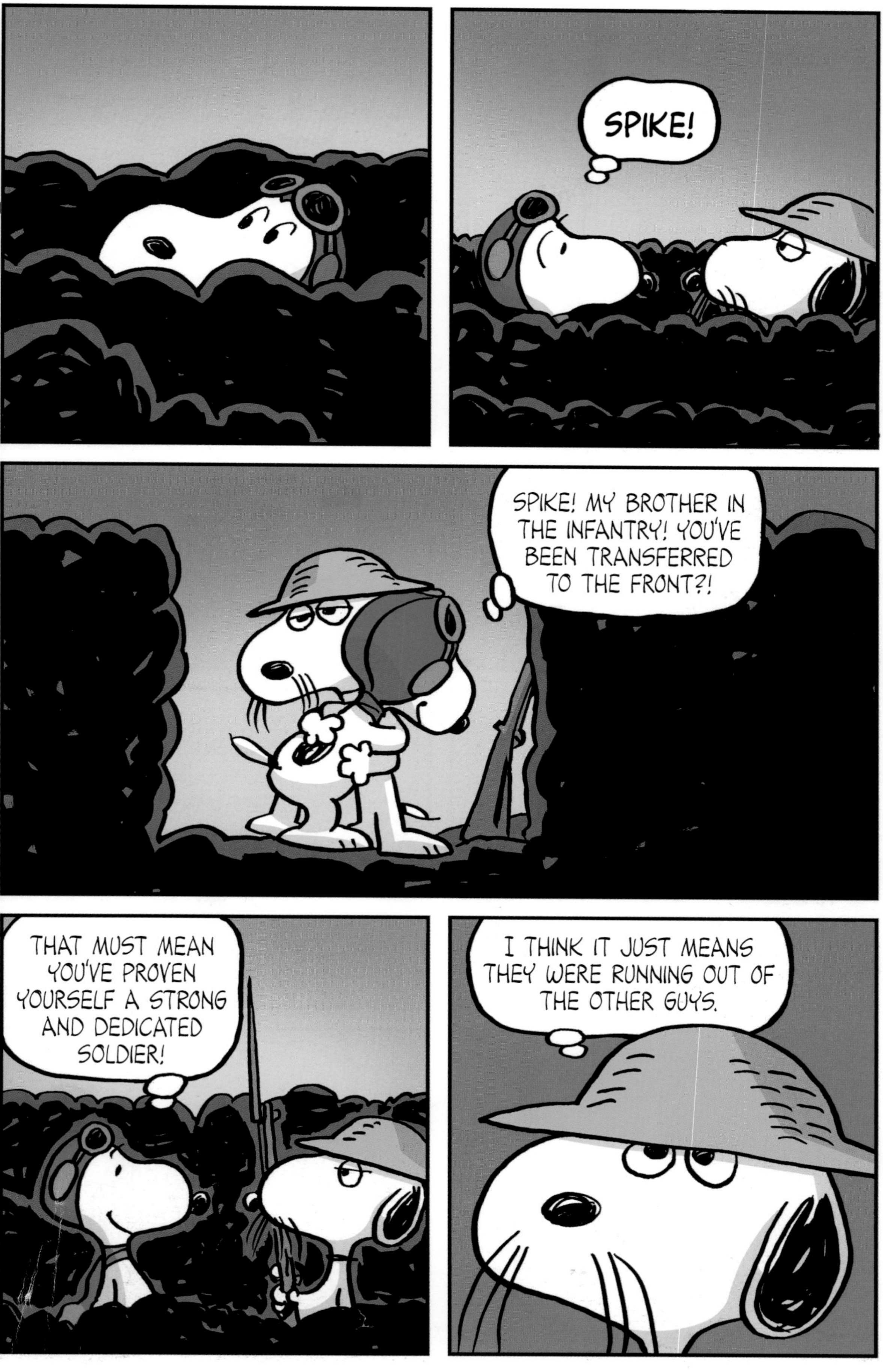
SPIKE!
SPIKE! MY BROTHER IN THE INFANTRY! YOU'VE BEEN TRANSFERRED TO THE FRONT?!
THAT MUST MEAN YOU'VE PROVEN YOURSELF A STRONG AND DEDICATED SOLDIER!
I THINK IT JUST MEANS THEY WERE RUNNING OUT OF THE OTHER GUYS.

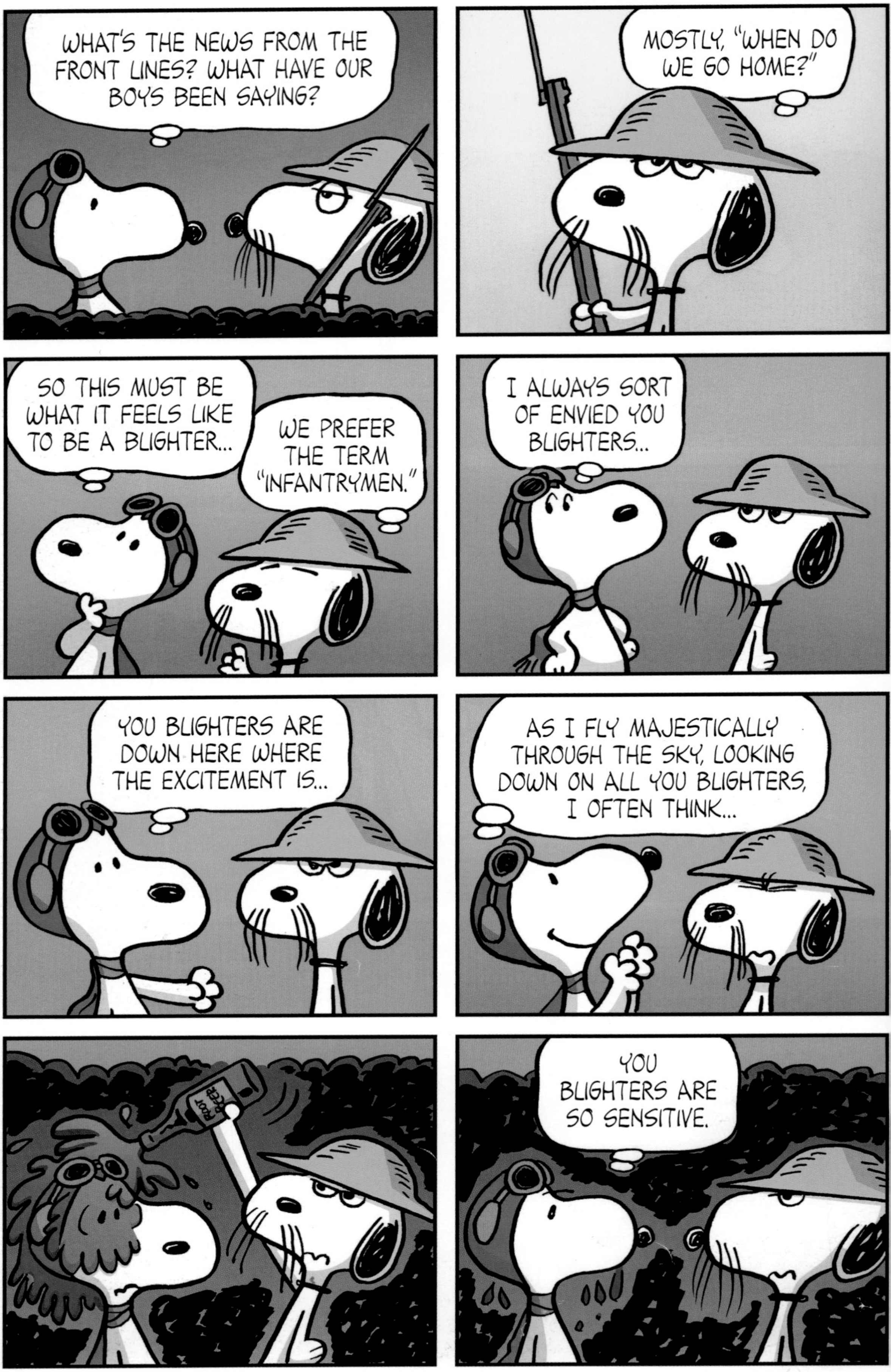
WHAT'S THE NEWS FROM THE FRONT LINES? WHAT HAVE OUR BOYS BEEN SAYING?
MOSTLY, "WHEN DO WE GO HOME?"
SO THIS MUST BE WHAT IT FEELS LIKE TO BE A BLIGHTER...
WE PREFER THE TERM "INFANTRYMEN."
I ALWAYS SORT OF ENVIED YOU BLIGHTERS...
YOU BLIGHTERS ARE DOWN HERE WHERE THE EXCITEMENT IS...
AS I FLY MAJESTICALLY THROUGH THE SKY, LOOKING DOWN ON ALL YOU BLIGHTERS, I OFTEN THINK...
ROOT BEER
YOU BLIGHTERS ARE SO SENSITIVE.

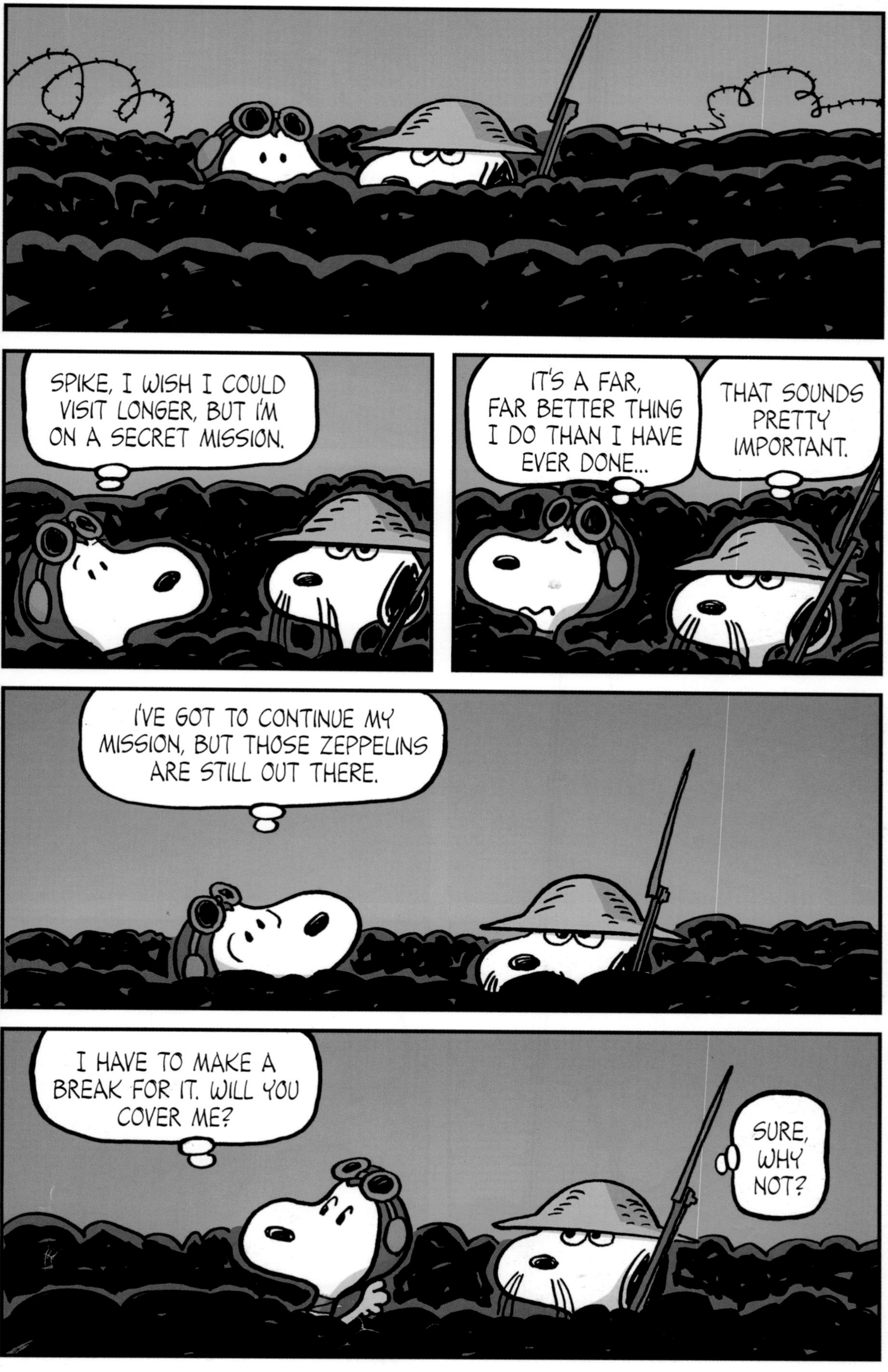
SPIKE, I WISH I COULD VISIT LONGER, BUT I'M ON A SECRET MISSION.
IT'S A FAR, FAR BETTER THING I DO THAN I HAVE EVER DONE...
THAT SOUNDS PRETTY IMPORTANT.
I'VE GOT TO CONTINUE MY MISSION, BUT THOSE ZEPPELINS ARE STILL OUT THERE.
I HAVE TO MAKE A BREAK FOR IT. WILL YOU COVER ME?
SURE, WHY NOT?

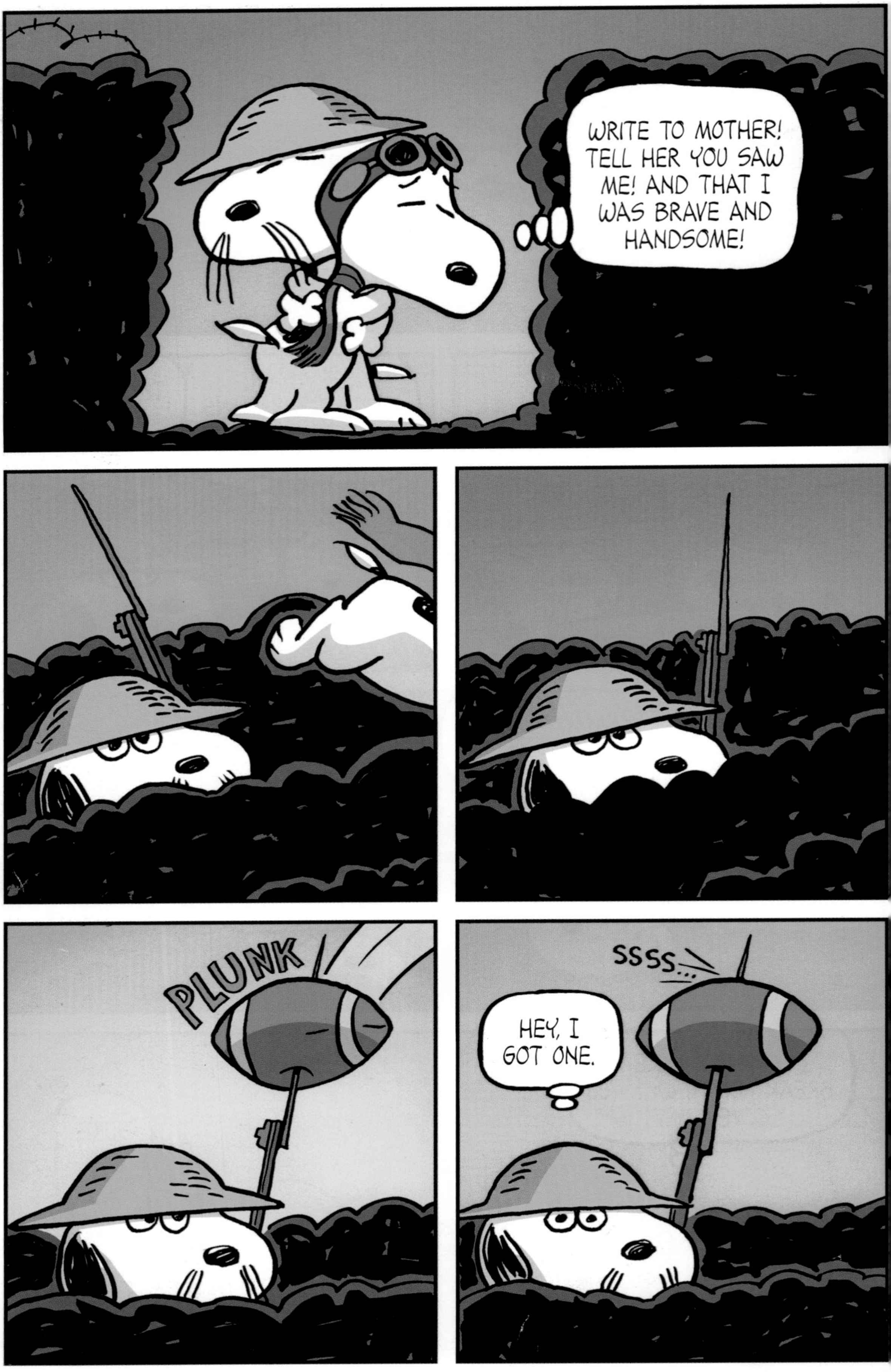
WRITE TO MOTHER! TELL HER YOU SAW ME! AND THAT I WAS BRAVE AND HANDSOME!
PLUNK
SSSS...
HEY, I GOT ONE.

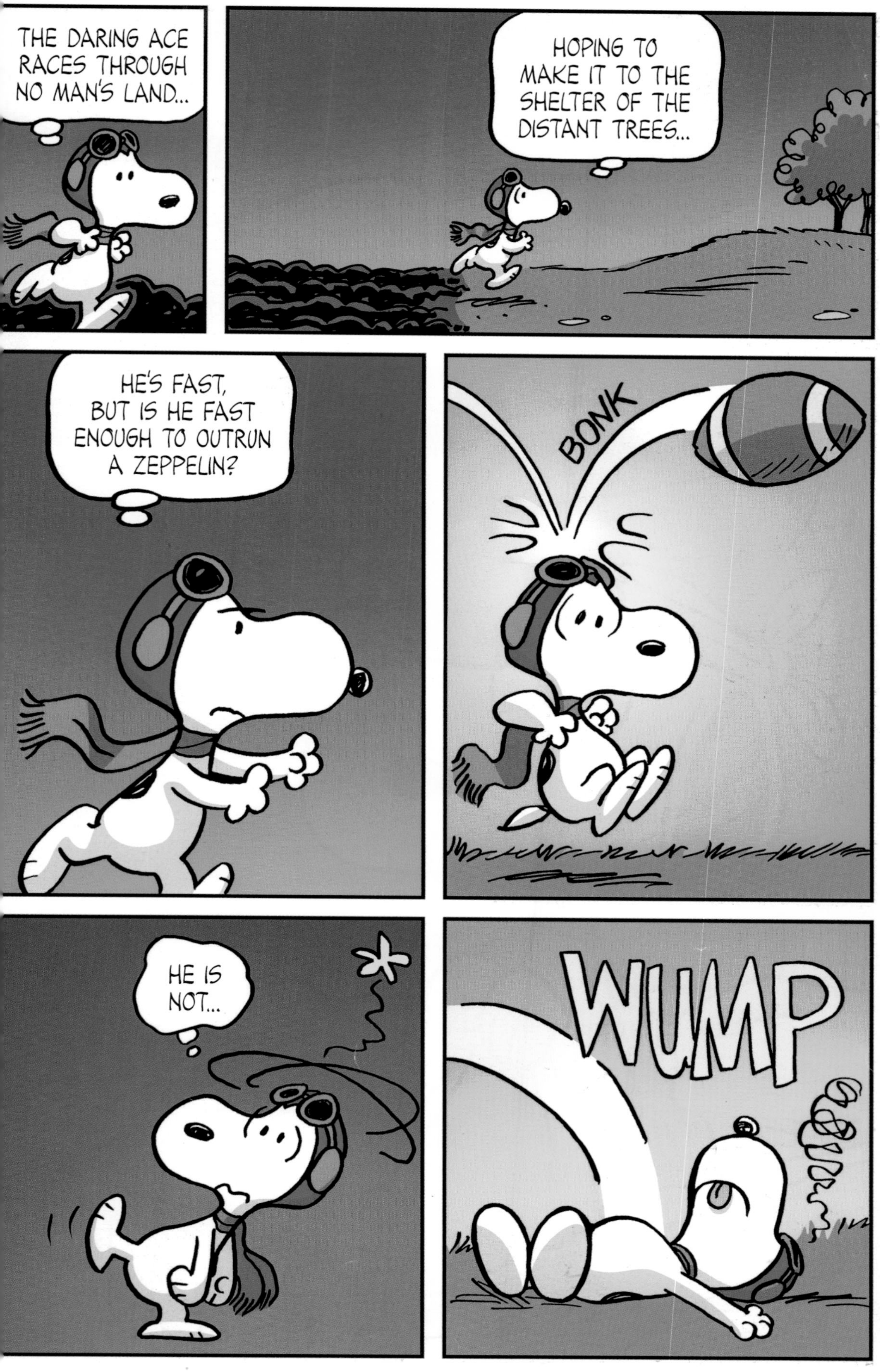
THE DARING ACE RACES THROUGH NO MAN'S LAND...
HOPING TO MAKE IT TO THE SHELTER OF THE DISTANT TREES...
HE'S FAST, BUT IS HE FAST ENOUGH TO OUTRUN A ZEPPELIN?
BONK
HE IS NOT...
WUMP

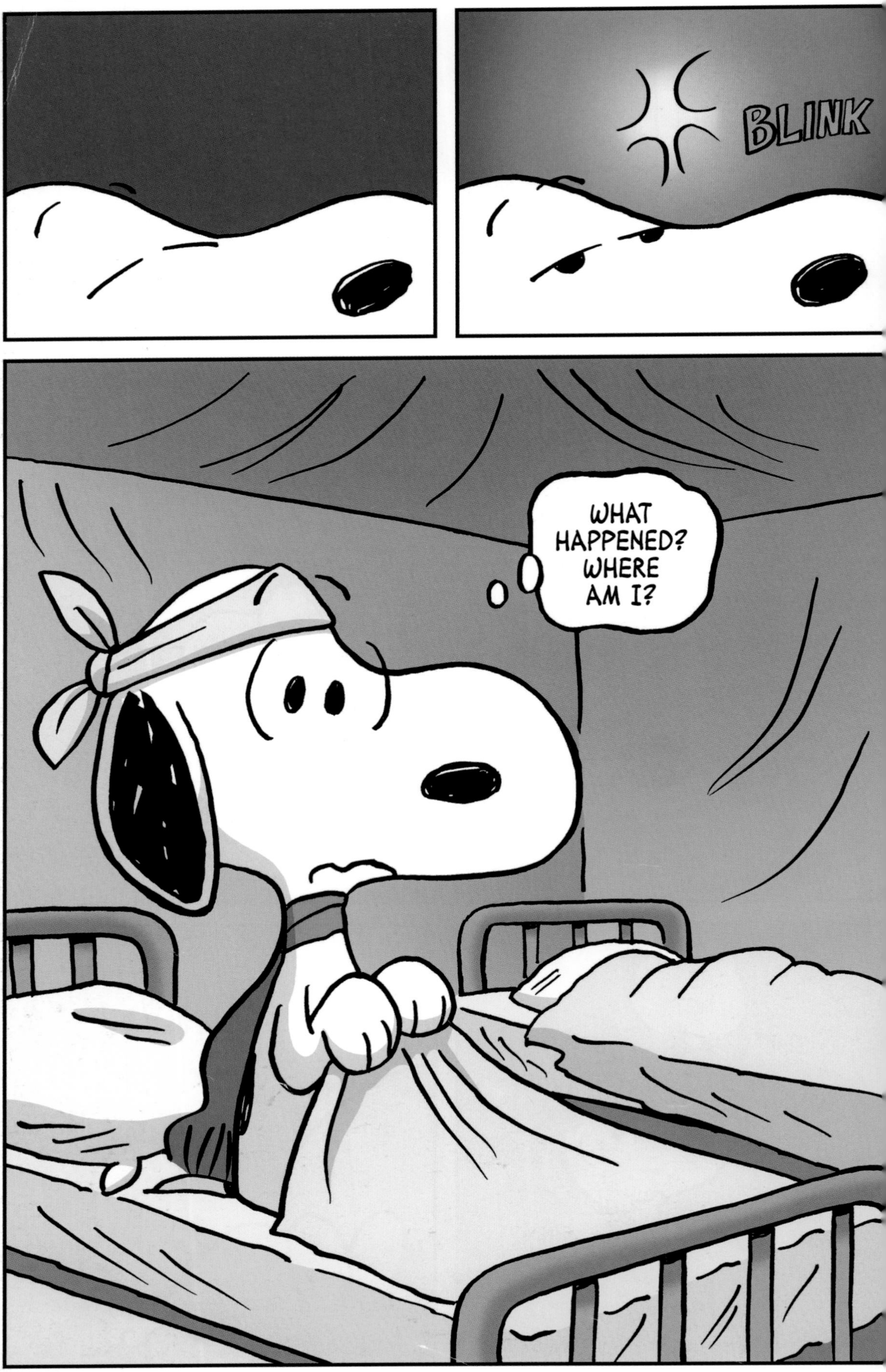
BLINK
WHAT HAPPENED? WHERE AM I?

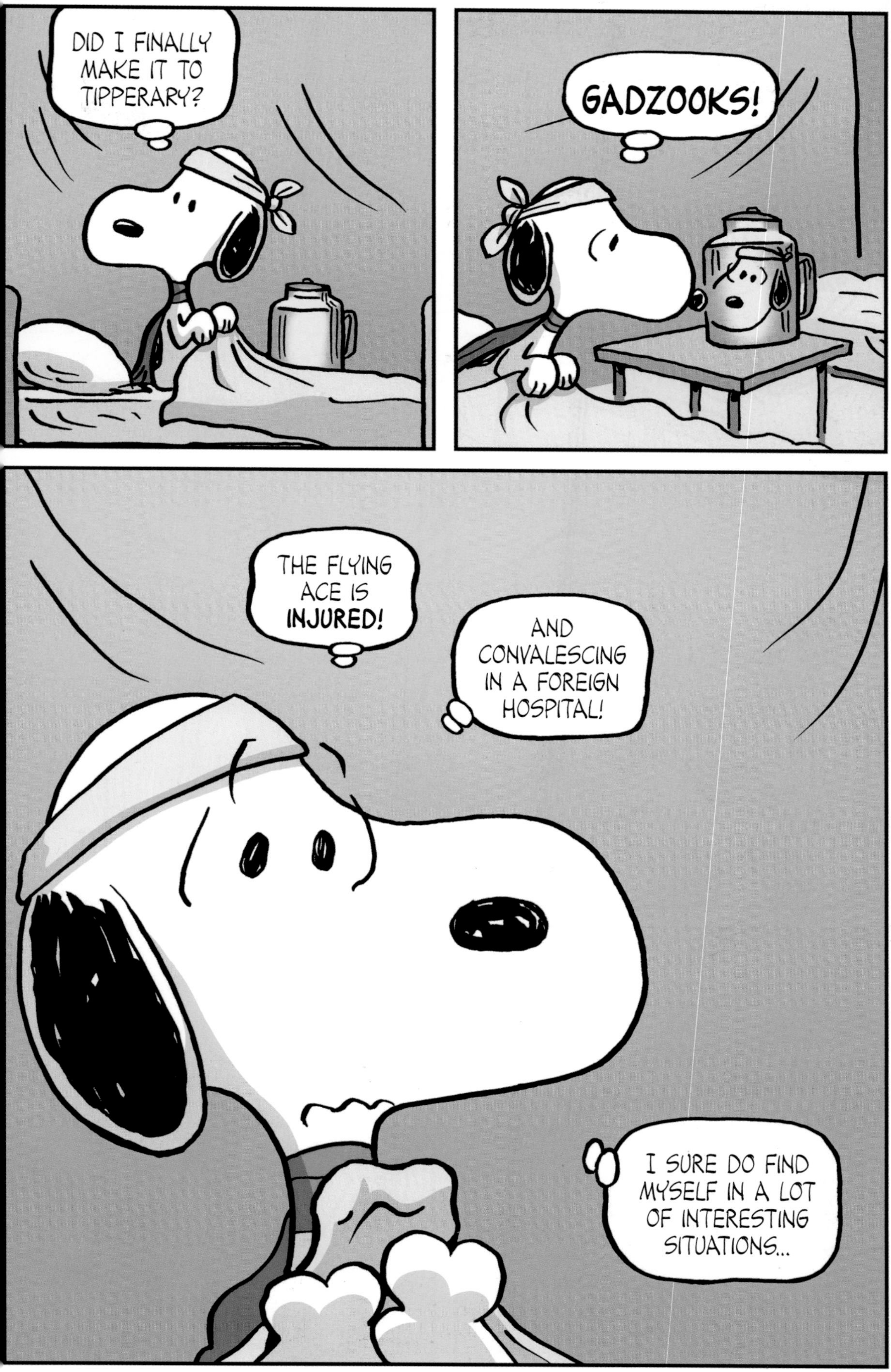
DID I FINALLY MAKE IT TO TIPPERARY?
GADZOOKS!
THE FLYING ACE IS **INJURED!**
AND CONVALESCING IN A FOREIGN HOSPITAL!
I SURE DO FIND MYSELF IN A LOT OF INTERESTING SITUATIONS...

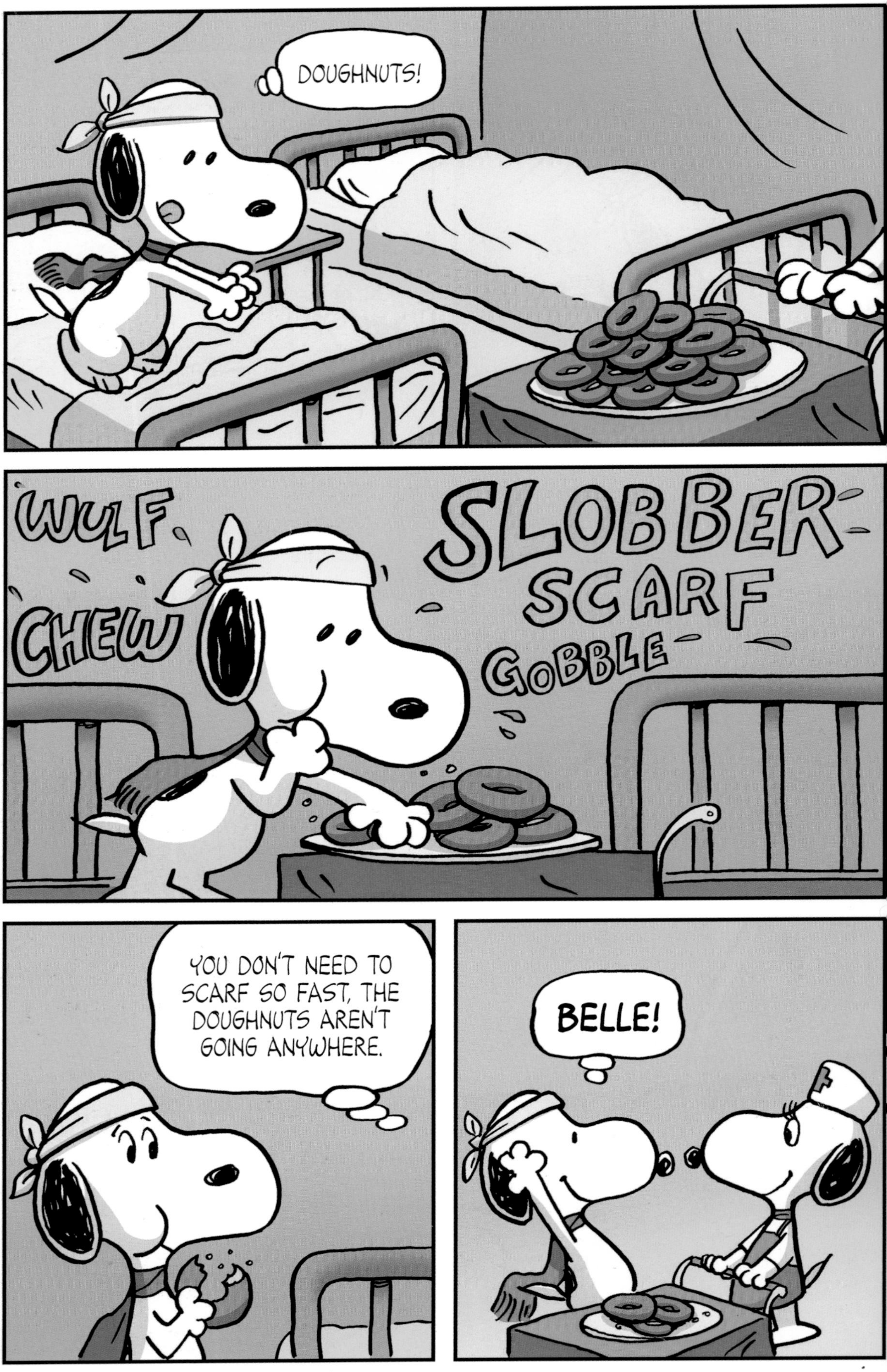
DOUGHNUTS!
WULF
CHEW
SLOBBER
SCARF
GOBBLE
YOU DON'T NEED TO SCARF SO FAST, THE DOUGHNUTS AREN'T GOING ANYWHERE.
BELLE!

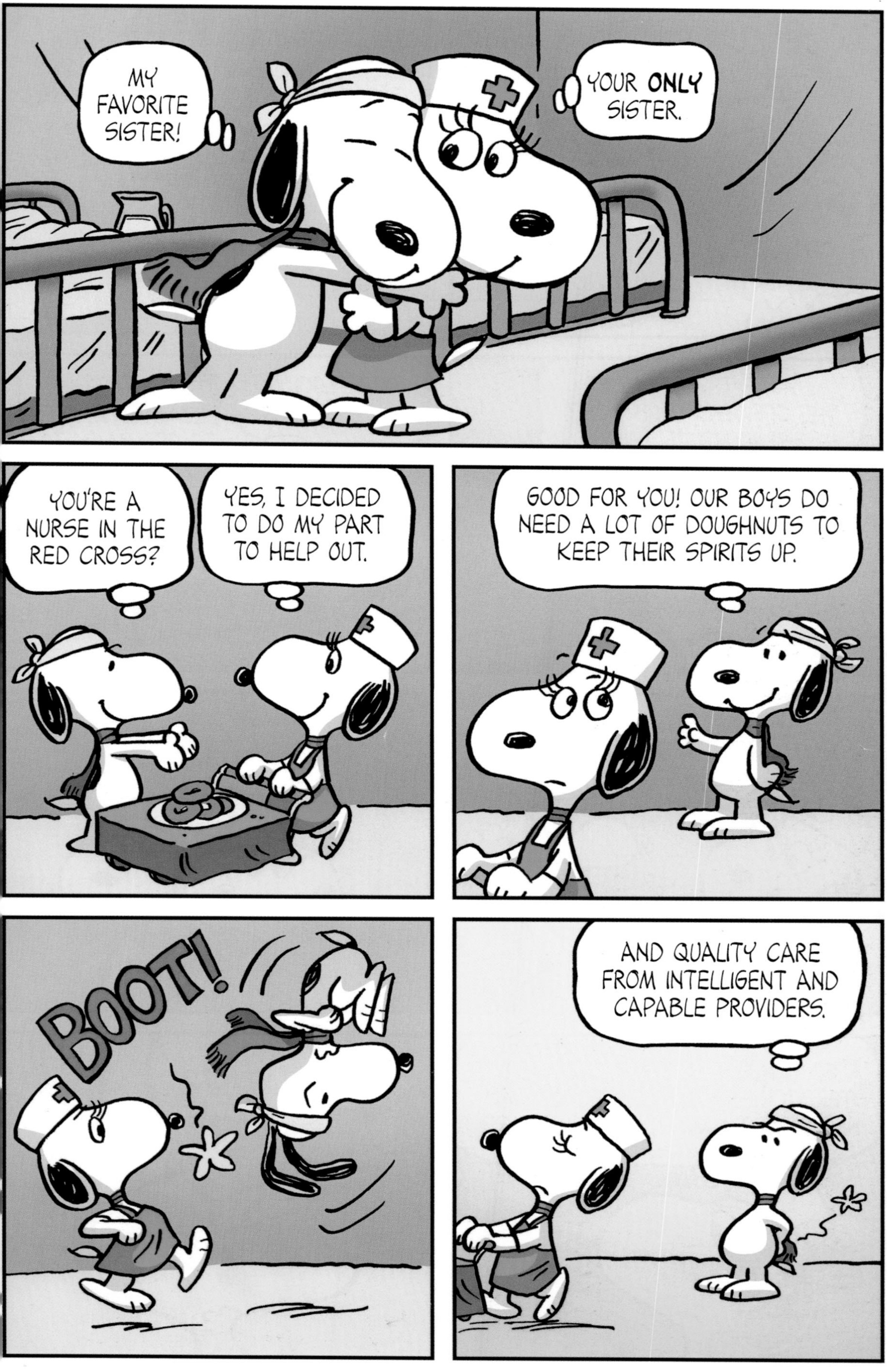
MY FAVORITE SISTER!
YOUR ONLY SISTER.
YOU'RE A NURSE IN THE RED CROSS?
YES, I DECIDED TO DO MY PART TO HELP OUT.
GOOD FOR YOU! OUR BOYS DO NEED A LOT OF DOUGHNUTS TO KEEP THEIR SPIRITS UP.
BOOT!
AND QUALITY CARE FROM INTELLIGENT AND CAPABLE PROVIDERS.

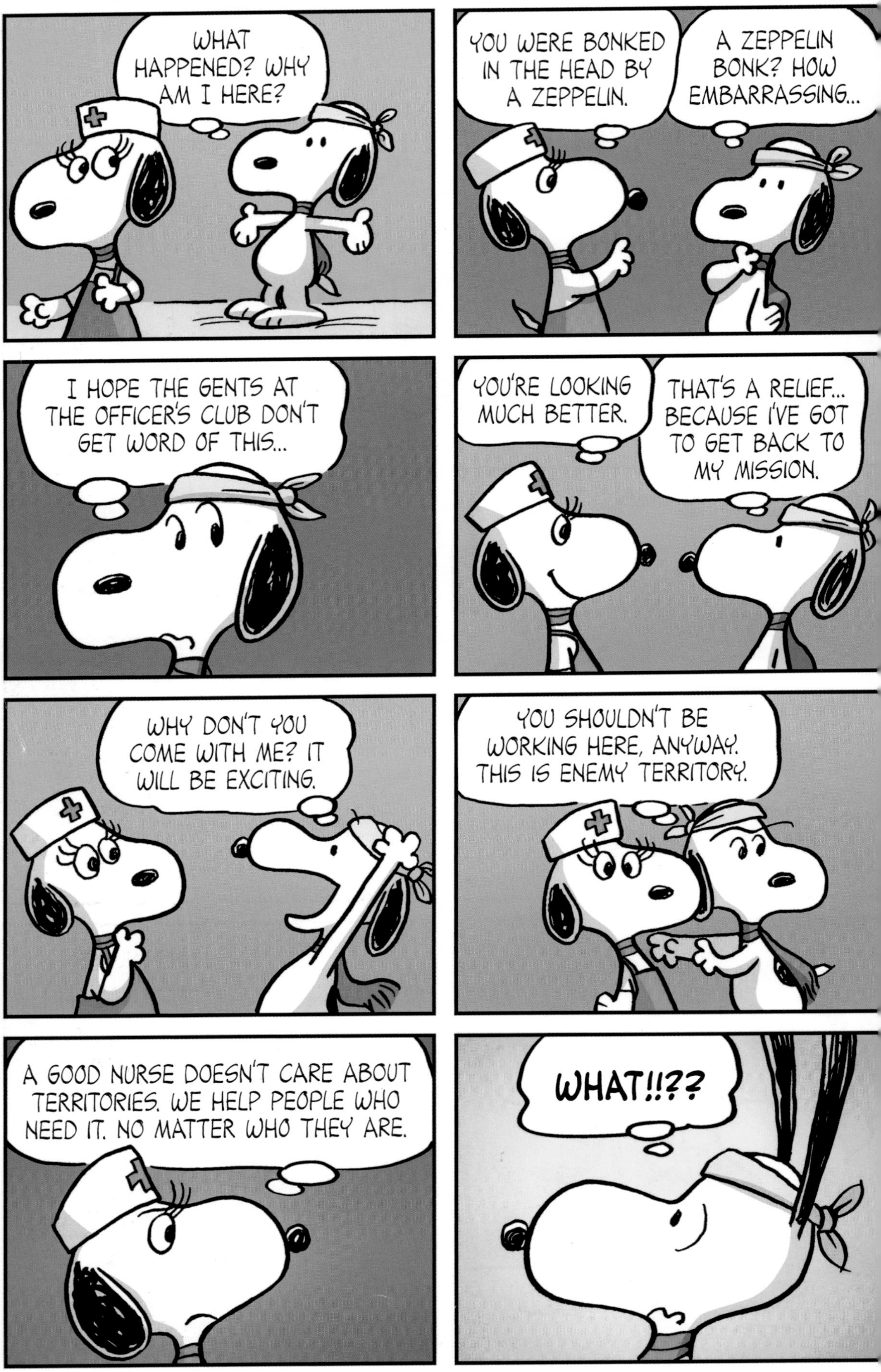
WHAT HAPPENED? WHY AM I HERE?
YOU WERE BONKED IN THE HEAD BY A ZEPPELIN.
A ZEPPELIN BONK? HOW EMBARRASSING...
I HOPE THE GENTS AT THE OFFICER'S CLUB DON'T GET WORD OF THIS...
YOU'RE LOOKING MUCH BETTER.
THAT'S A RELIEF... BECAUSE I'VE GOT TO GET BACK TO MY MISSION.
WHY DON'T YOU COME WITH ME? IT WILL BE EXCITING.
YOU SHOULDN'T BE WORKING HERE, ANYWAY. THIS IS ENEMY TERRITORY.
A GOOD NURSE DOESN'T CARE ABOUT TERRITORIES. WE HELP PEOPLE WHO NEED IT. NO MATTER WHO THEY ARE.
WHAT!!??

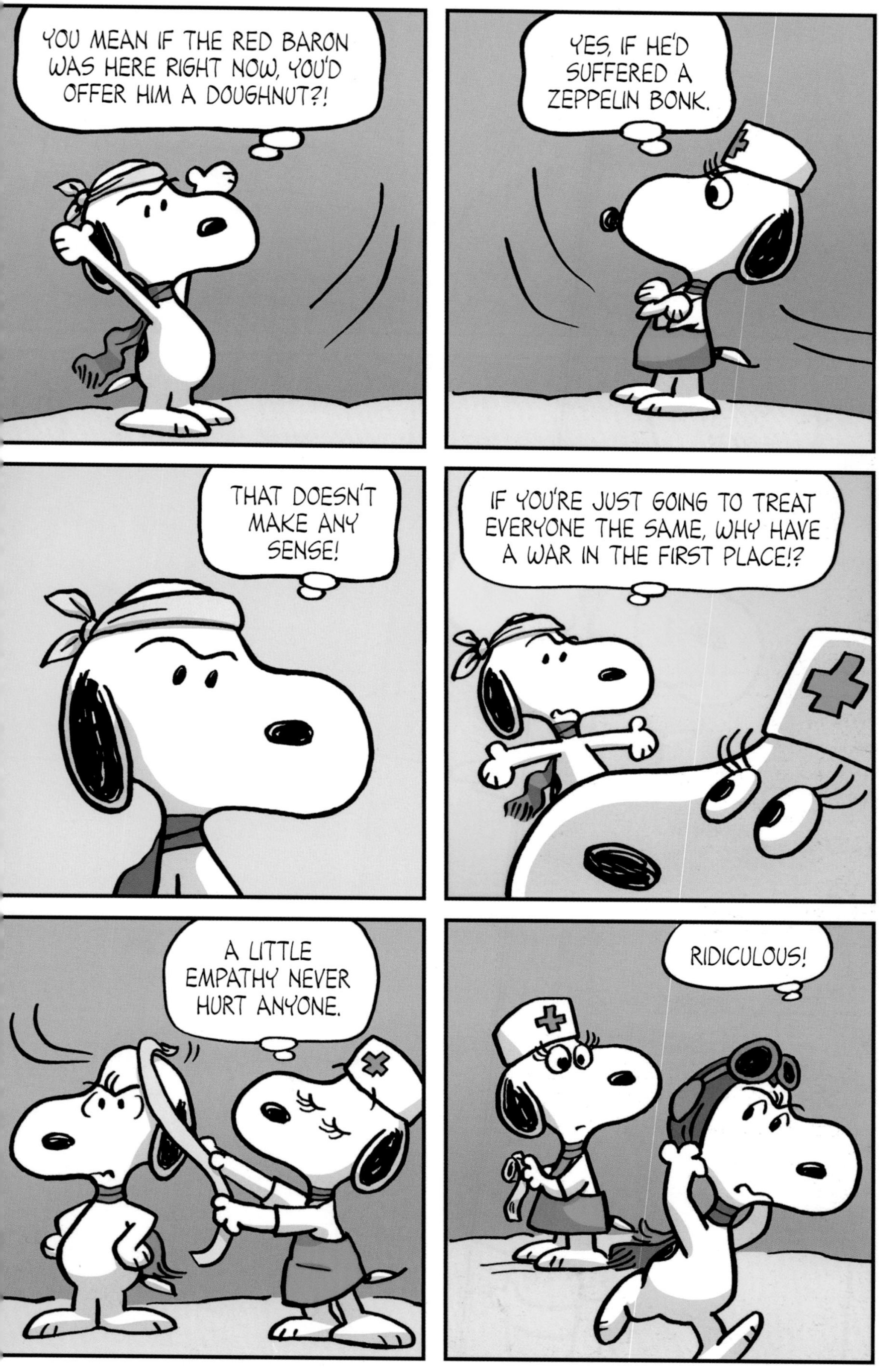
YOU MEAN IF THE RED BARON WAS HERE RIGHT NOW, YOU'D OFFER HIM A DOUGHNUT?!
YES, IF HE'D SUFFERED A ZEPPELIN BONK.
THAT DOESN'T MAKE ANY SENSE!
IF YOU'RE JUST GOING TO TREAT EVERYONE THE SAME, WHY HAVE A WAR IN THE FIRST PLACE!?
A LITTLE EMPATHY NEVER HURT ANYONE.
RIDICULOUS!

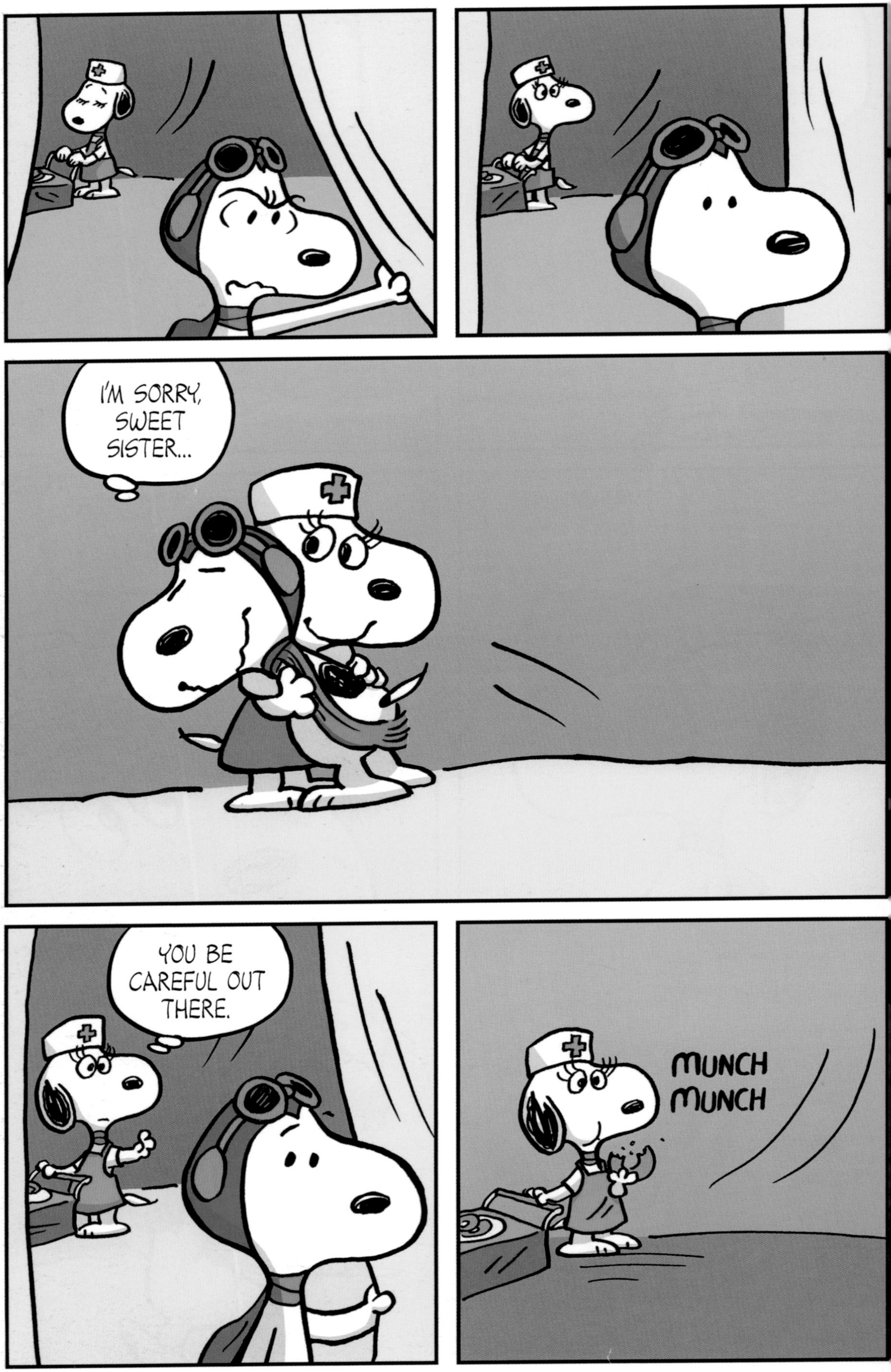
I'M SORRY, SWEET SISTER...
YOU BE CAREFUL OUT THERE.
MUNCH MUNCH

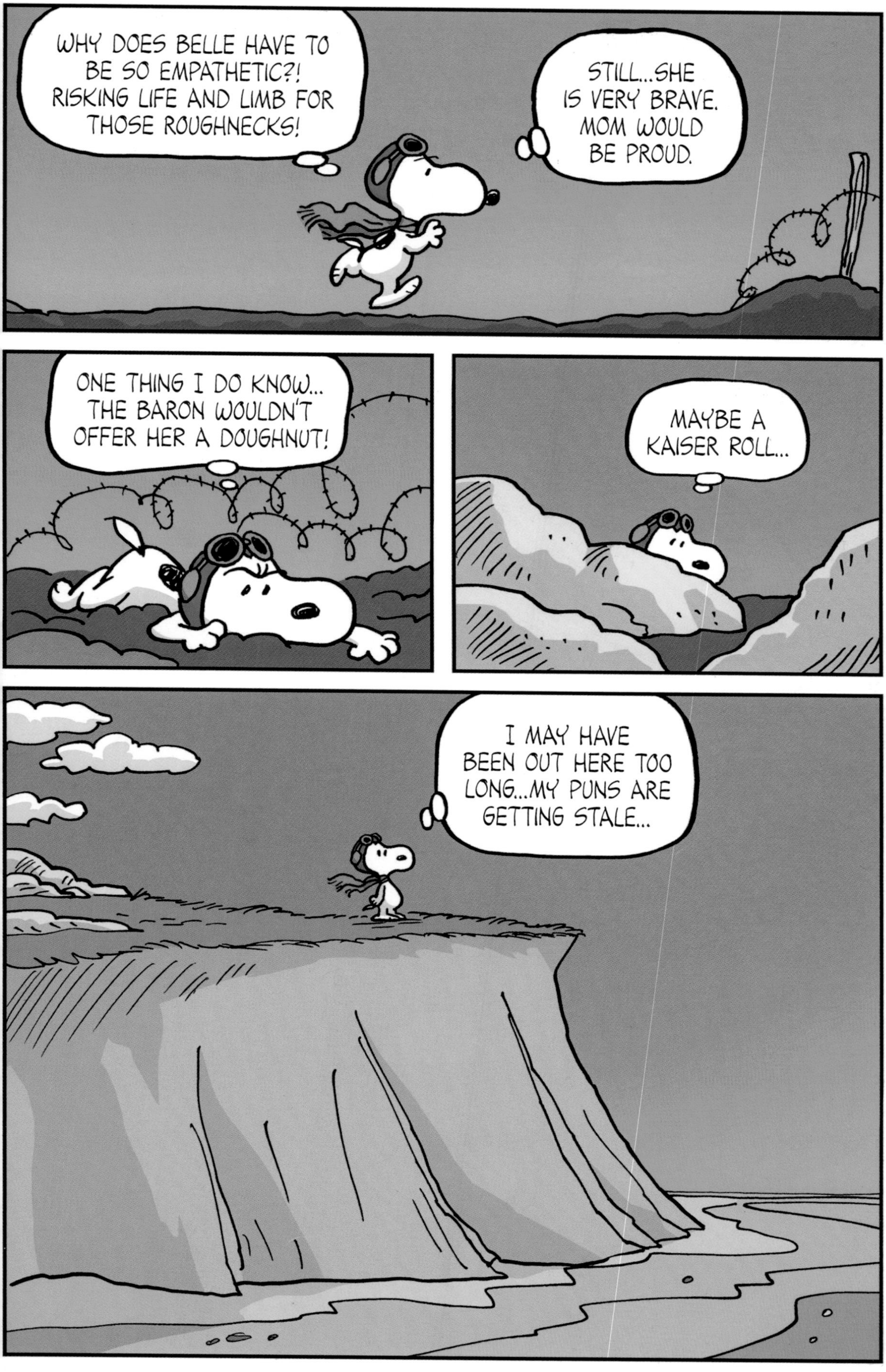
WHY DOES BELLE HAVE TO BE SO EMPATHETIC?! RISKING LIFE AND LIMB FOR THOSE ROUGHNECKS!
STILL...SHE IS VERY BRAVE. MOM WOULD BE PROUD.
ONE THING I DO KNOW... THE BARON WOULDN'T OFFER HER A DOUGHNUT!
MAYBE A KAISER ROLL...
I MAY HAVE BEEN OUT HERE TOO LONG...MY PUNS ARE GETTING STALE...

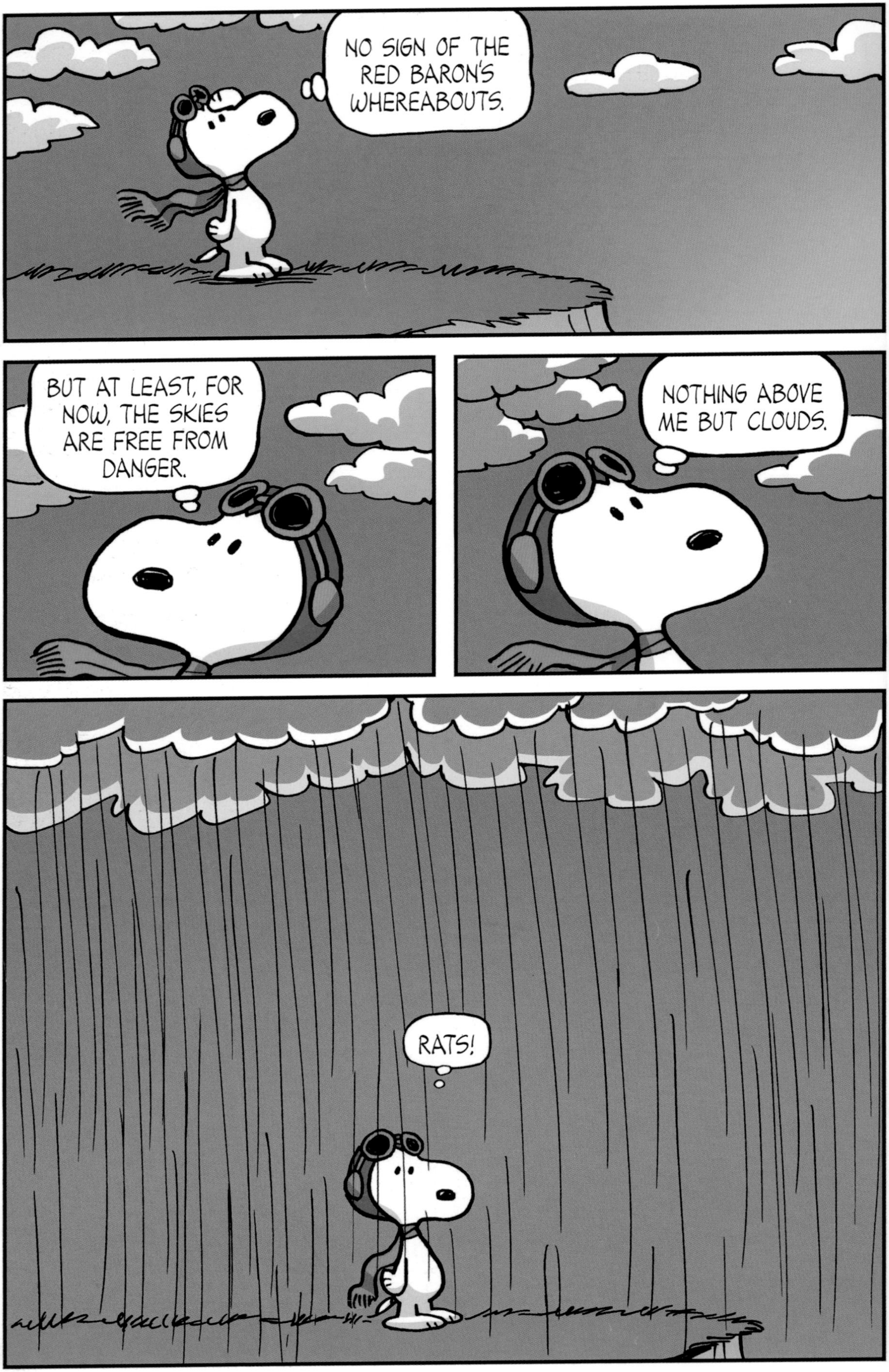
NO SIGN OF THE RED BARON'S WHEREABOUTS.
BUT AT LEAST, FOR NOW, THE SKIES ARE FREE FROM DANGER.
NOTHING ABOVE ME BUT CLOUDS.
RATS!

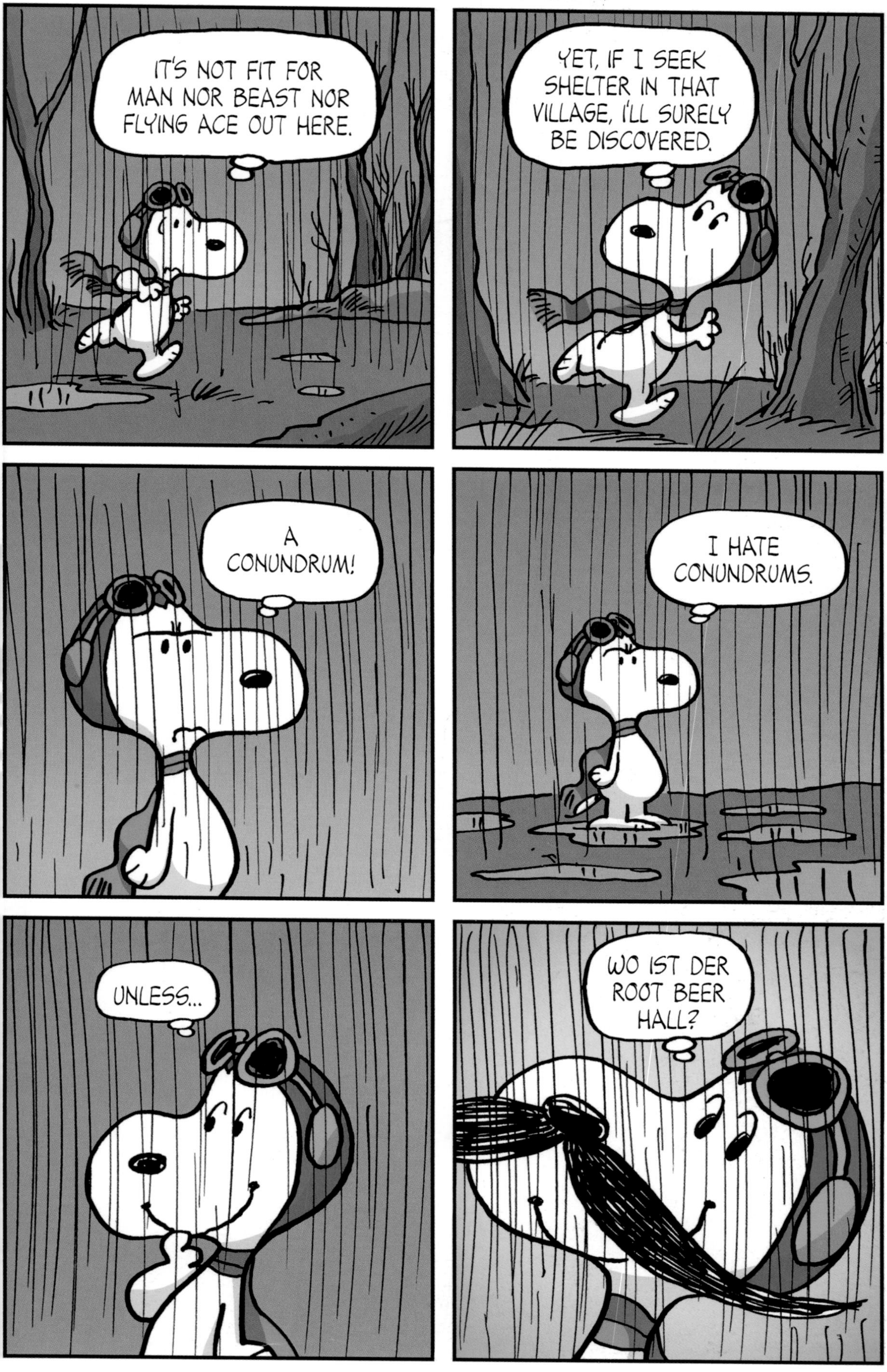
IT'S NOT FIT FOR MAN NOR BEAST NOR FLYING ACE OUT HERE.
YET, IF I SEEK SHELTER IN THAT VILLAGE, I'LL SURELY BE DISCOVERED.
A CONUNDRUM!
I HATE CONUNDRUMS.
UNLESS...
WO IST DER ROOT BEER HALL?

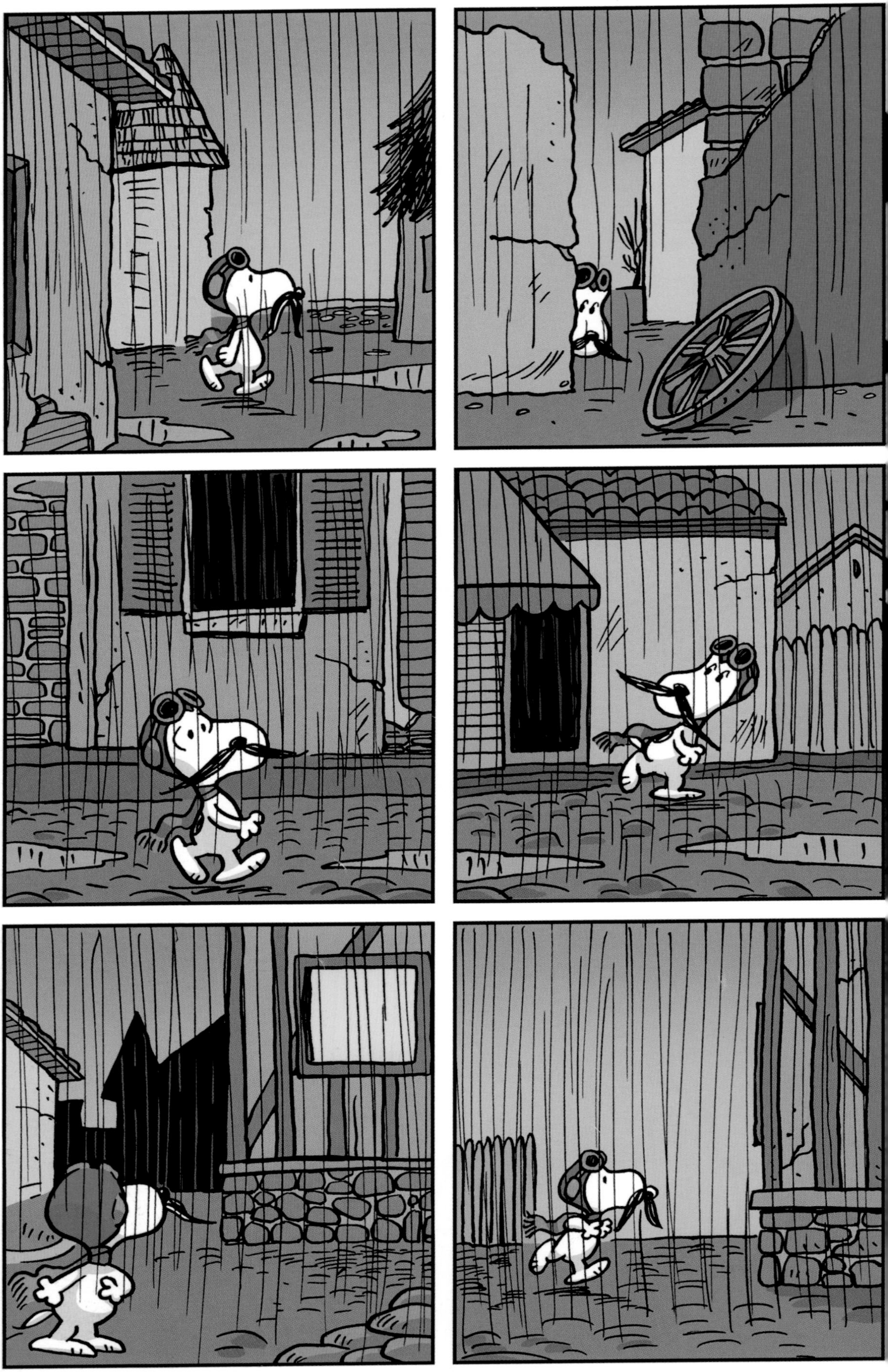

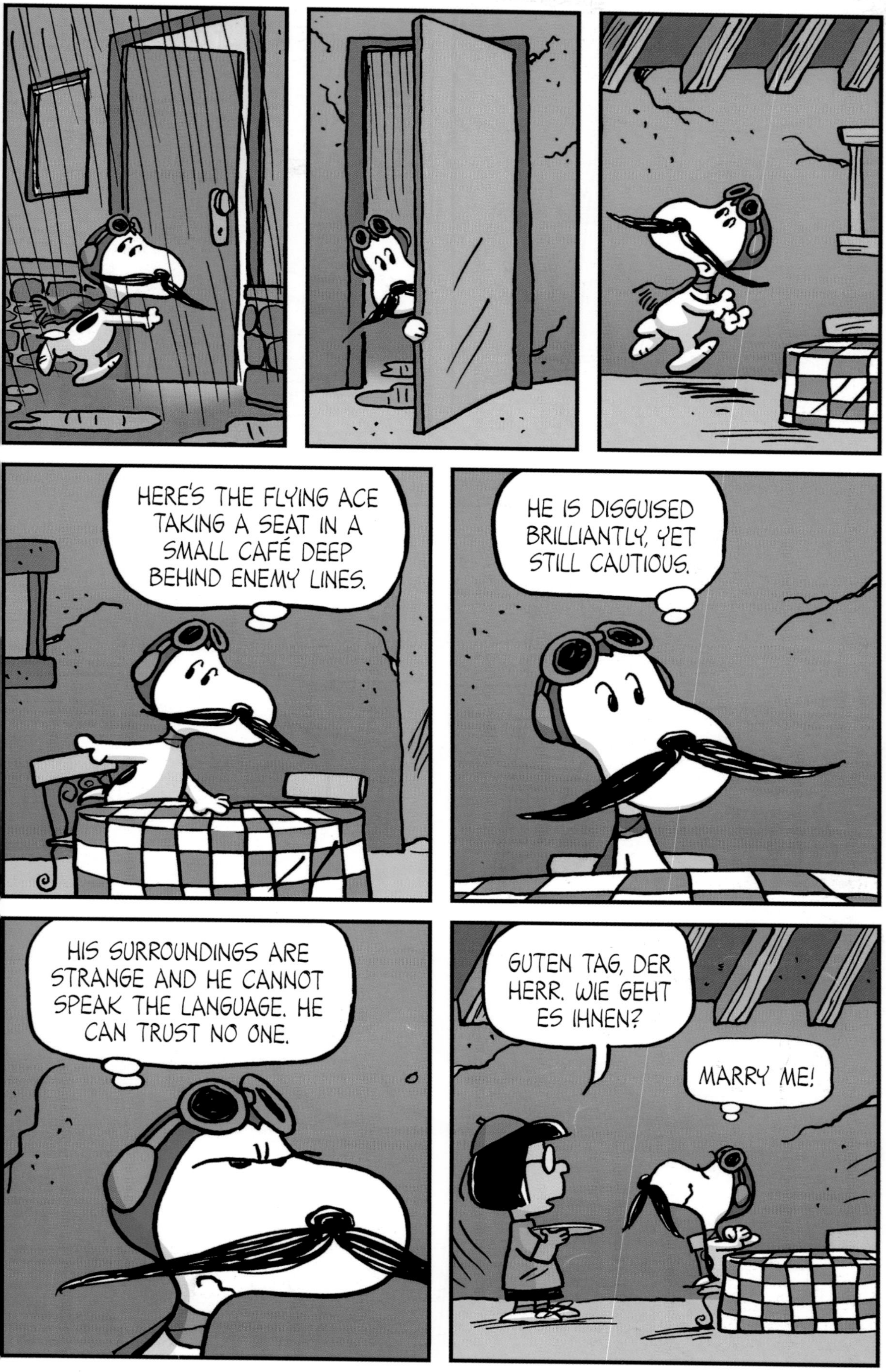
HERE'S THE FLYING ACE TAKING A SEAT IN A SMALL CAFÉ DEEP BEHIND ENEMY LINES.
HE IS DISGUISED BRILLIANTLY, YET STILL CAUTIOUS.
HIS SURROUNDINGS ARE STRANGE AND HE CANNOT SPEAK THE LANGUAGE. HE CAN TRUST NO ONE.
GUTEN TAG, DER HERR. WIE GEHT ES IHNEN?
MARRY ME!

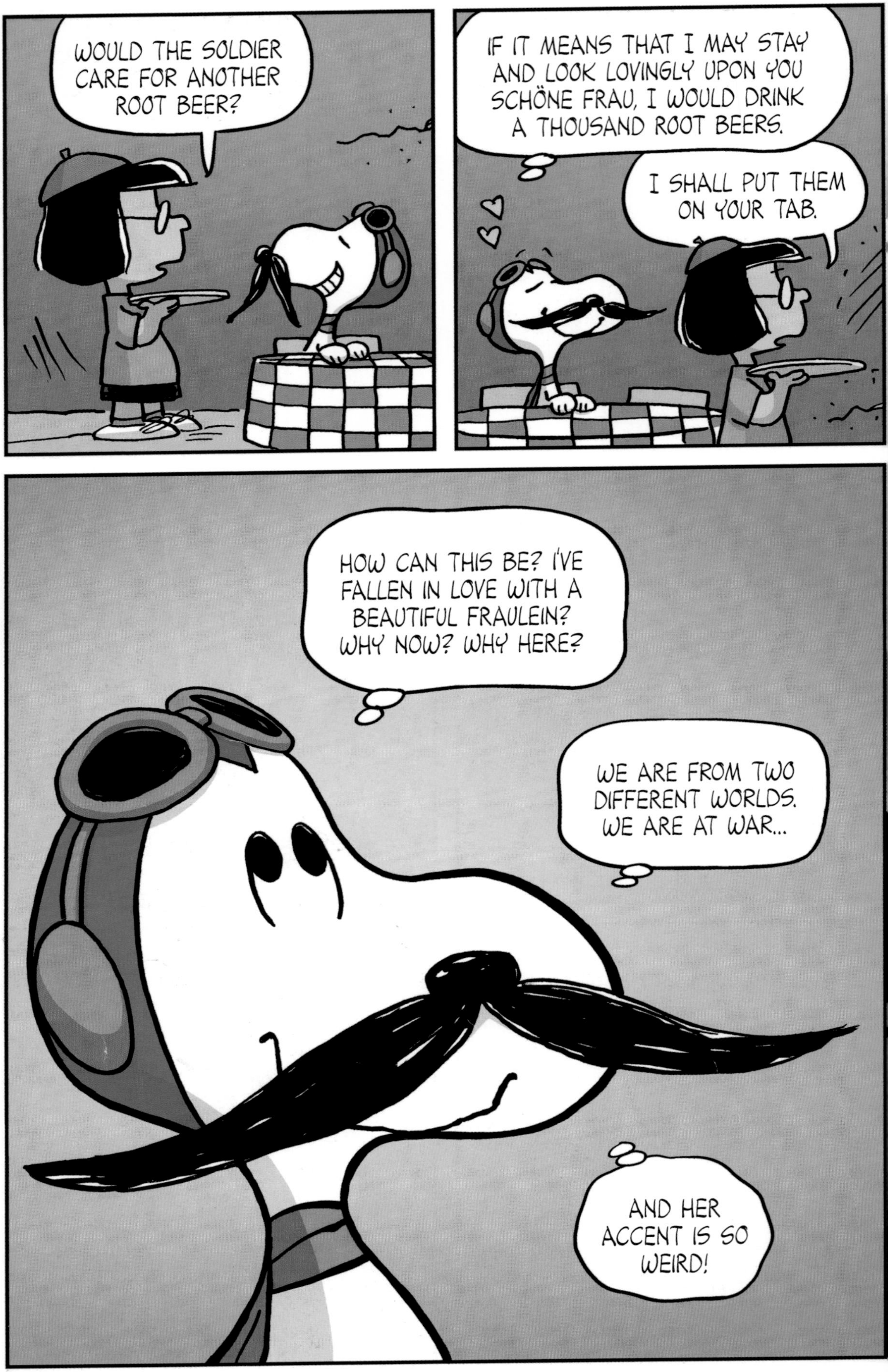
WOULD THE SOLDIER CARE FOR ANOTHER ROOT BEER?
IF IT MEANS THAT I MAY STAY AND LOOK LOVINGLY UPON YOU SCHÖNE FRAU, I WOULD DRINK A THOUSAND ROOT BEERS.
I SHALL PUT THEM ON YOUR TAB.
HOW CAN THIS BE? I'VE FALLEN IN LOVE WITH A BEAUTIFUL FRAULEIN? WHY NOW? WHY HERE?
WE ARE FROM TWO DIFFERENT WORLDS. WE ARE AT WAR...
AND HER ACCENT IS SO WEIRD!

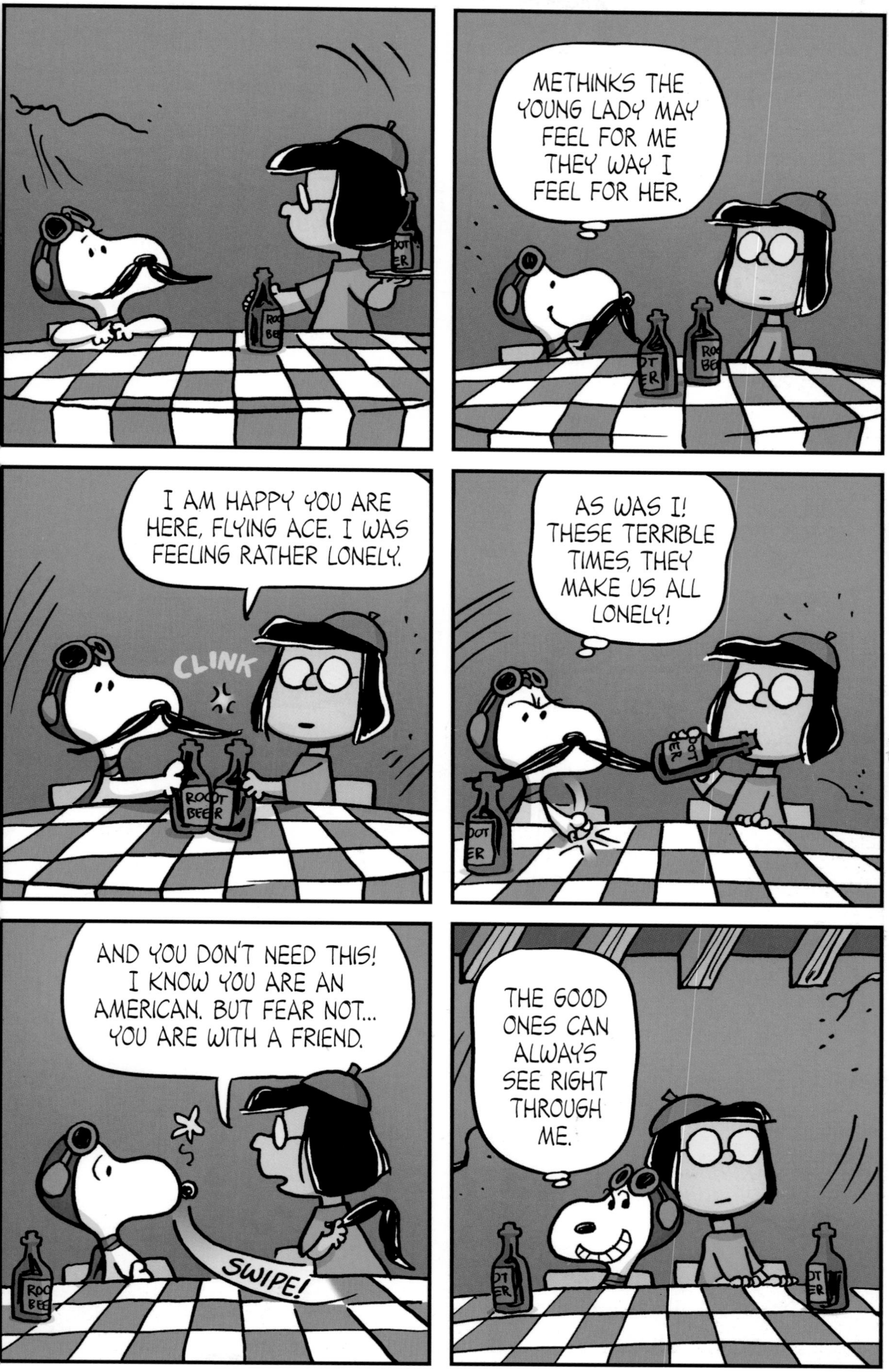
METHINKS THE YOUNG LADY MAY FEEL FOR ME THEY WAY I FEEL FOR HER.
I AM HAPPY YOU ARE HERE, FLYING ACE. I WAS FEELING RATHER LONELY.
CLINK
AS WAS I! THESE TERRIBLE TIMES, THEY MAKE US ALL LONELY!
AND YOU DON'T NEED THIS! I KNOW YOU ARE AN AMERICAN. BUT FEAR NOT... YOU ARE WITH A FRIEND.
SWIPE!
THE GOOD ONES CAN ALWAYS SEE RIGHT THROUGH ME.

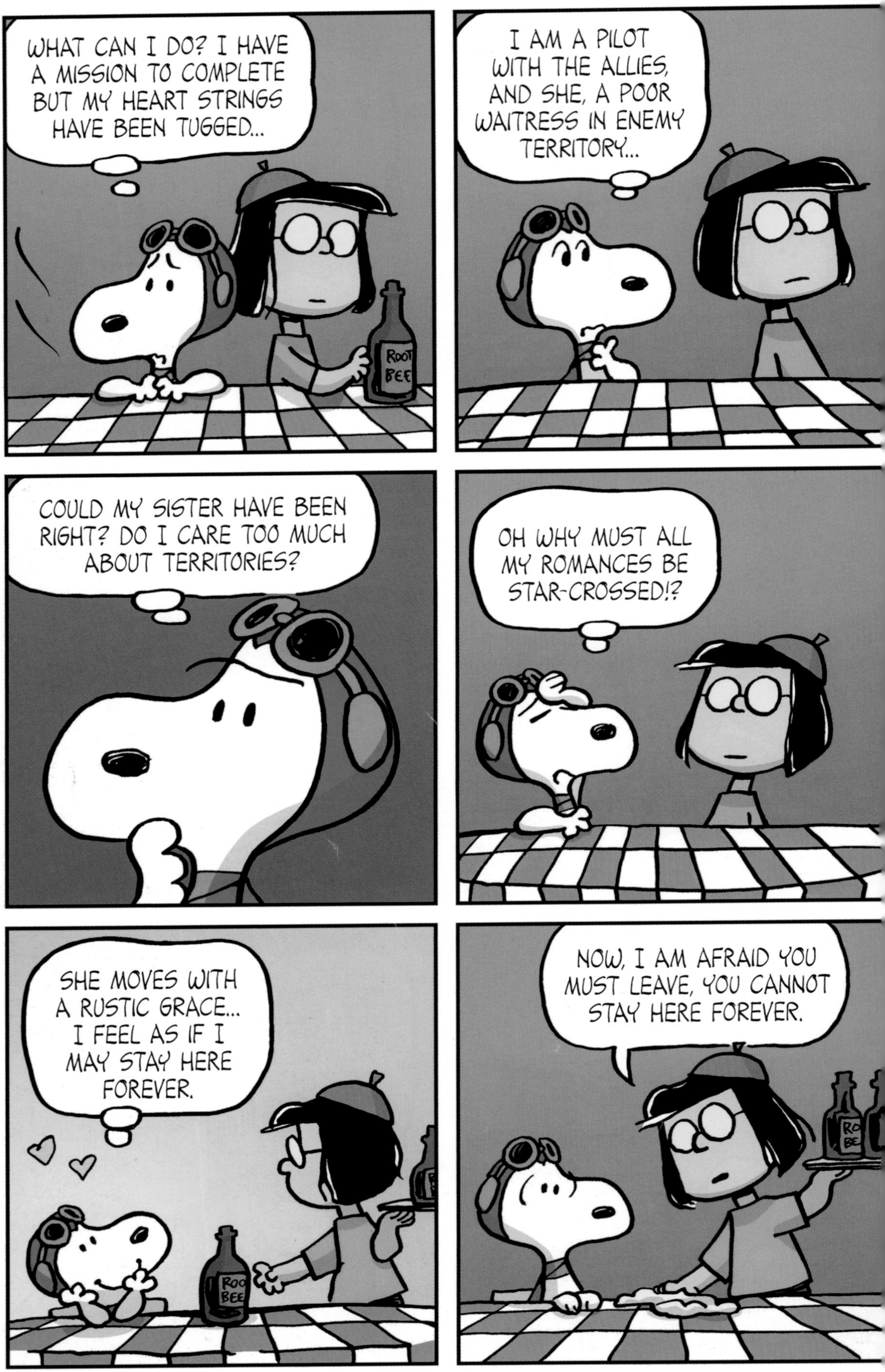

WHAT CAN I DO? I HAVE A MISSION TO COMPLETE BUT MY HEART STRINGS HAVE BEEN TUGGED...
ROOT BEE
I AM A PILOT WITH THE ALLIES, AND SHE, A POOR WAITRESS IN ENEMY TERRITORY...
COULD MY SISTER HAVE BEEN RIGHT? DO I CARE TOO MUCH ABOUT TERRITORIES?
OH WHY MUST ALL MY ROMANCES BE STAR-CROSSED!?
SHE MOVES WITH A RUSTIC GRACE... I FEEL AS IF I MAY STAY HERE FOREVER.
NOW, I AM AFRAID YOU MUST LEAVE, YOU CANNOT STAY HERE FOREVER.

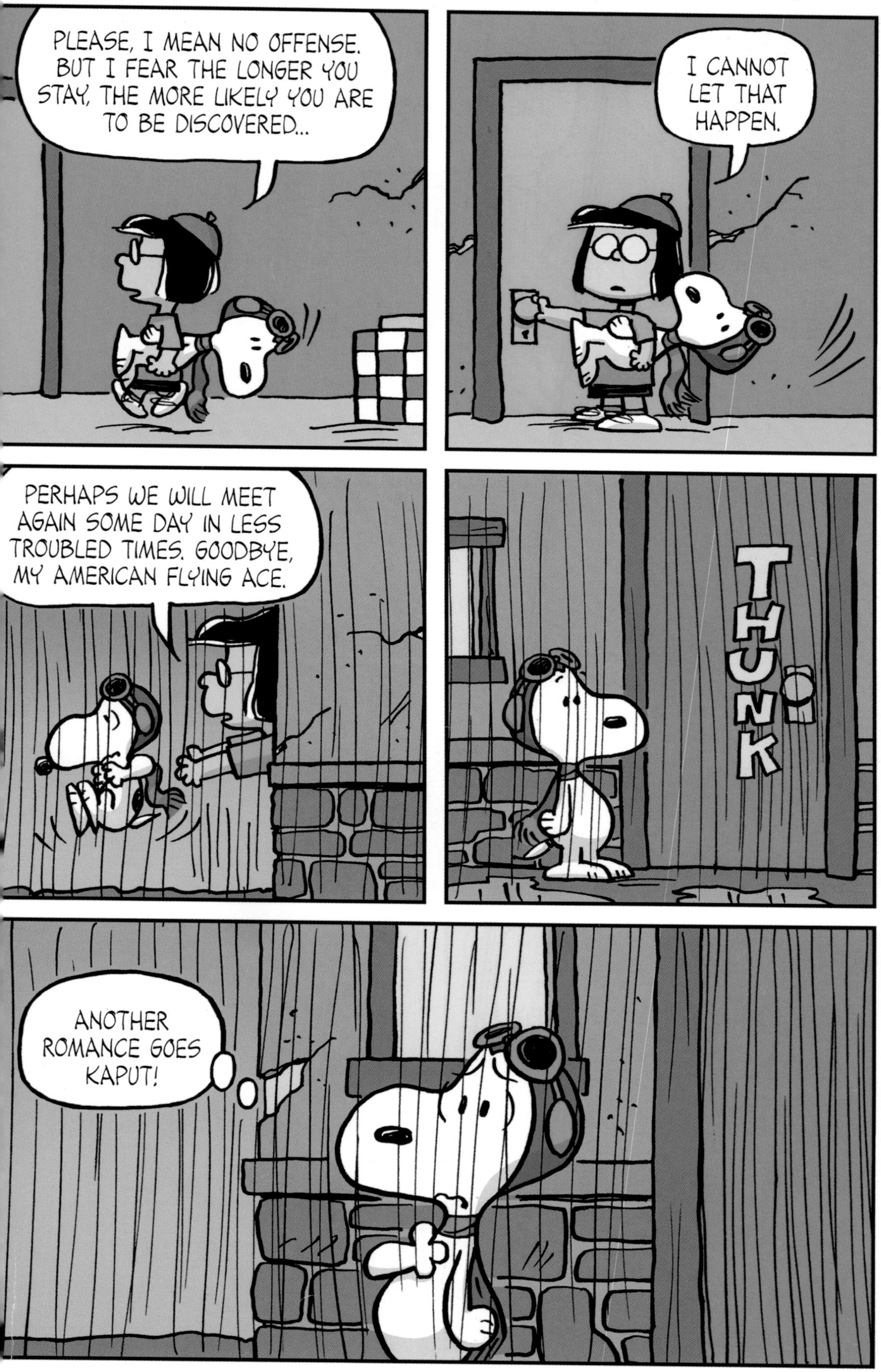
PLEASE, I MEAN NO OFFENSE. BUT I FEAR THE LONGER YOU STAY, THE MORE LIKELY YOU ARE TO BE DISCOVERED...
I CANNOT LET THAT HAPPEN.
PERHAPS WE WILL MEET AGAIN SOME DAY IN LESS TROUBLED TIMES. GOODBYE, MY AMERICAN FLYING ACE.
THUNK
ANOTHER ROMANCE GOES KAPUT!

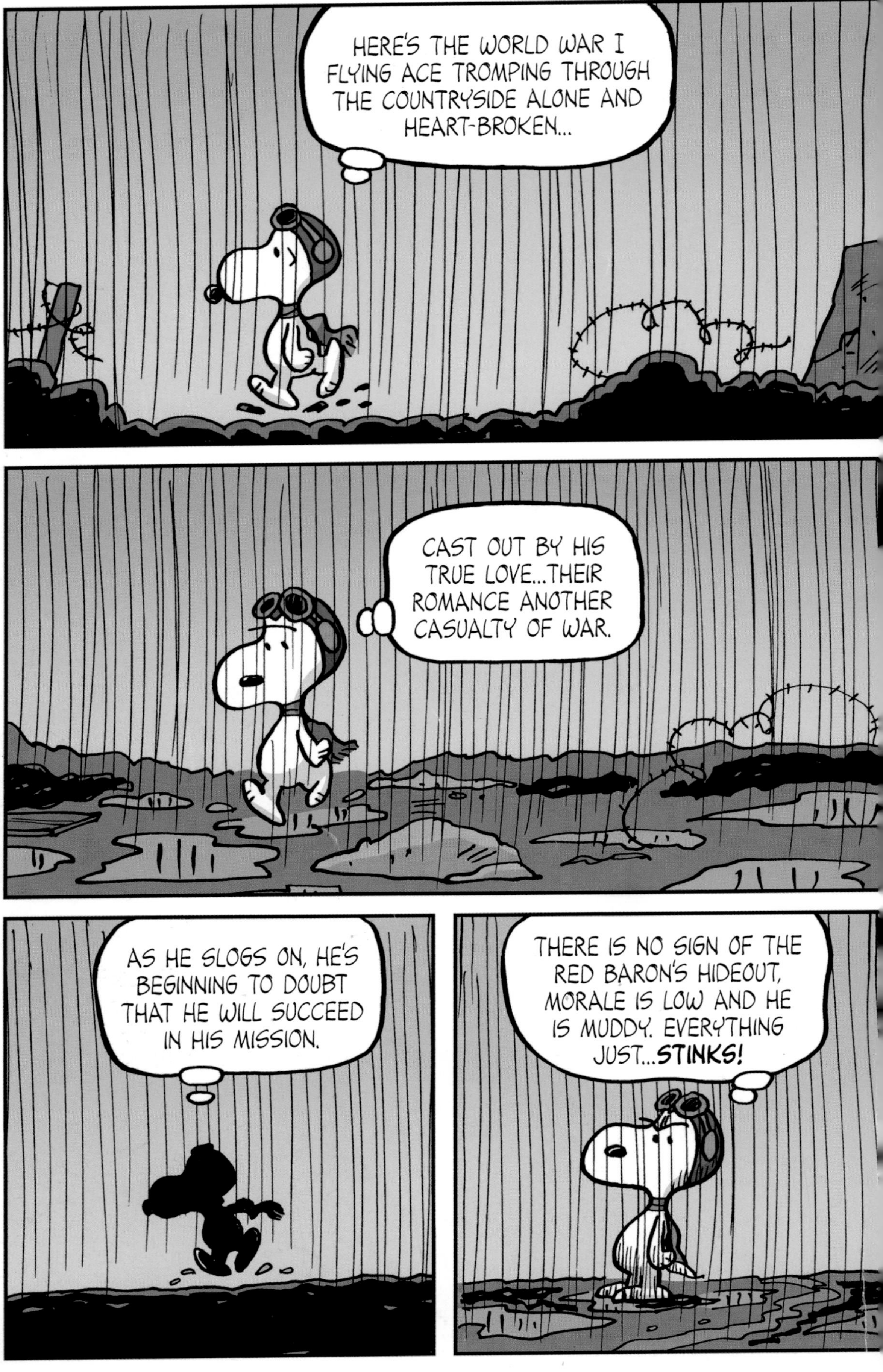
HERE'S THE WORLD WAR I FLYING ACE TROMPING THROUGH THE COUNTRYSIDE ALONE AND HEART-BROKEN...
CAST OUT BY HIS TRUE LOVE...THEIR ROMANCE ANOTHER CASUALTY OF WAR.
AS HE SLOGS ON, HE'S BEGINNING TO DOUBT THAT HE WILL SUCCEED IN HIS MISSION.
THERE IS NO SIGN OF THE RED BARON'S HIDEOUT, MORALE IS LOW AND HE IS MUDDY. EVERYTHING JUST...**STINKS!**

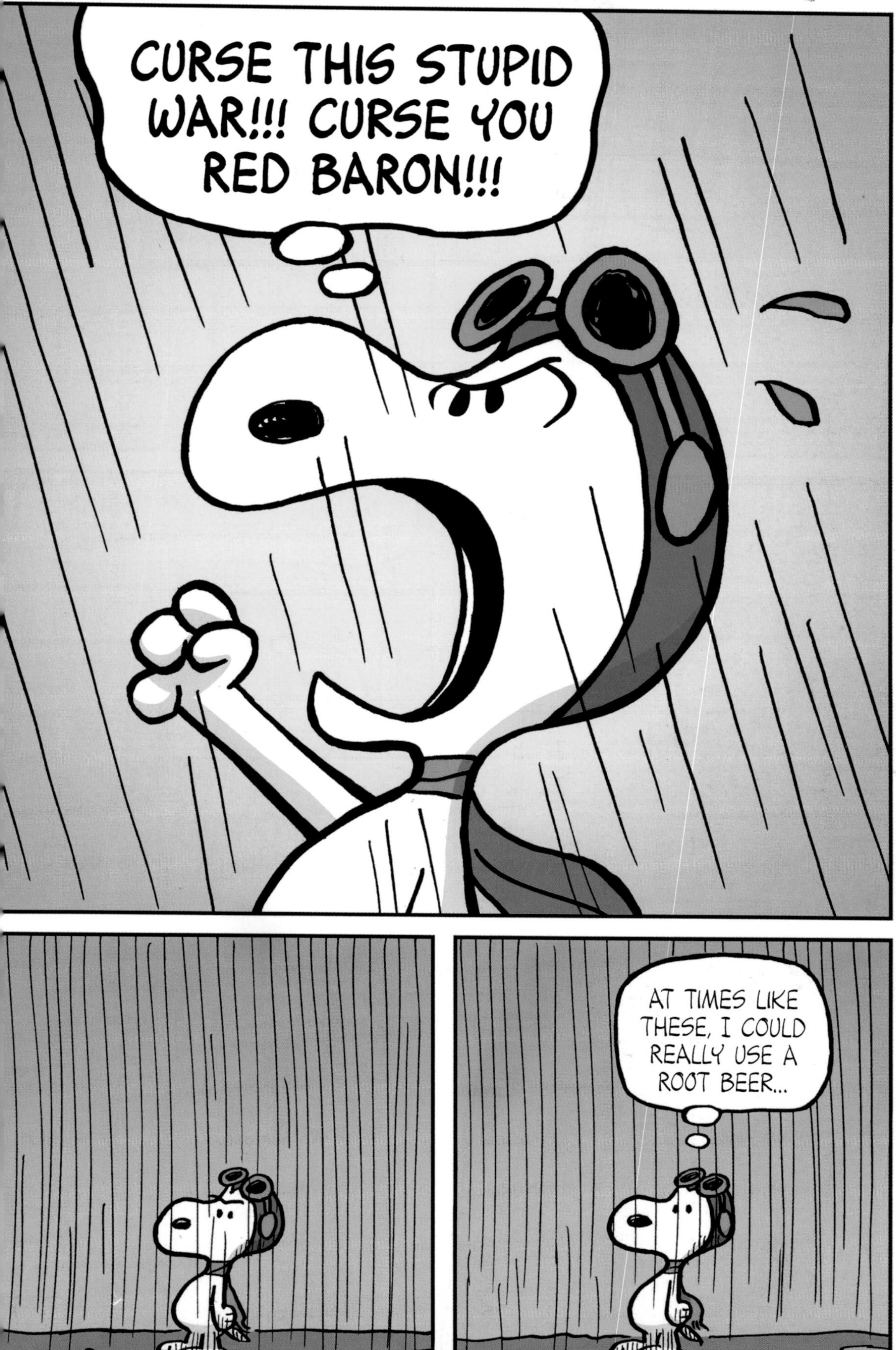
CURSE THIS STUPID WAR!!! CURSE YOU RED BARON!!!
AT TIMES LIKE THESE, I COULD REALLY USE A ROOT BEER...

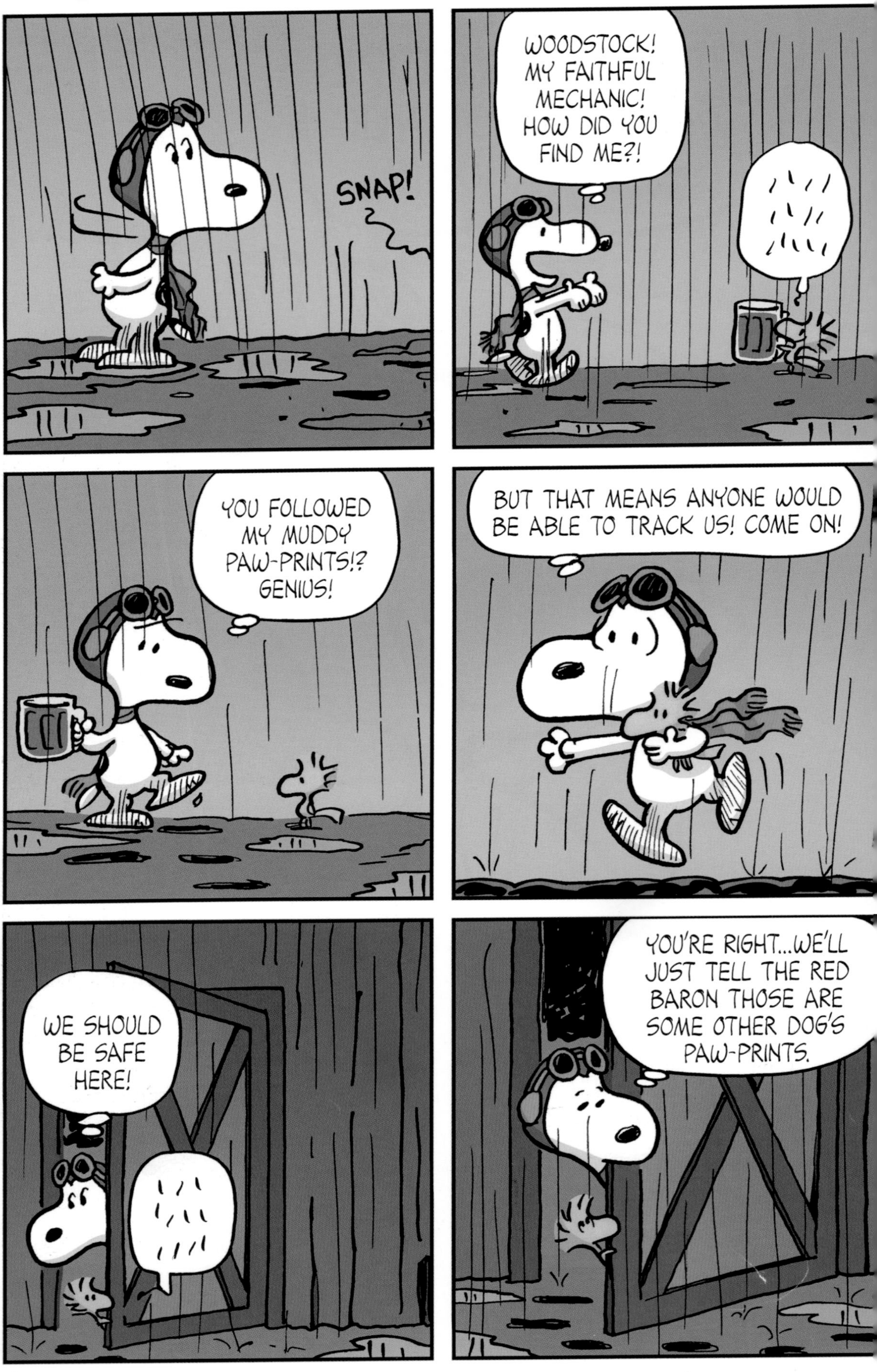
SNAP!
WOODSTOCK! MY FAITHFUL MECHANIC! HOW DID YOU FIND ME?!
YOU FOLLOWED MY MUDDY PAW-PRINTS!? GENIUS!
BUT THAT MEANS ANYONE WOULD BE ABLE TO TRACK US! COME ON!
WE SHOULD BE SAFE HERE!
YOU'RE RIGHT...WE'LL JUST TELL THE RED BARON THOSE ARE SOME OTHER DOG'S PAW-PRINTS.

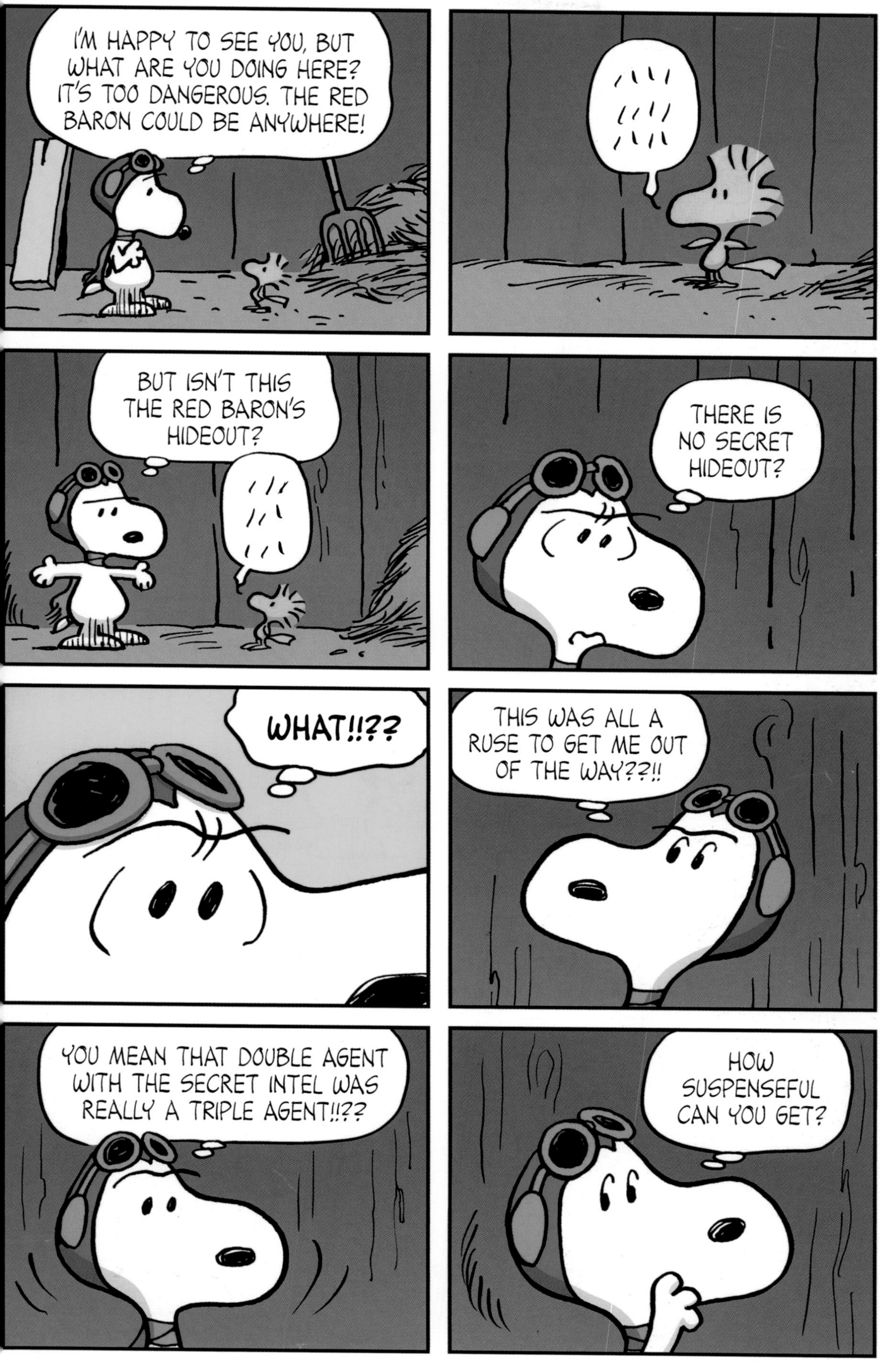
I'M HAPPY TO SEE YOU, BUT WHAT ARE YOU DOING HERE? IT'S TOO DANGEROUS. THE RED BARON COULD BE ANYWHERE!
BUT ISN'T THIS THE RED BARON'S HIDEOUT?
THERE IS NO SECRET HIDEOUT?
WHAT!!??
THIS WAS ALL A RUSE TO GET ME OUT OF THE WAY??!!
YOU MEAN THAT DOUBLE AGENT WITH THE SECRET INTEL WAS REALLY A TRIPLE AGENT!!??
HOW SUSPENSEFUL CAN YOU GET?

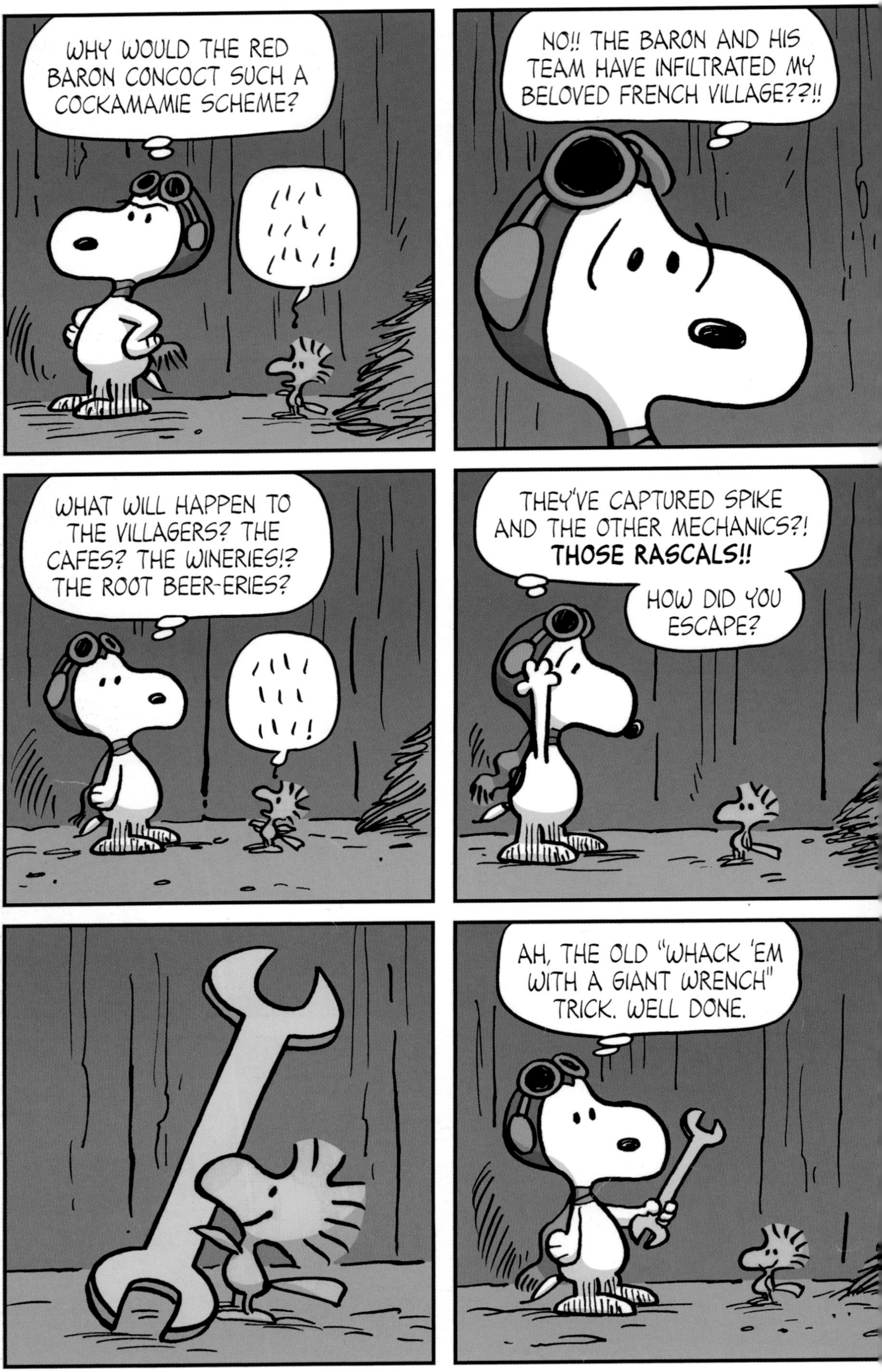

WHY WOULD THE RED BARON CONCOCT SUCH A COCKAMAMIE SCHEME?
NO!! THE BARON AND HIS TEAM HAVE INFILTRATED MY BELOVED FRENCH VILLAGE??!!
WHAT WILL HAPPEN TO THE VILLAGERS? THE CAFES? THE WINERIES!? THE ROOT BEER-ERIES?
THEY'VE CAPTURED SPIKE AND THE OTHER MECHANICS?! **THOSE RASCALS!!**
HOW DID YOU ESCAPE?
AH, THE OLD "WHACK 'EM WITH A GIANT WRENCH" TRICK. WELL DONE.

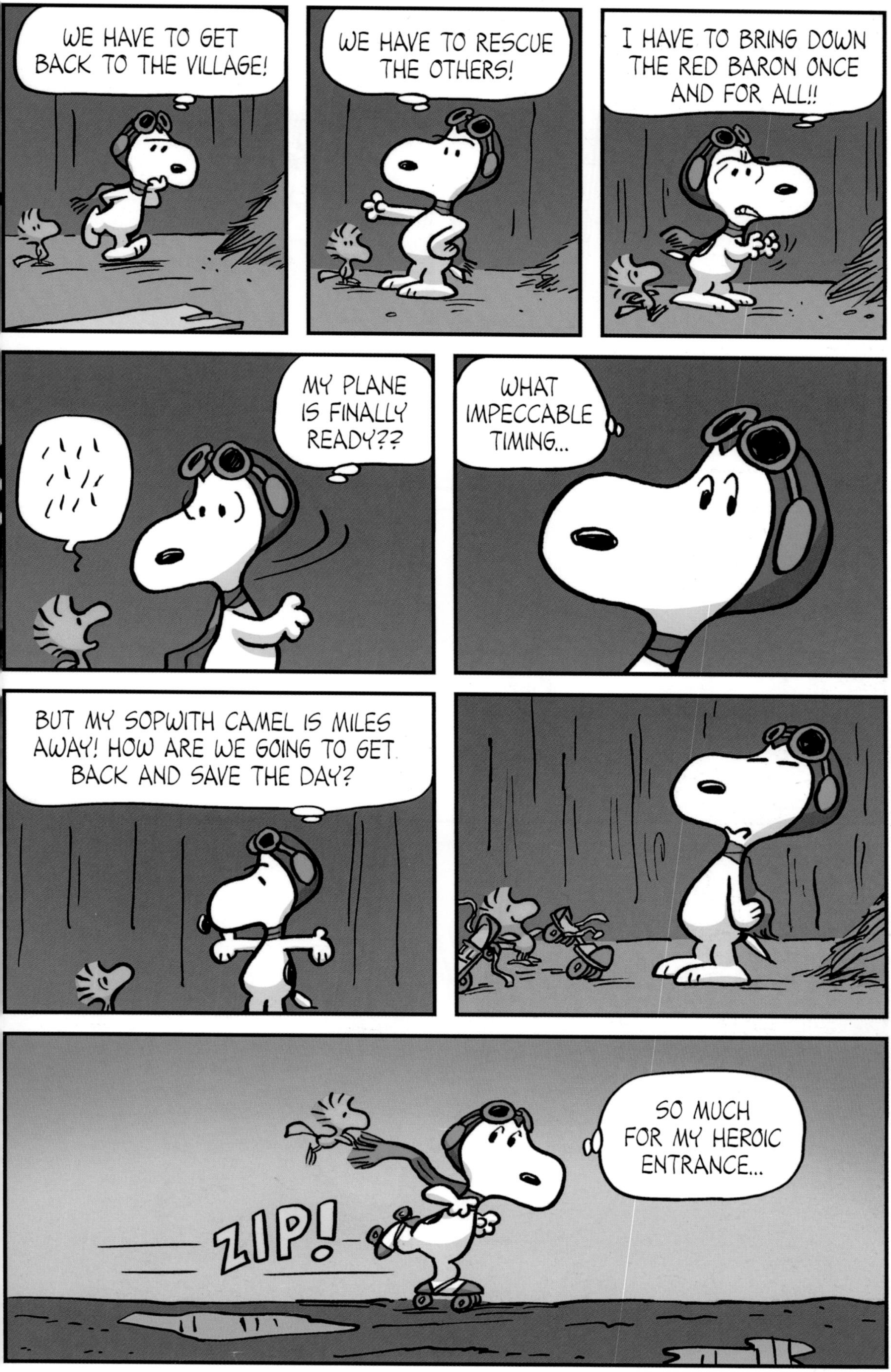
WE HAVE TO GET BACK TO THE VILLAGE!
WE HAVE TO RESCUE THE OTHERS!
I HAVE TO BRING DOWN THE RED BARON ONCE AND FOR ALL!!
MY PLANE IS FINALLY READY??
WHAT IMPECCABLE TIMING...
BUT MY SOPWITH CAMEL IS MILES AWAY! HOW ARE WE GOING TO GET BACK AND SAVE THE DAY?
ZIP!
SO MUCH FOR MY HEROIC ENTRANCE...

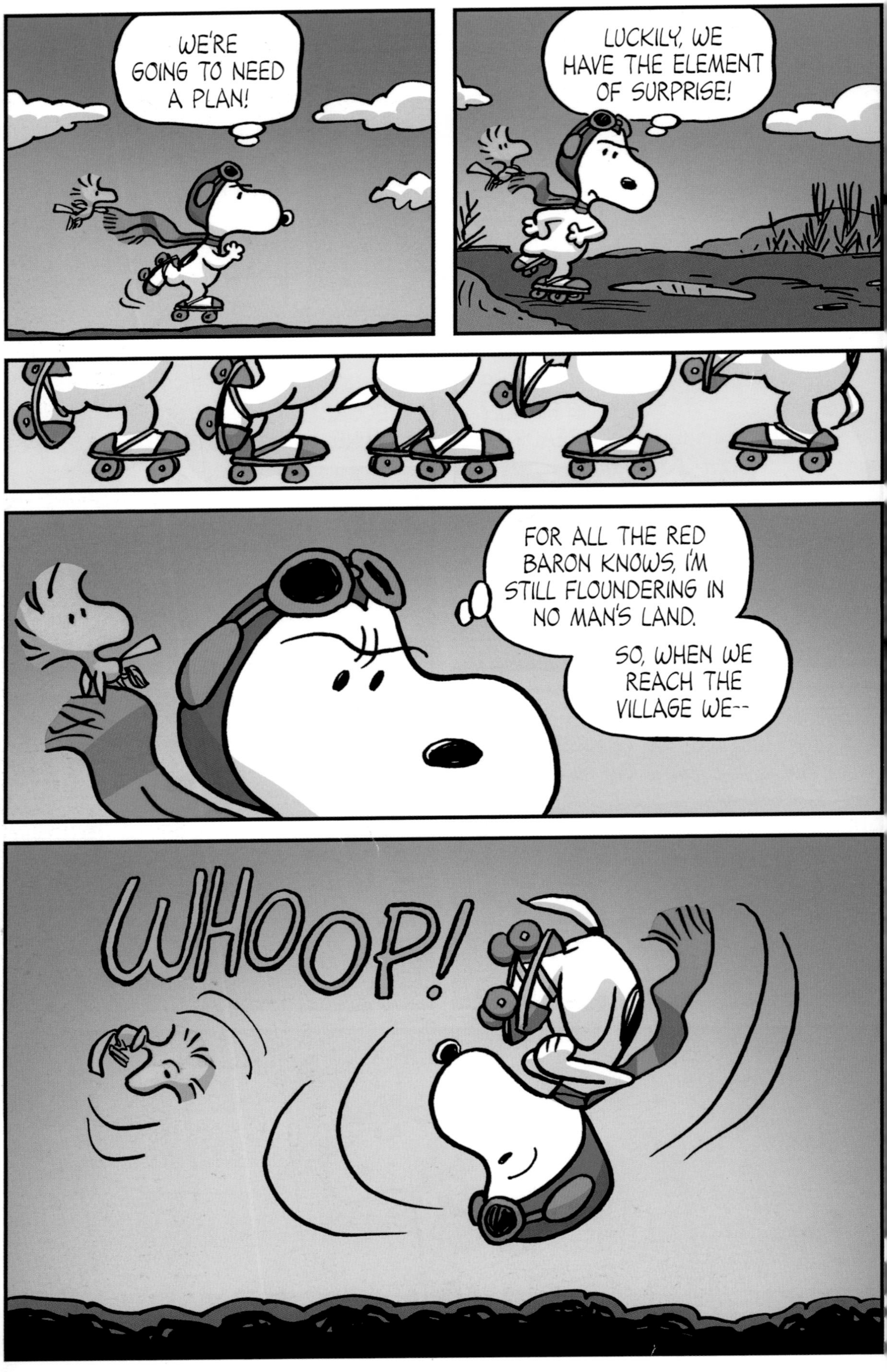
WE'RE GOING TO NEED A PLAN!
LUCKILY, WE HAVE THE ELEMENT OF SURPRISE!
FOR ALL THE RED BARON KNOWS, I'M STILL FLOUNDERING IN NO MAN'S LAND.
SO, WHEN WE REACH THE VILLAGE WE--
WHOOP!

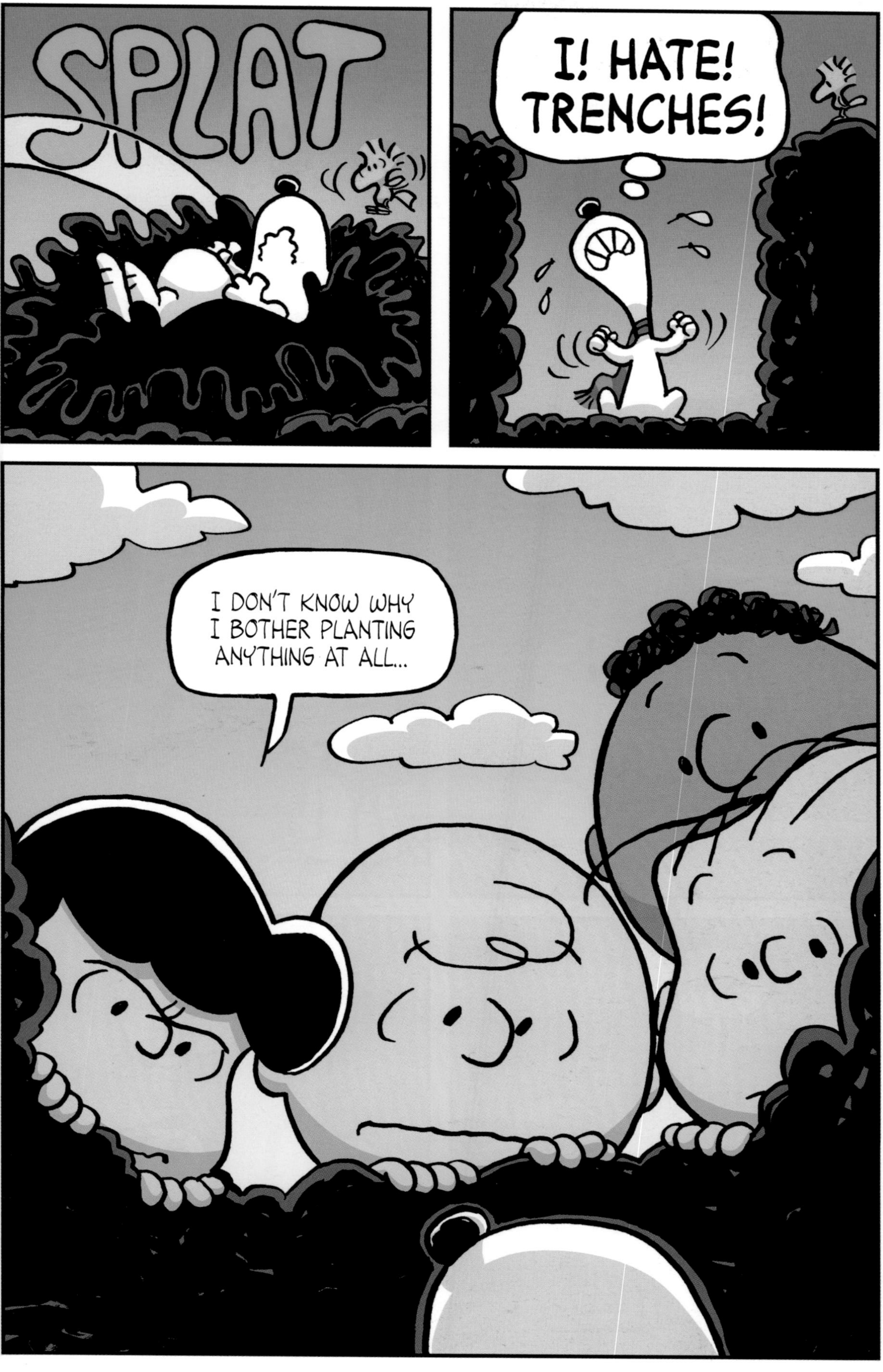
SPLAT
I! HATE! TRENCHES!
I DON'T KNOW WHY I BOTHER PLANTING ANYTHING AT ALL...

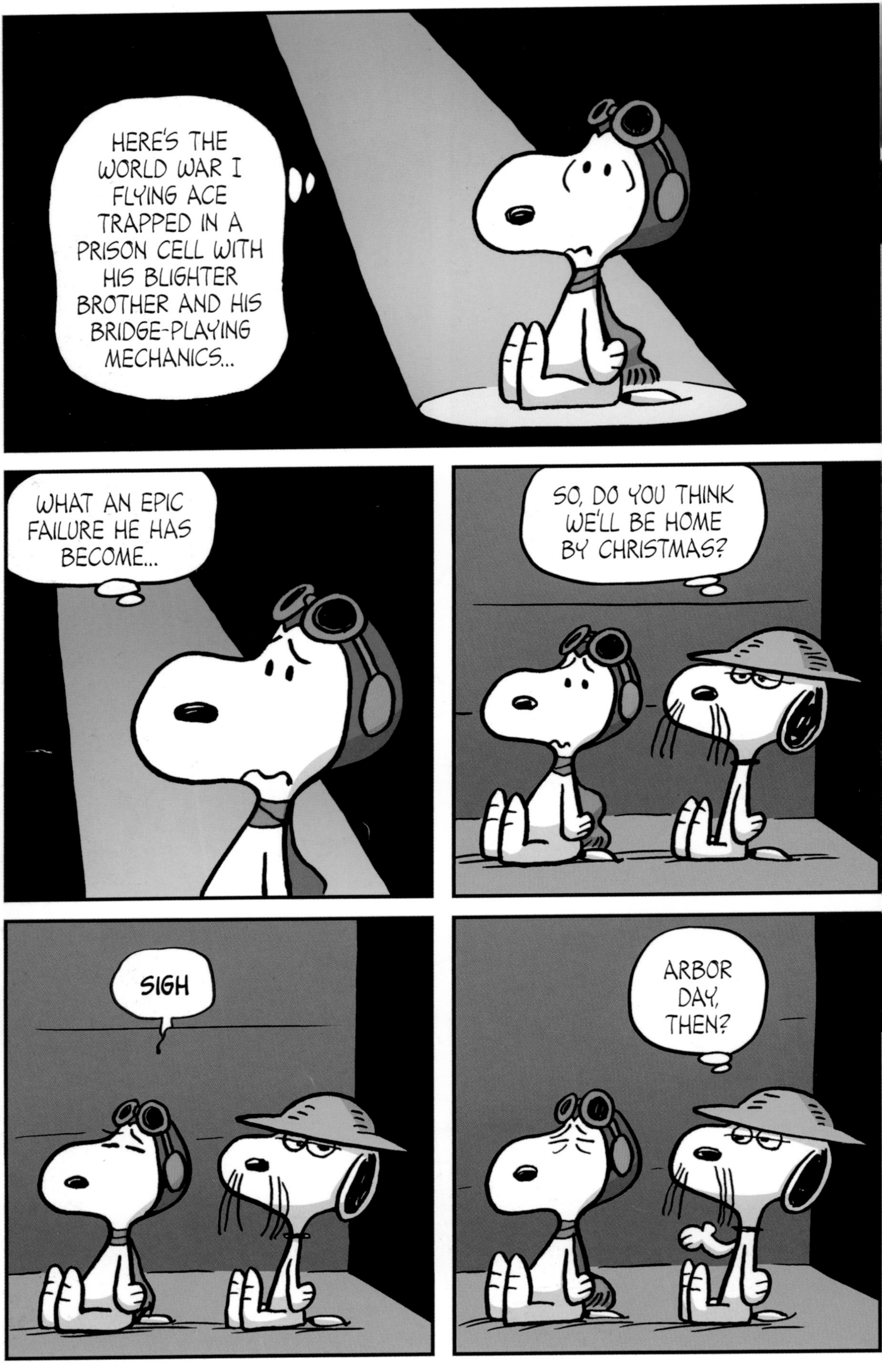
HERE'S THE WORLD WAR I FLYING ACE TRAPPED IN A PRISON CELL WITH HIS BLIGHTER BROTHER AND HIS BRIDGE-PLAYING MECHANICS...
WHAT AN EPIC FAILURE HE HAS BECOME...
SO, DO YOU THINK WE'LL BE HOME BY CHRISTMAS?
SIGH
ARBOR DAY, THEN?

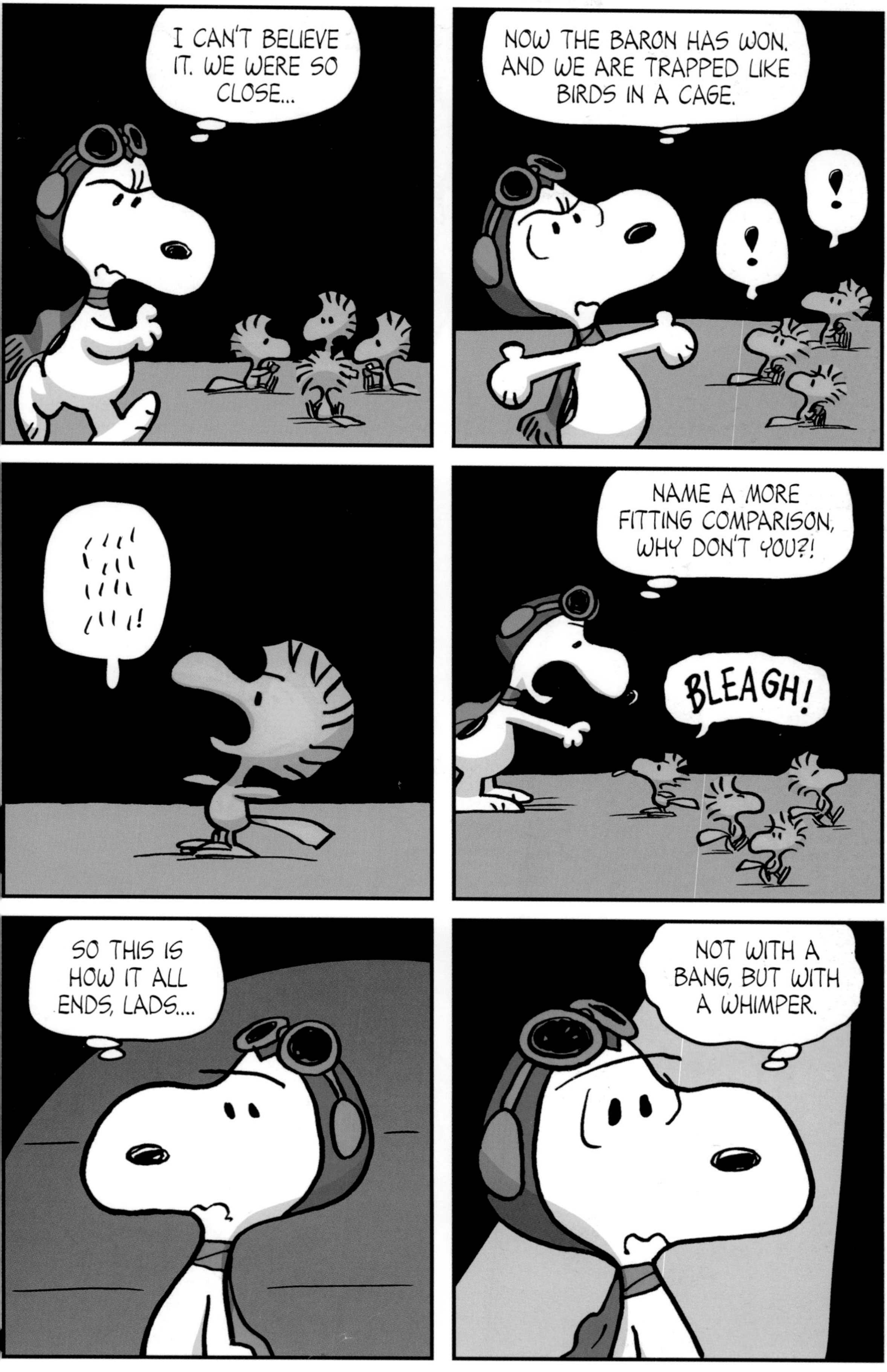
I CAN'T BELIEVE IT. WE WERE SO CLOSE...
NOW THE BARON HAS WON. AND WE ARE TRAPPED LIKE BIRDS IN A CAGE.
!
!
NAME A MORE FITTING COMPARISON, WHY DON'T YOU?!
BLEAGH!
SO THIS IS HOW IT ALL ENDS, LADS....
NOT WITH A BANG, BUT WITH A WHIMPER.

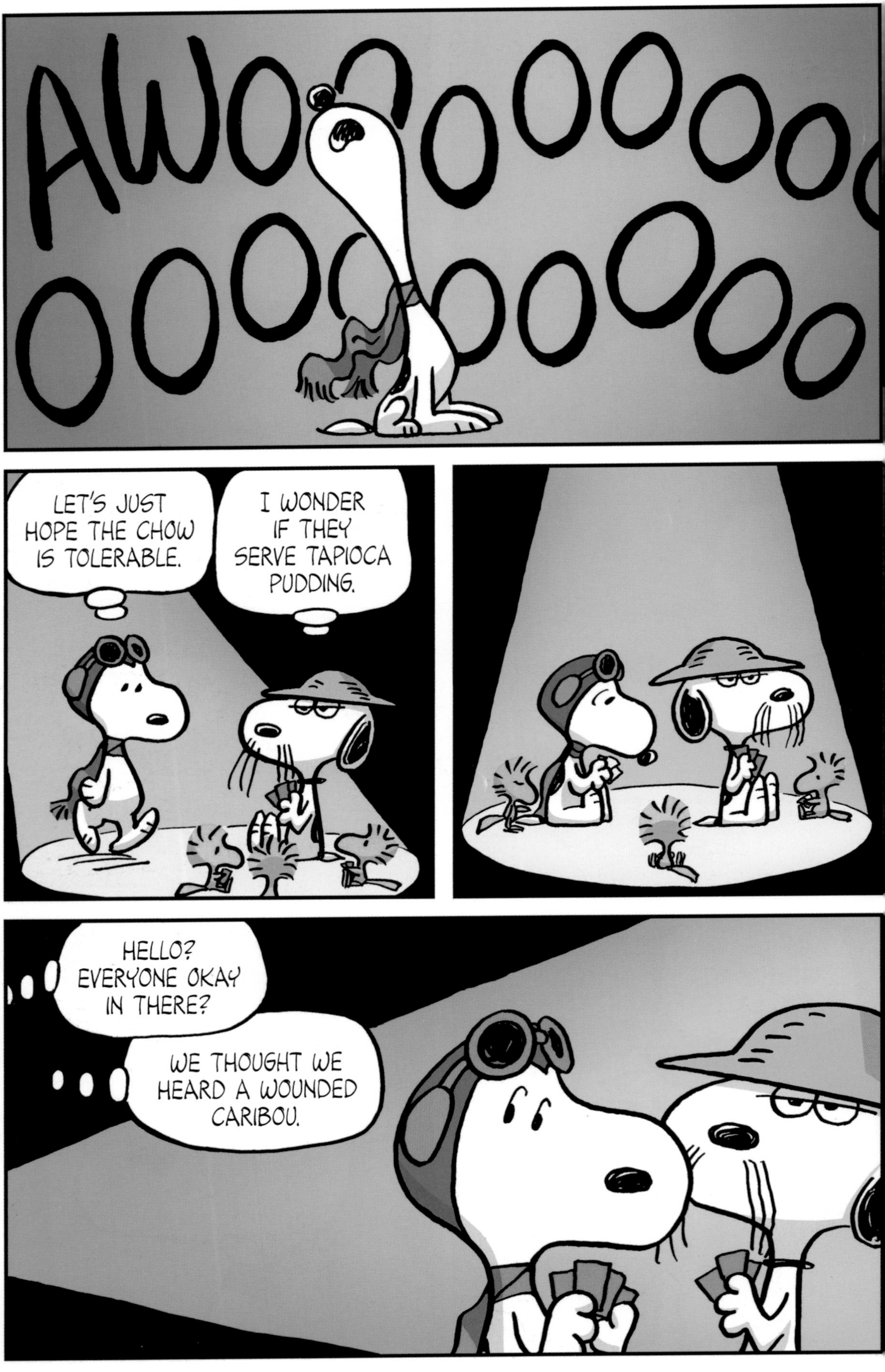
AWOOOOOOOOOOOOOOOOOO
LET'S JUST HOPE THE CHOW IS TOLERABLE.
I WONDER IF THEY SERVE TAPIOCA PUDDING.
HELLO? EVERYONE OKAY IN THERE?
WE THOUGHT WE HEARD A WOUNDED CARIBOU.

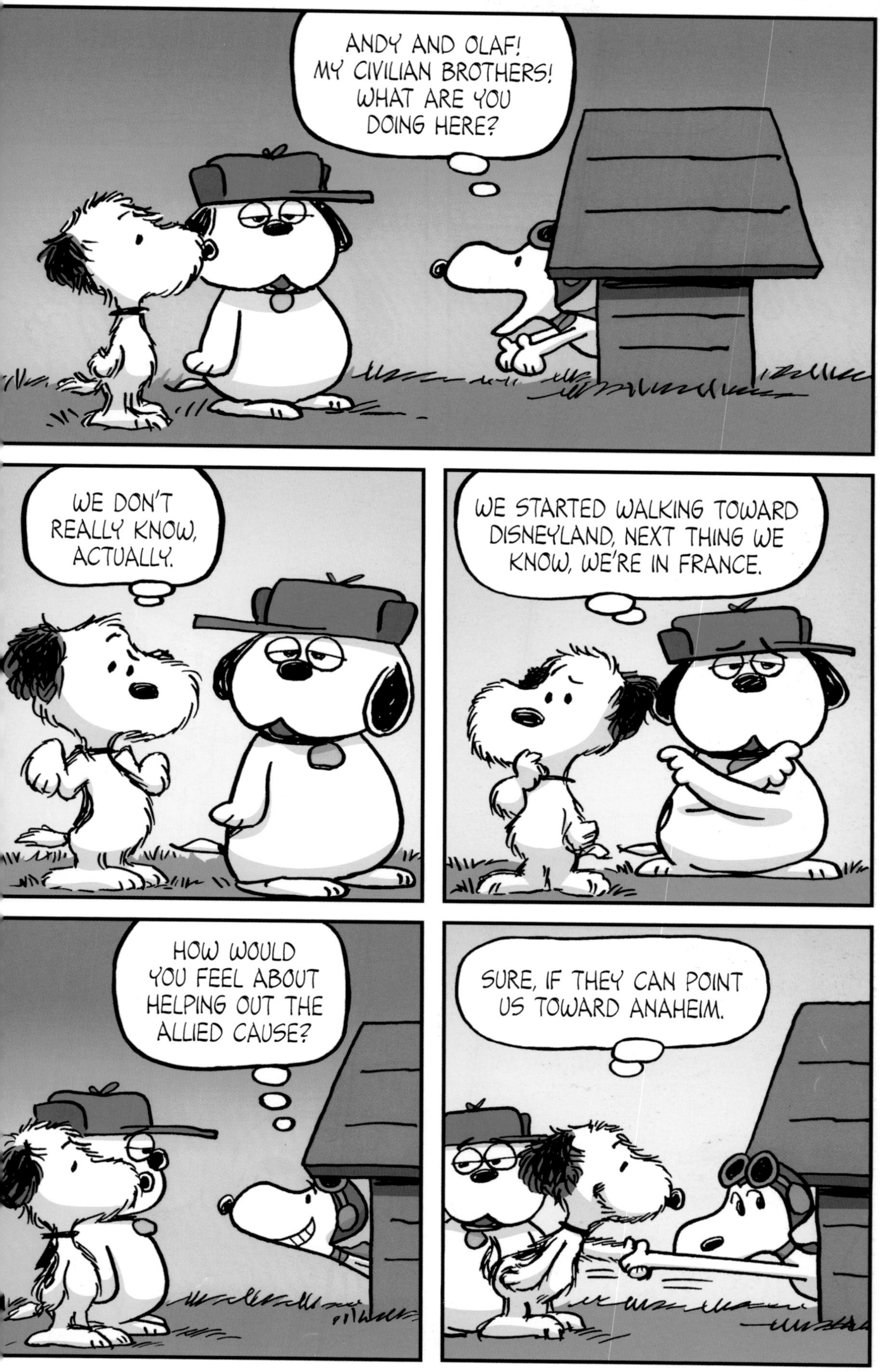
ANDY AND OLAF! MY CIVILIAN BROTHERS! WHAT ARE YOU DOING HERE?
WE DON'T REALLY KNOW, ACTUALLY.
WE STARTED WALKING TOWARD DISNEYLAND, NEXT THING WE KNOW, WE'RE IN FRANCE.
HOW WOULD YOU FEEL ABOUT HELPING OUT THE ALLIED CAUSE?
SURE, IF THEY CAN POINT US TOWARD ANAHEIM.

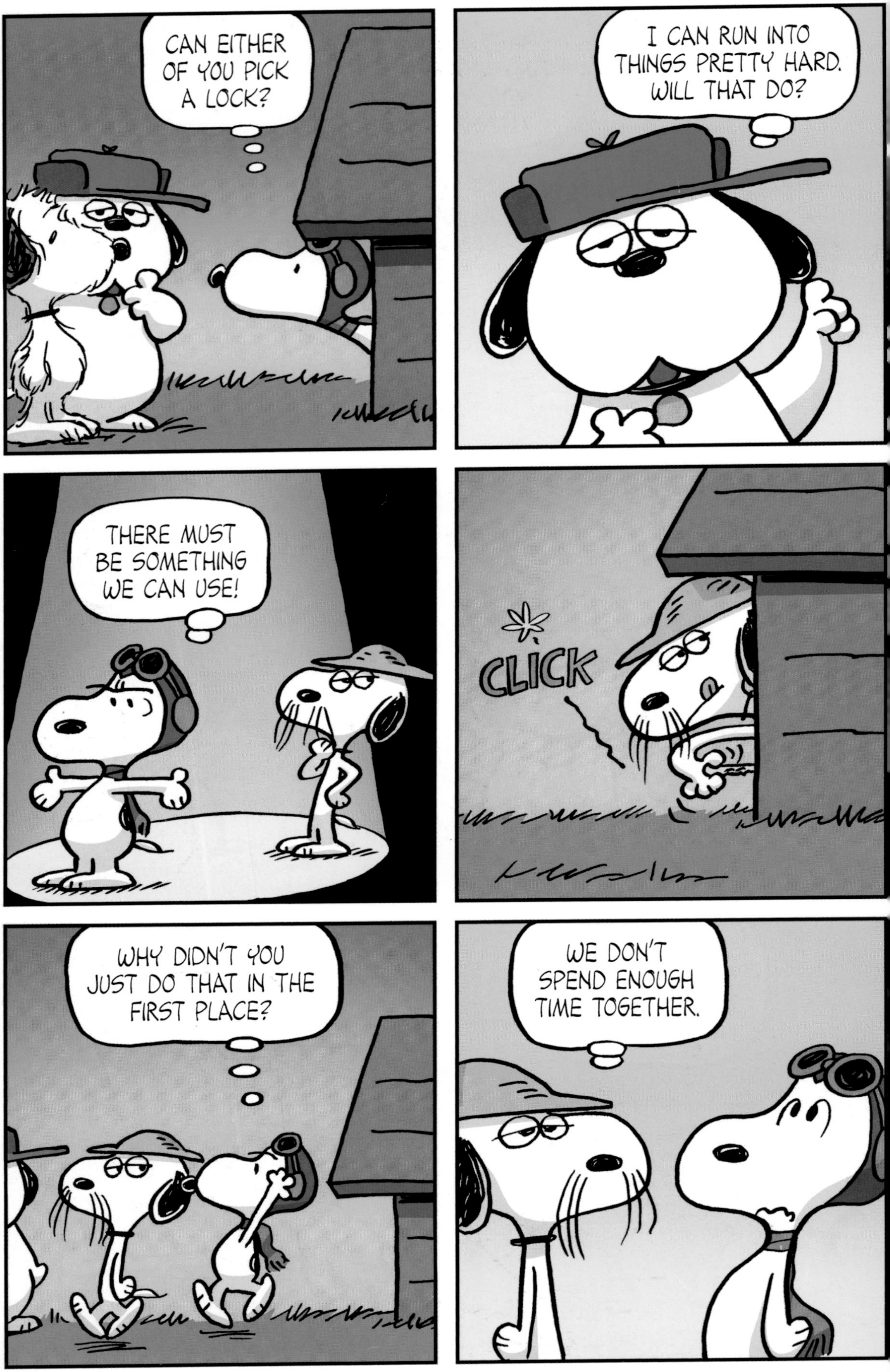
CAN EITHER OF YOU PICK A LOCK?
I CAN RUN INTO THINGS PRETTY HARD. WILL THAT DO?
THERE MUST BE SOMETHING WE CAN USE!
CLICK
WHY DIDN'T YOU JUST DO THAT IN THE FIRST PLACE?
WE DON'T SPEND ENOUGH TIME TOGETHER.

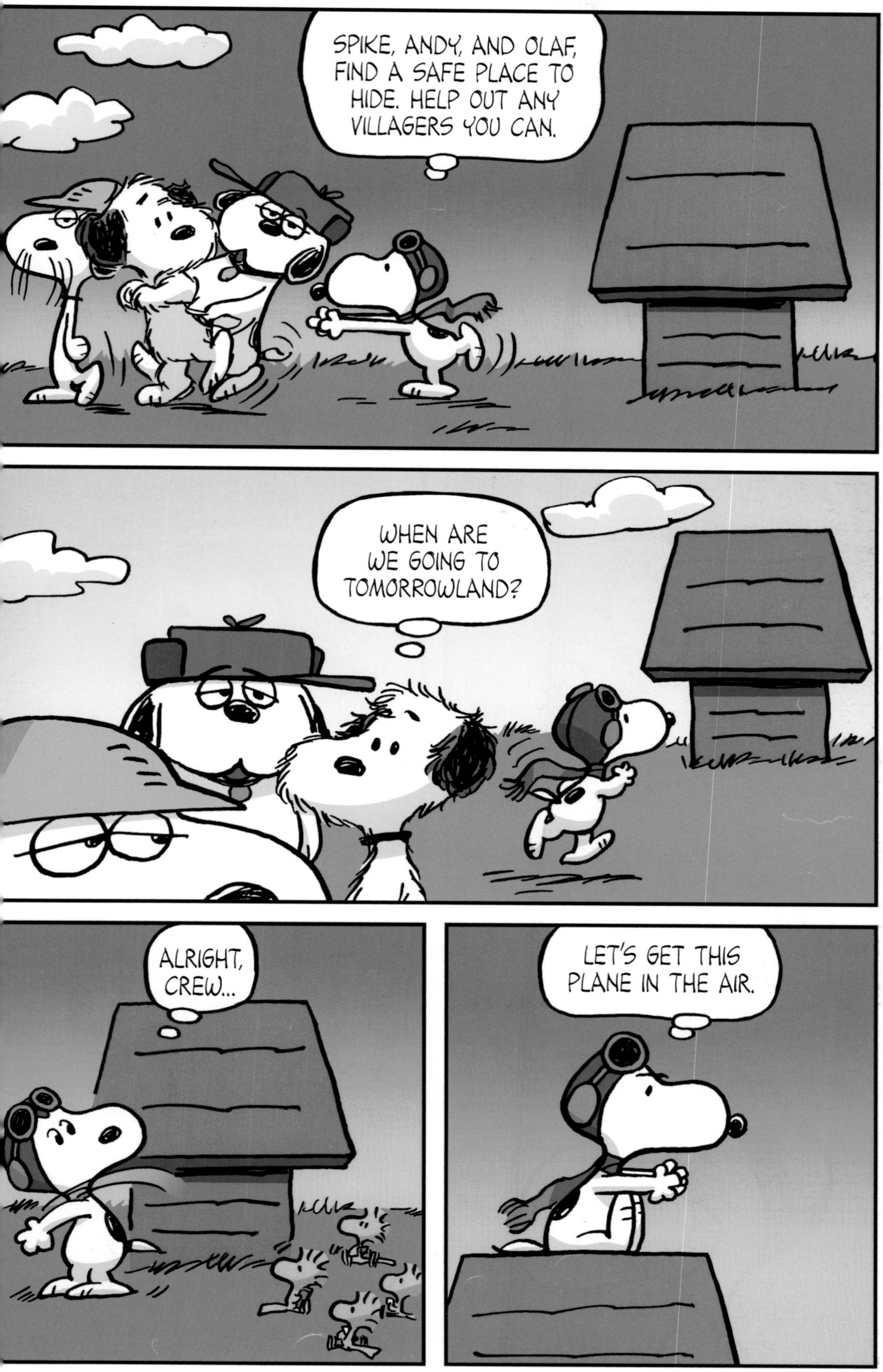
SPIKE, ANDY, AND OLAF, FIND A SAFE PLACE TO HIDE. HELP OUT ANY VILLAGERS YOU CAN.
WHEN ARE WE GOING TO TOMORROWLAND?
ALRIGHT, CREW...
LET'S GET THIS PLANE IN THE AIR.

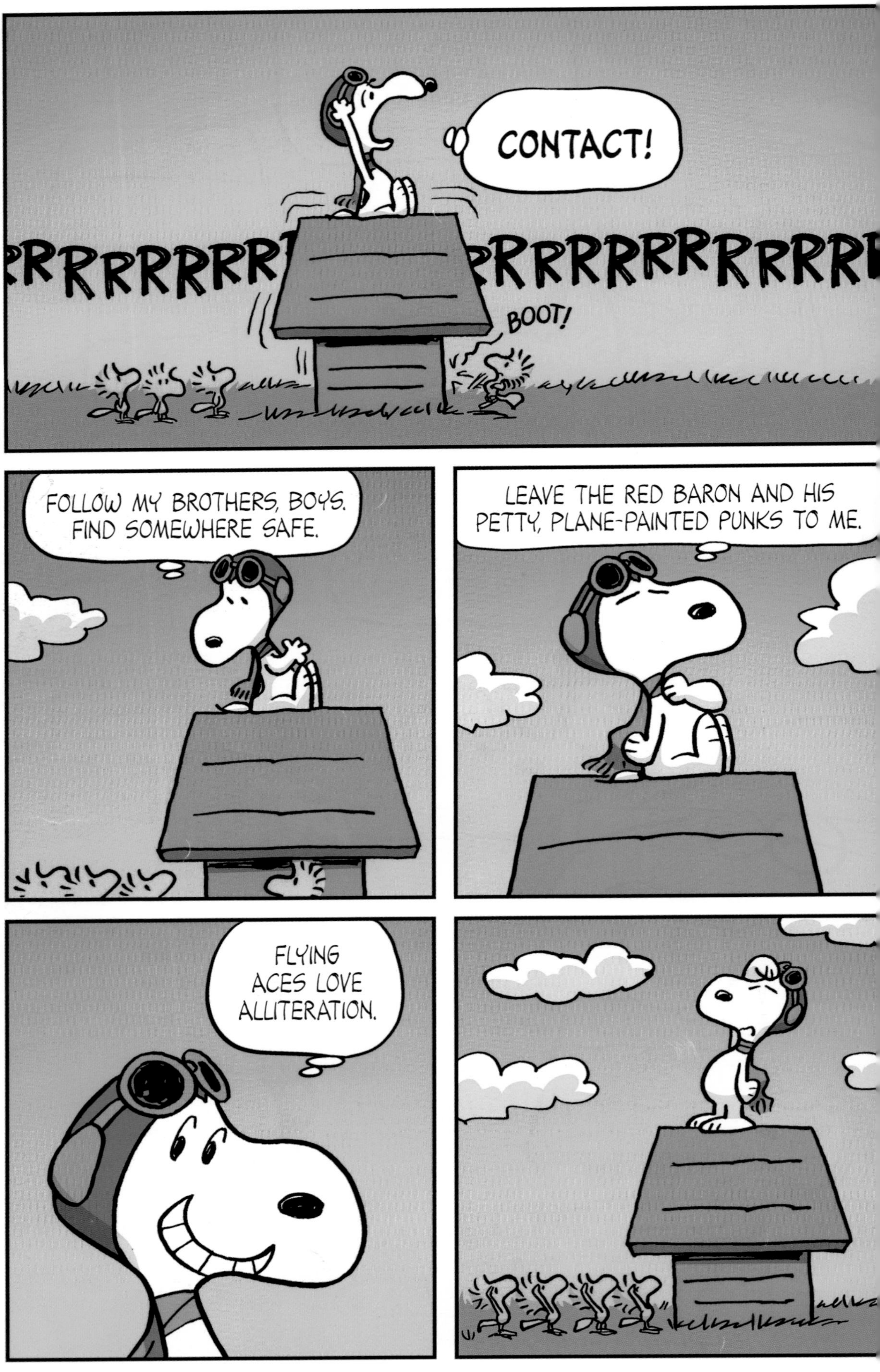
CONTACT!
RRRRRRRRRRRRRRRRRRRRRR
BOOT!
FOLLOW MY BROTHERS, BOYS. FIND SOMEWHERE SAFE.
LEAVE THE RED BARON AND HIS PETTY, PLANE-PAINTED PUNKS TO ME.
FLYING ACES LOVE ALLITERATION.

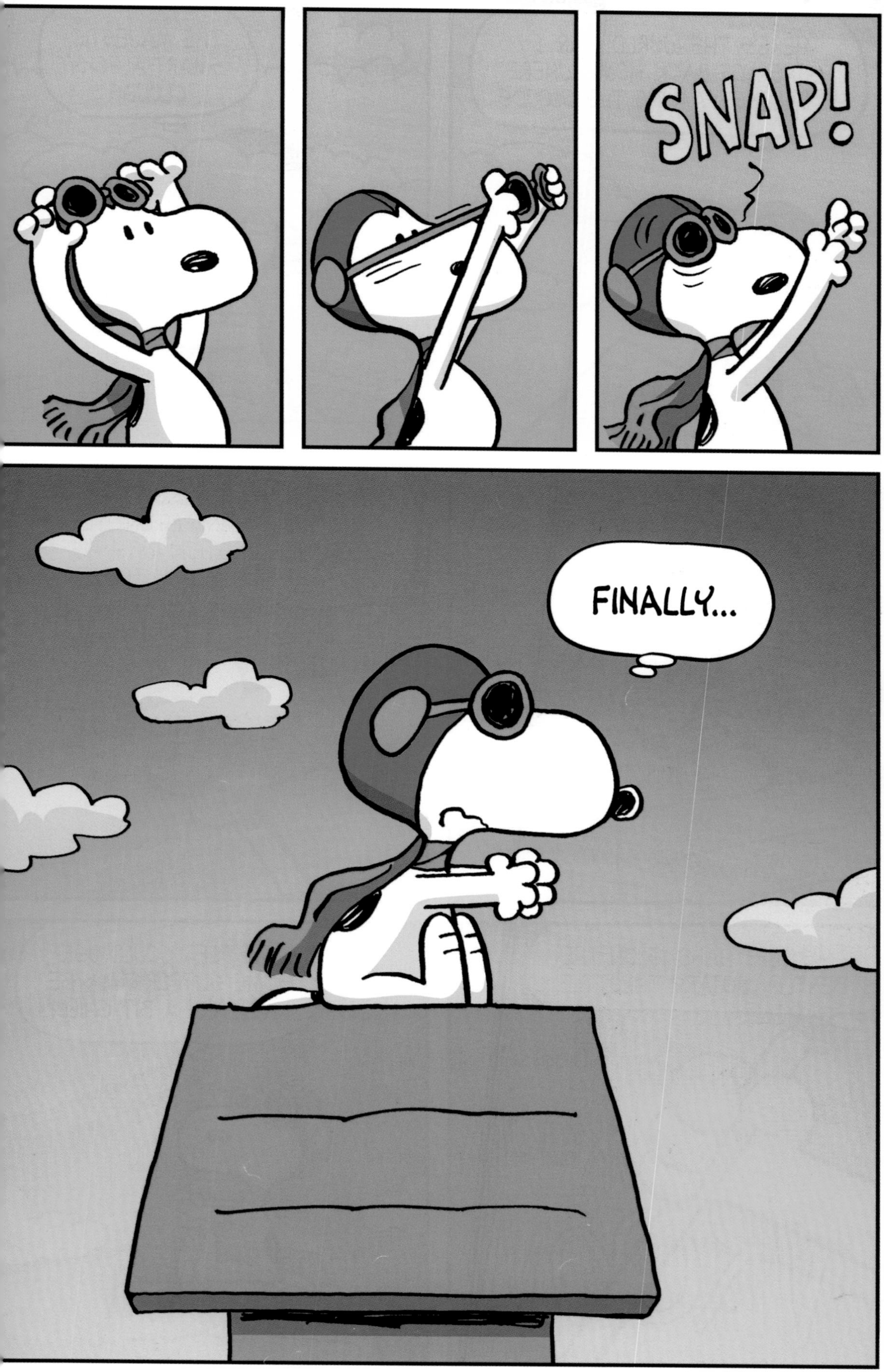
SNAP!
FINALLY...

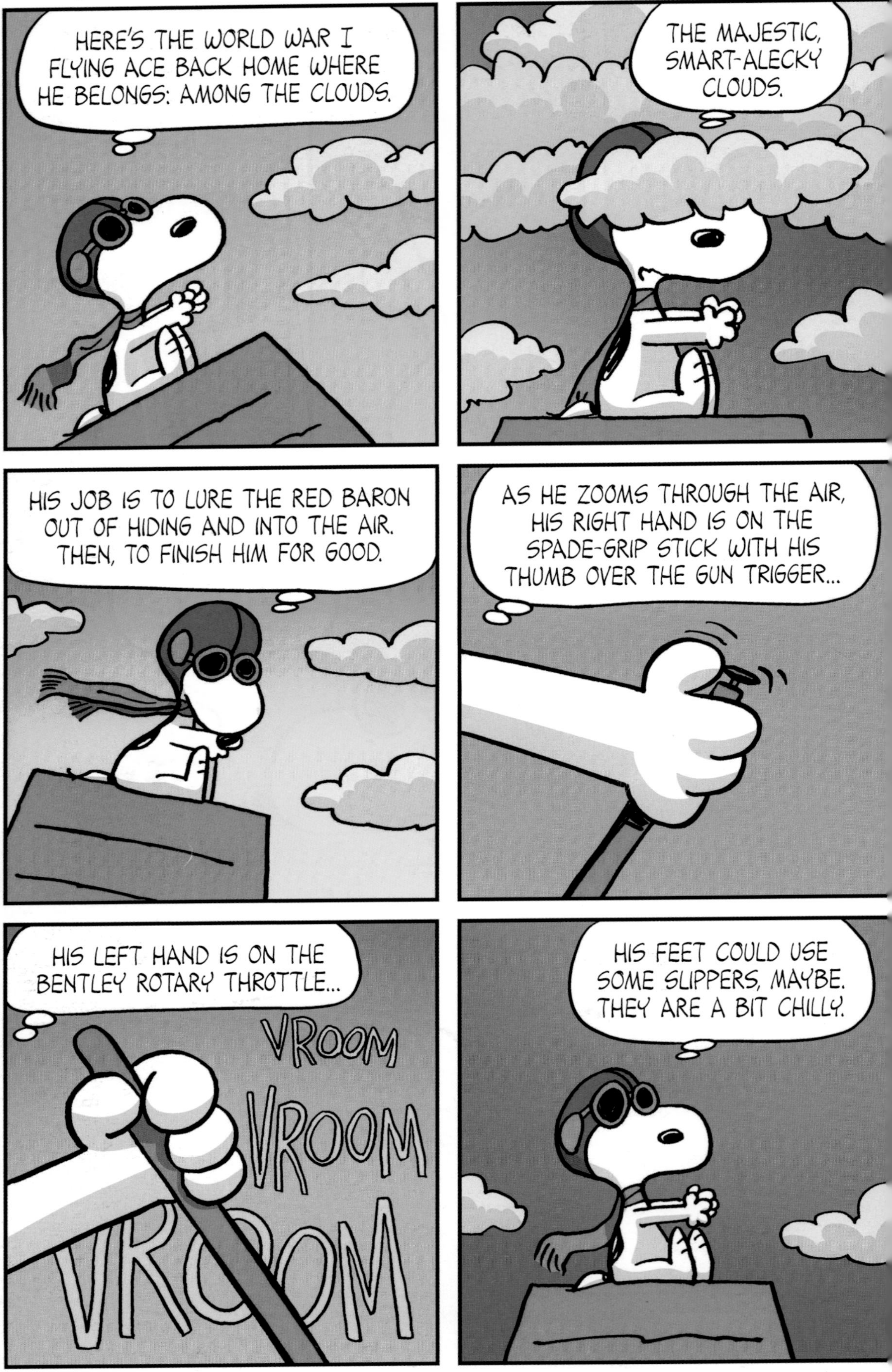
HERE'S THE WORLD WAR I FLYING ACE BACK HOME WHERE HE BELONGS: AMONG THE CLOUDS.
THE MAJESTIC, SMART-ALECKY CLOUDS.
HIS JOB IS TO LURE THE RED BARON OUT OF HIDING AND INTO THE AIR. THEN, TO FINISH HIM FOR GOOD.
AS HE ZOOMS THROUGH THE AIR, HIS RIGHT HAND IS ON THE SPADE-GRIP STICK WITH HIS THUMB OVER THE GUN TRIGGER...
HIS LEFT HAND IS ON THE BENTLEY ROTARY THROTTLE...
VROOM
VROOM
VROOM
HIS FEET COULD USE SOME SLIPPERS, MAYBE. THEY ARE A BIT CHILLY.

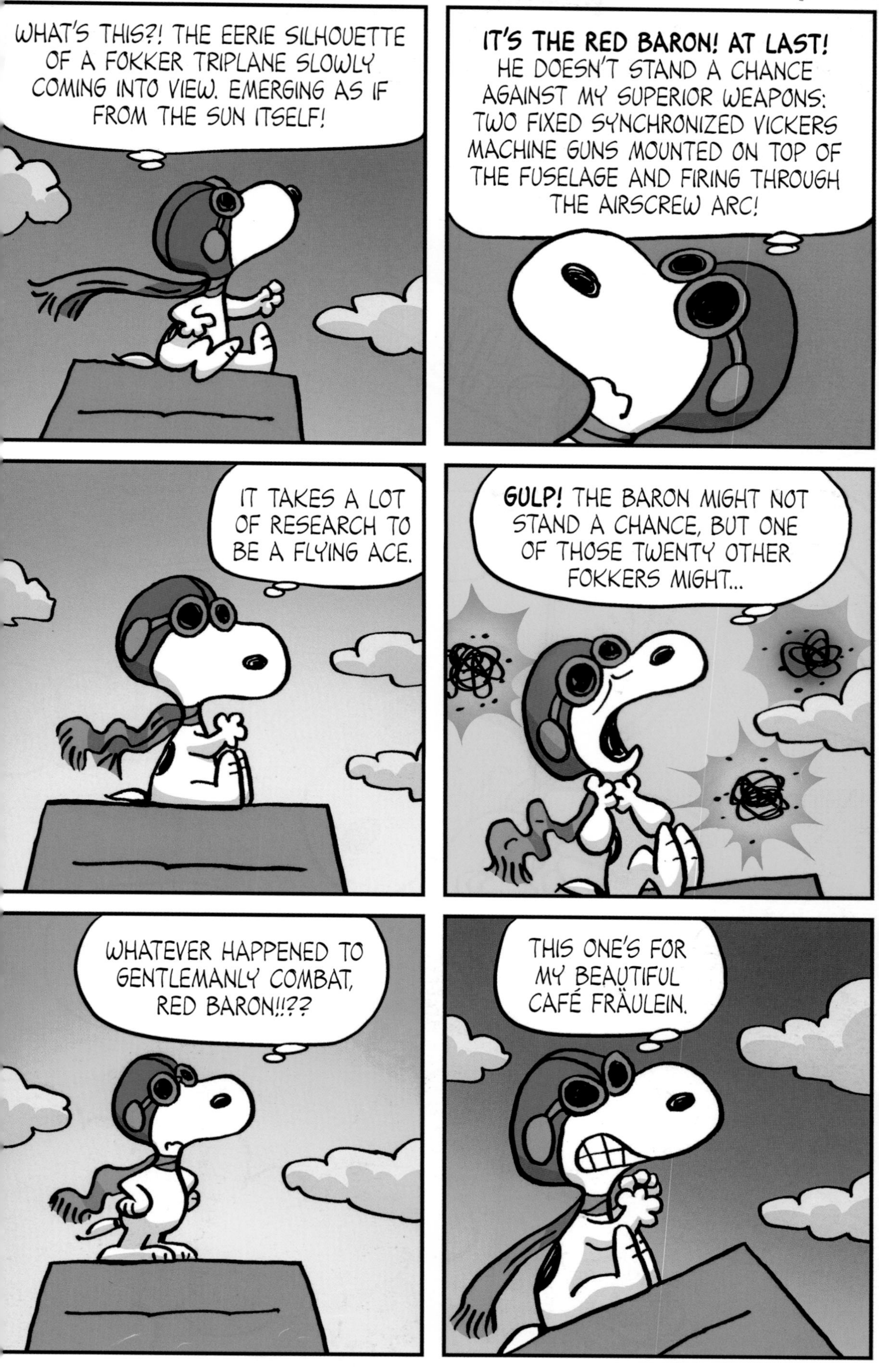
WHAT'S THIS?! THE EERIE SILHOUETTE OF A FOKKER TRIPLANE SLOWLY COMING INTO VIEW. EMERGING AS IF FROM THE SUN ITSELF!
IT'S THE RED BARON! AT LAST! HE DOESN'T STAND A CHANCE AGAINST MY SUPERIOR WEAPONS: TWO FIXED SYNCHRONIZED VICKERS MACHINE GUNS MOUNTED ON TOP OF THE FUSELAGE AND FIRING THROUGH THE AIRSCREW ARC!
IT TAKES A LOT OF RESEARCH TO BE A FLYING ACE.
GULP! THE BARON MIGHT NOT STAND A CHANCE, BUT ONE OF THOSE TWENTY OTHER FOKKERS MIGHT...
WHATEVER HAPPENED TO GENTLEMANLY COMBAT, RED BARON!!??
THIS ONE'S FOR MY BEAUTIFUL CAFÉ FRÄULEIN.

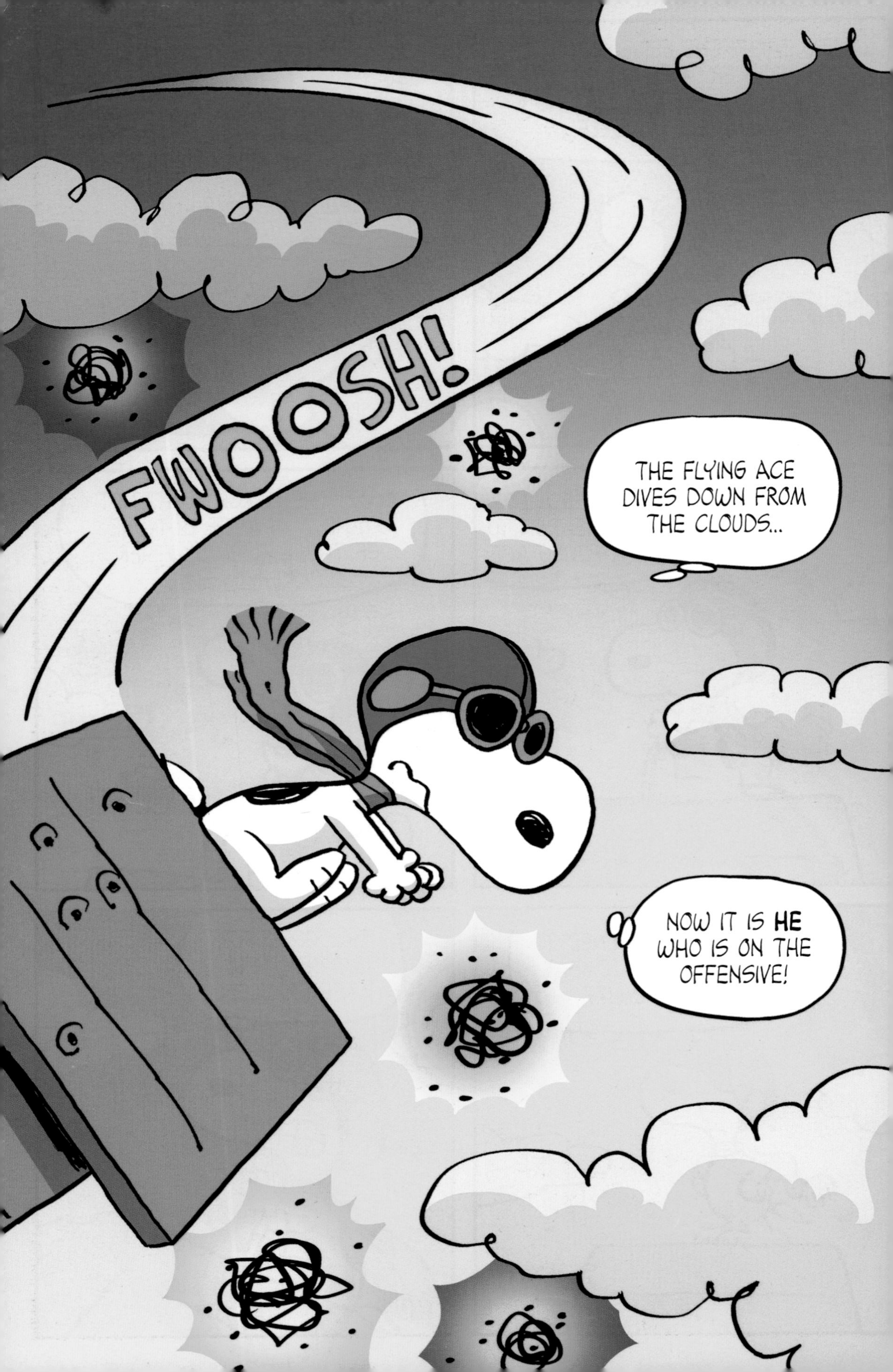
FWOOSH!
THE FLYING ACE DIVES DOWN FROM THE CLOUDS...
NOW IT IS **HE** WHO IS ON THE OFFENSIVE!

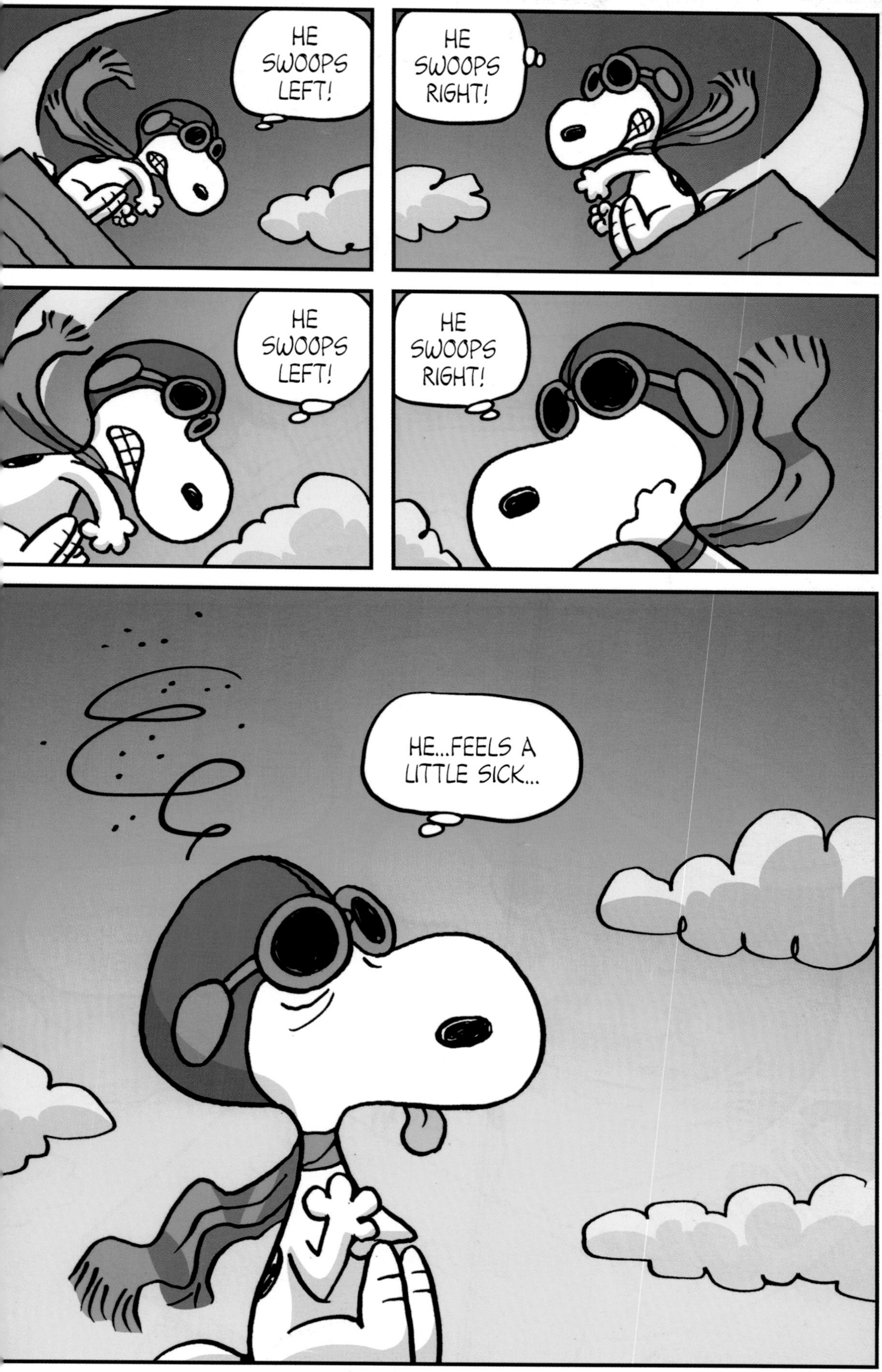
HE SWOOPS LEFT!
HE SWOOPS RIGHT!
HE SWOOPS LEFT!
HE SWOOPS RIGHT!
HE...FEELS A LITTLE SICK...

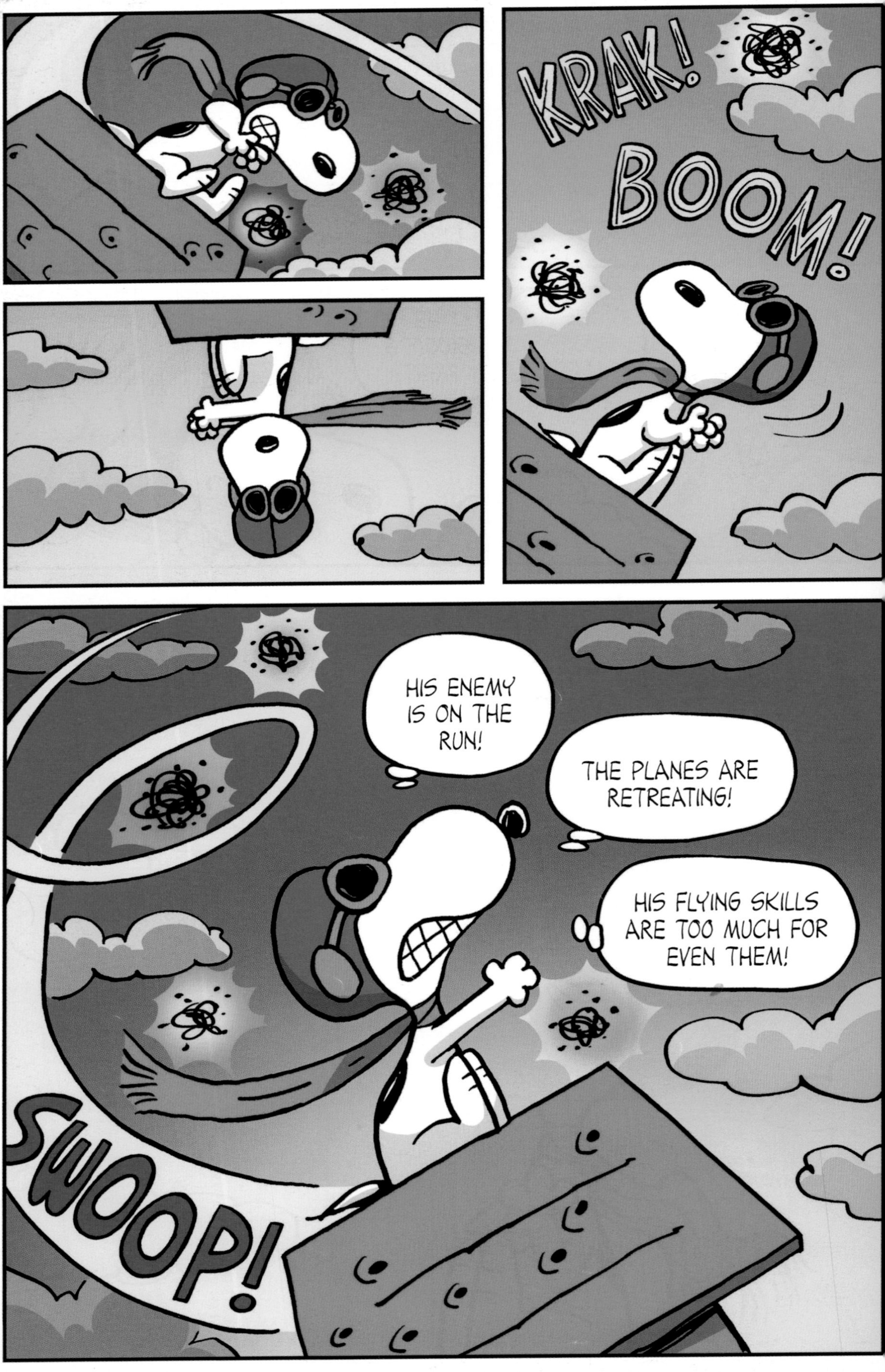
KRAK!
BOOM!
HIS ENEMY IS ON THE RUN!
THE PLANES ARE RETREATING!
HIS FLYING SKILLS ARE TOO MUCH FOR EVEN THEM!
SWOOP!

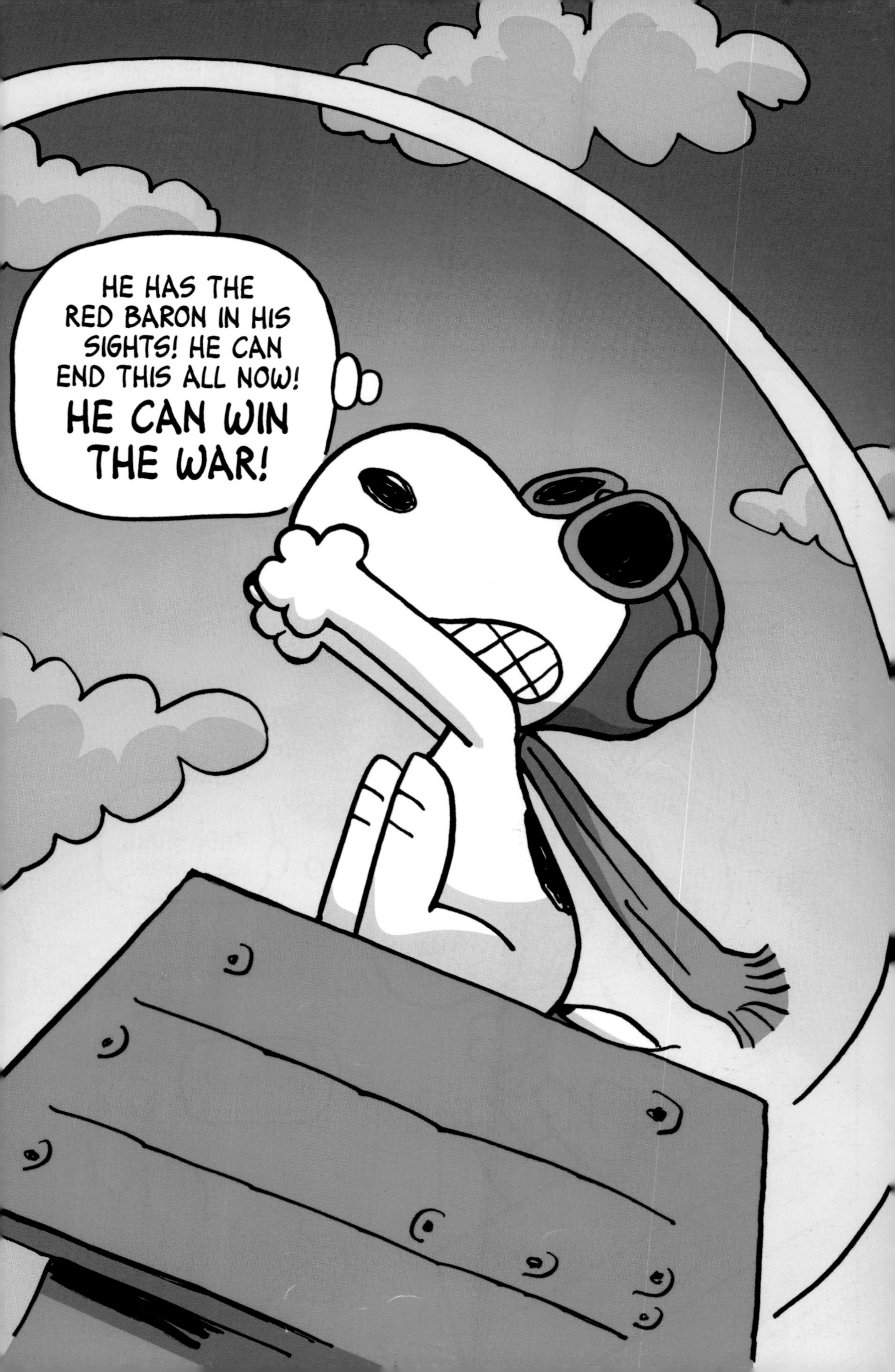
HE HAS THE RED BARON IN HIS SIGHTS! HE CAN END THIS ALL NOW! HE CAN WIN THE WAR!

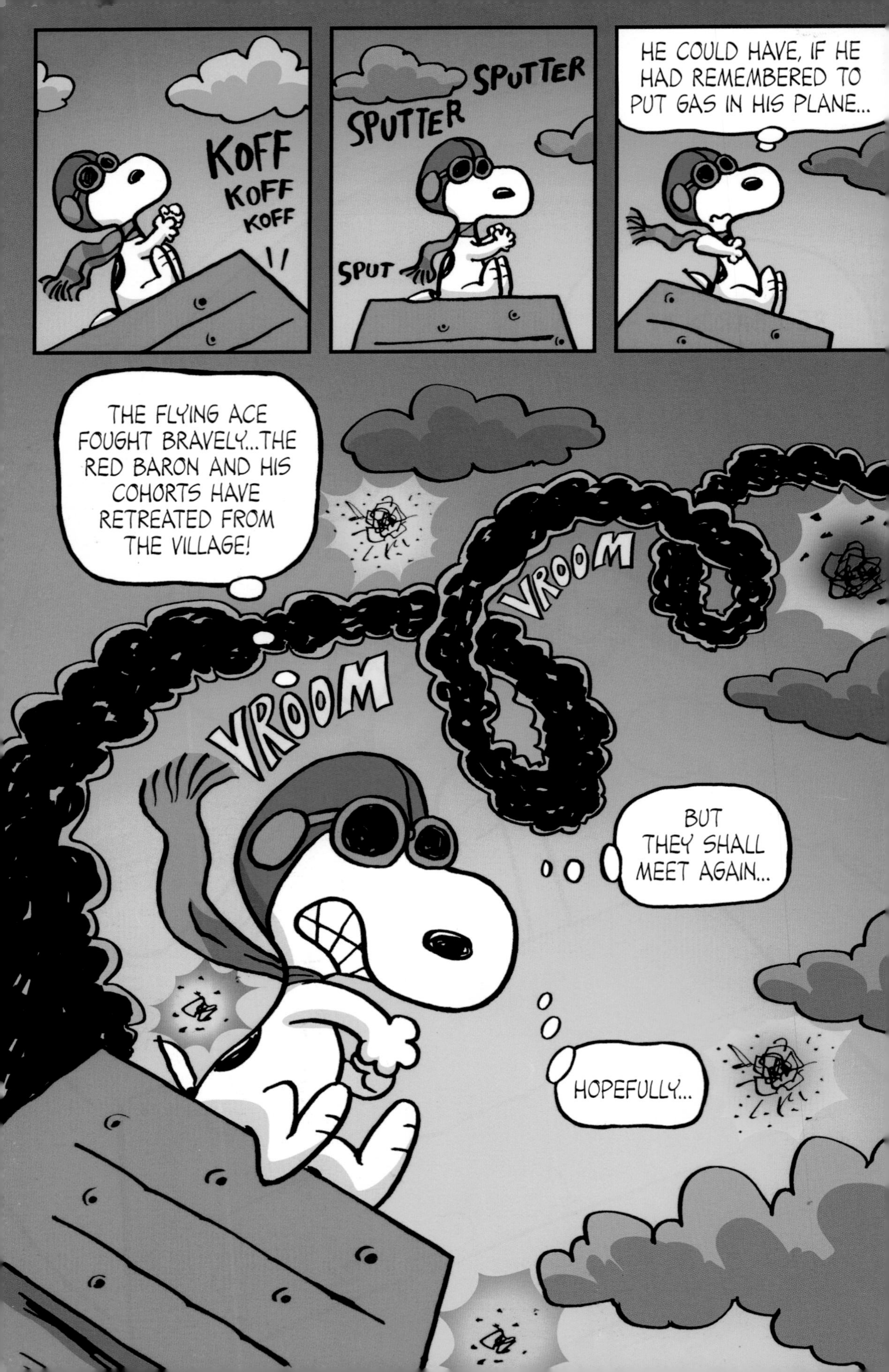
KOFF
KOFF
KOFF
SPUTTER
SPUTTER
SPUT
HE COULD HAVE, IF HE HAD REMEMBERED TO PUT GAS IN HIS PLANE...
THE FLYING ACE FOUGHT BRAVELY...THE RED BARON AND HIS COHORTS HAVE RETREATED FROM THE VILLAGE!
VROOM
VROOM
BUT THEY SHALL MEET AGAIN...
HOPEFULLY...

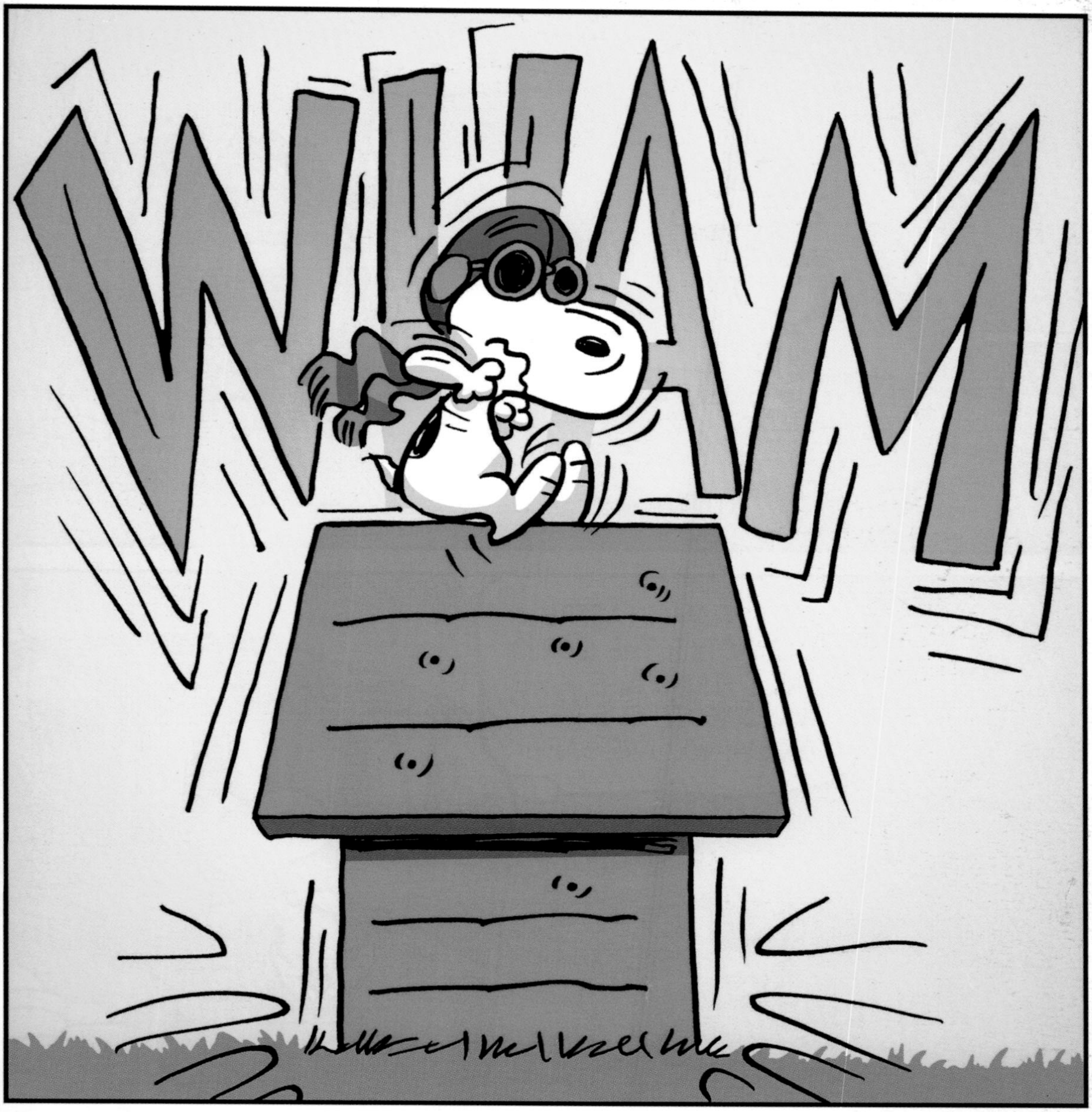
WHAM

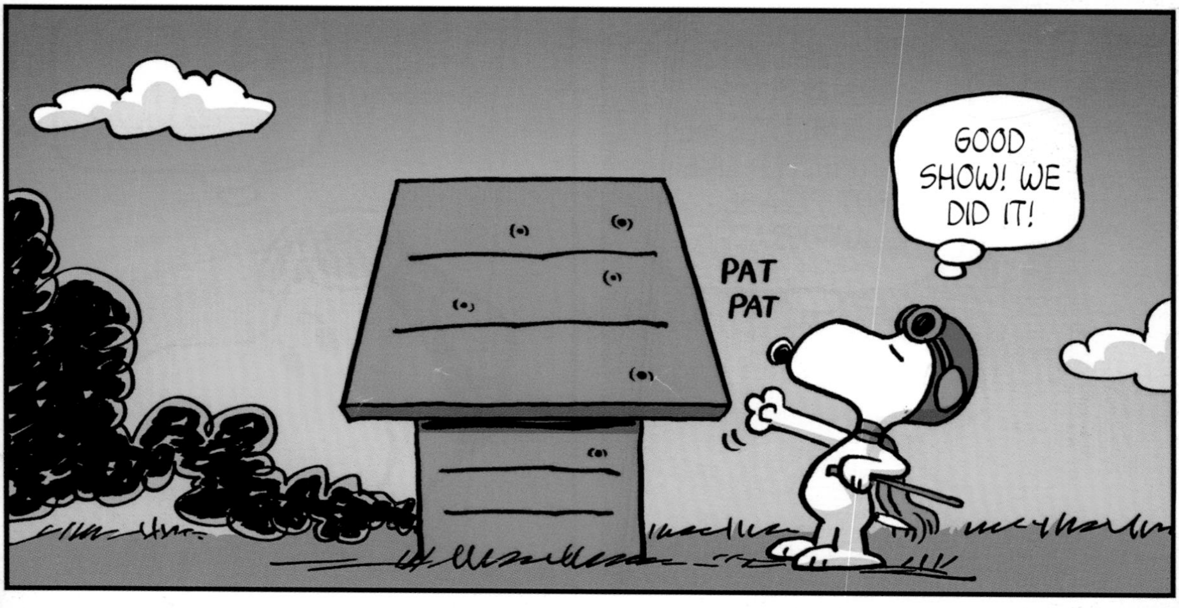
PAT
PAT
GOOD SHOW! WE DID IT!

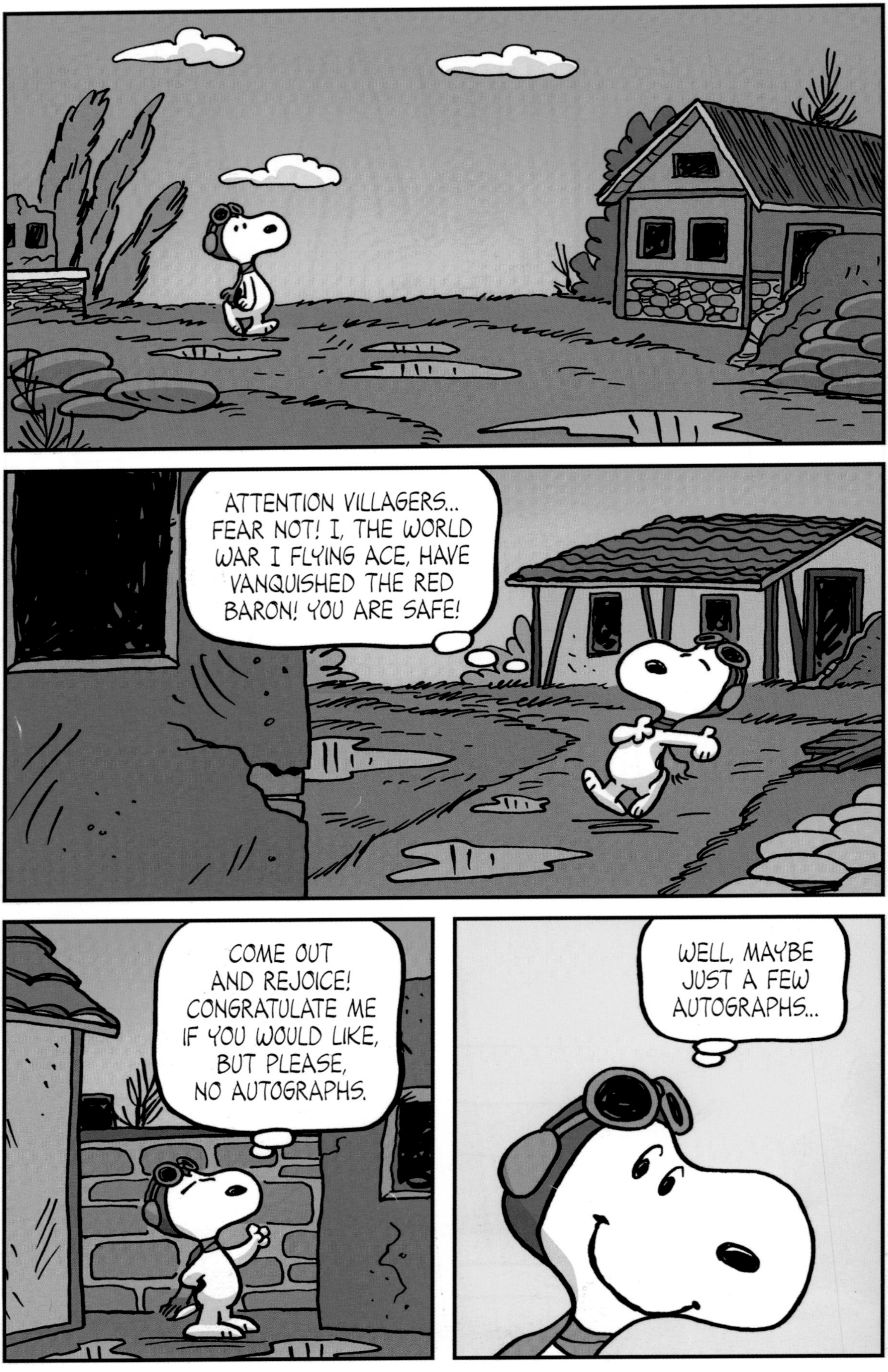
ATTENTION VILLAGERS... FEAR NOT! I, THE WORLD WAR I FLYING ACE, HAVE VANQUISHED THE RED BARON! YOU ARE SAFE!
COME OUT AND REJOICE! CONGRATULATE ME IF YOU WOULD LIKE, BUT PLEASE, NO AUTOGRAPHS.
WELL, MAYBE JUST A FEW AUTOGRAPHS...

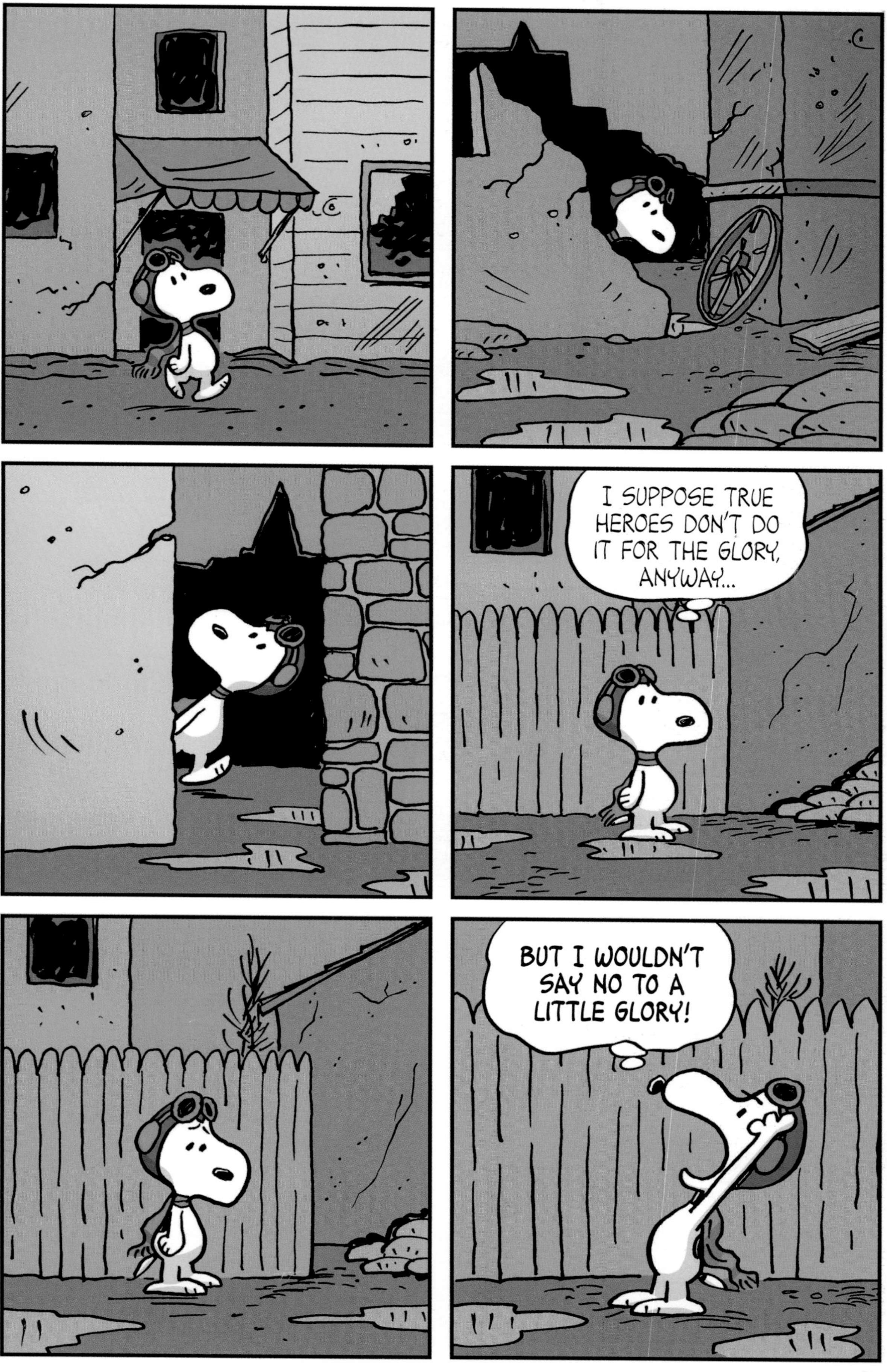
I SUPPOSE TRUE HEROES DON'T DO IT FOR THE GLORY, ANYWAY...
BUT I WOULDN'T SAY NO TO A LITTLE GLORY!

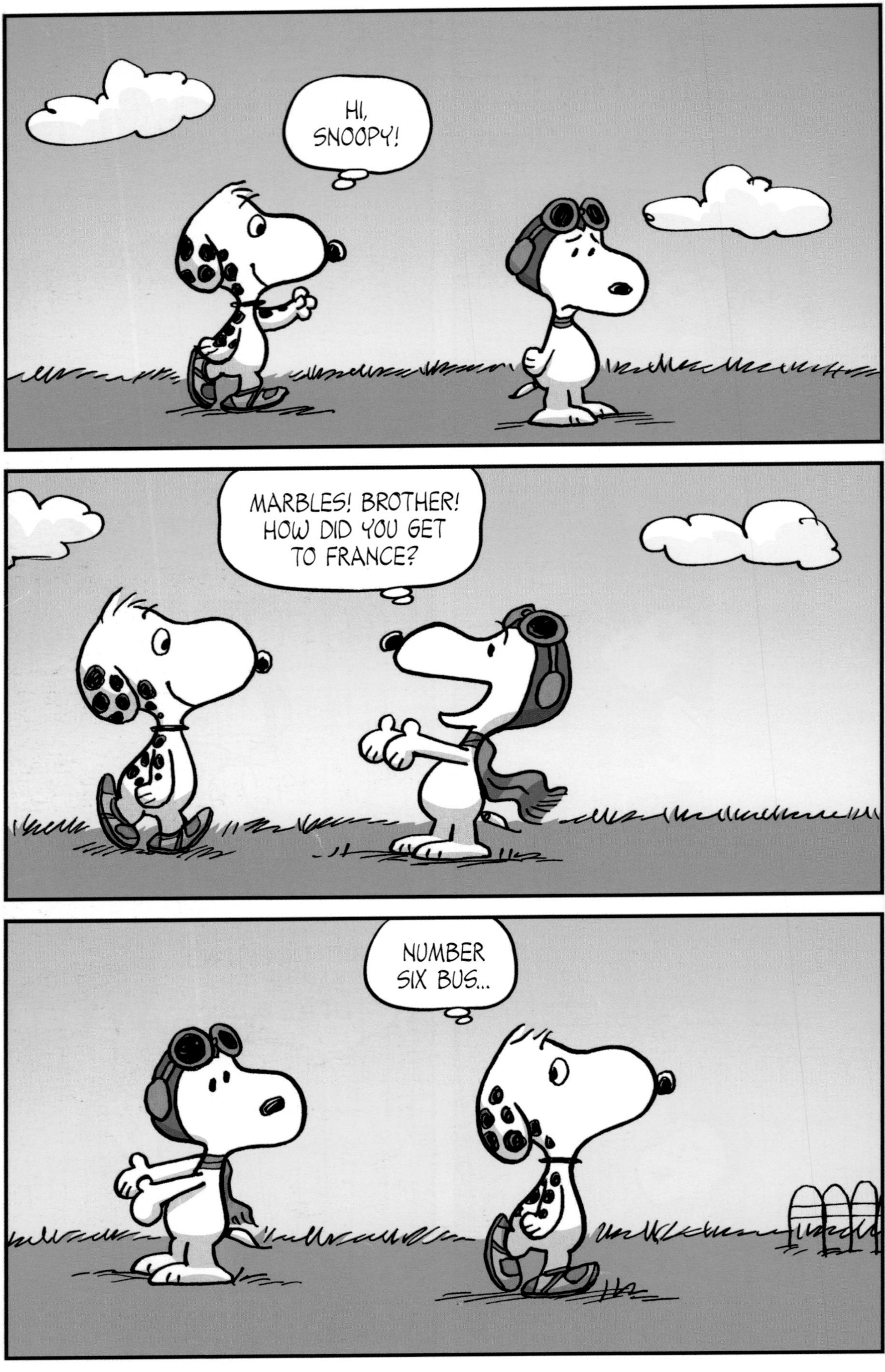
HI, SNOOPY!
MARBLES! BROTHER! HOW DID YOU GET TO FRANCE?
NUMBER SIX BUS...

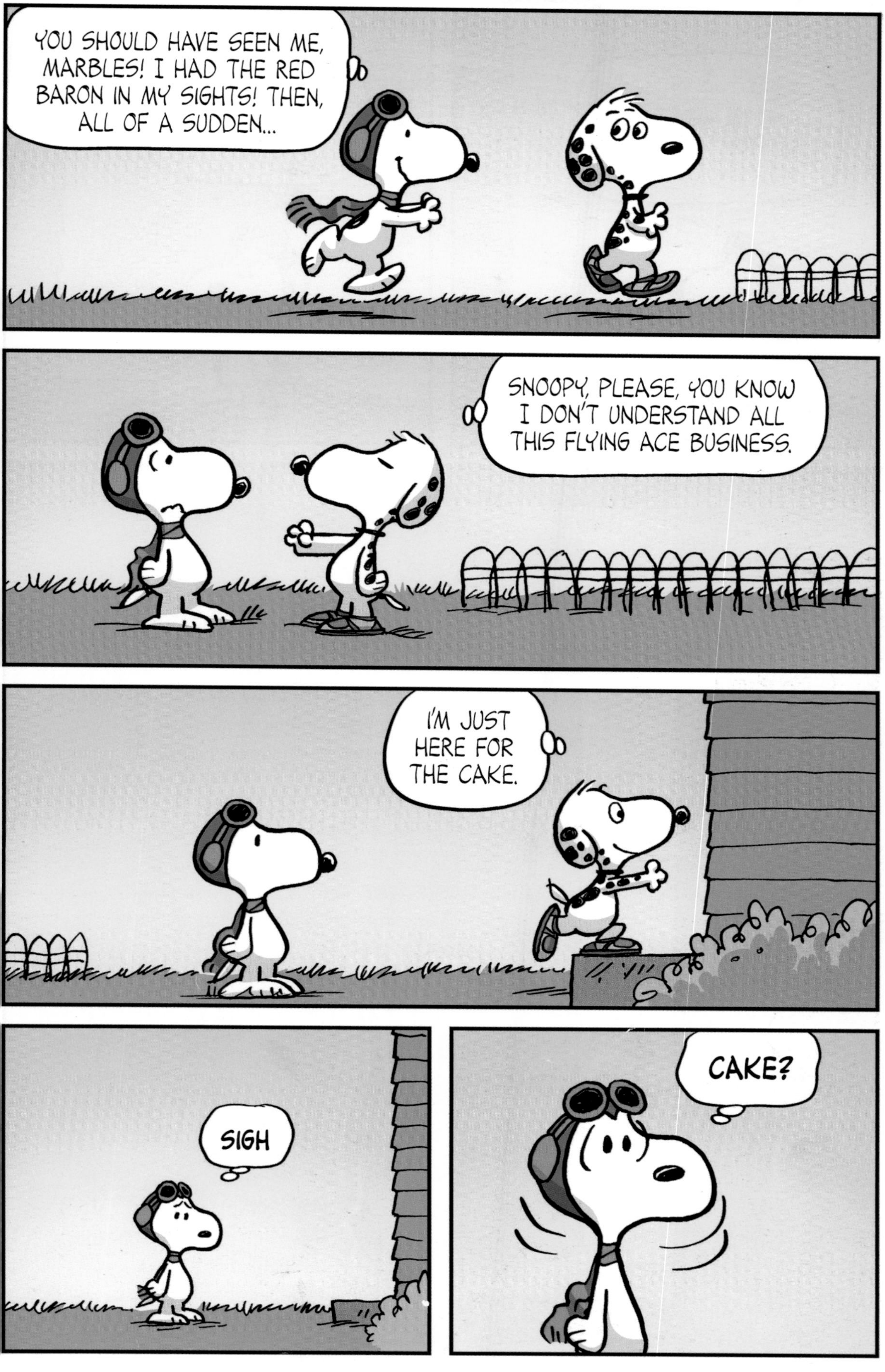
YOU SHOULD HAVE SEEN ME, MARBLES! I HAD THE RED BARON IN MY SIGHTS! THEN, ALL OF A SUDDEN...
SNOOPY, PLEASE, YOU KNOW I DON'T UNDERSTAND ALL THIS FLYING ACE BUSINESS.
I'M JUST HERE FOR THE CAKE.
SIGH
CAKE?

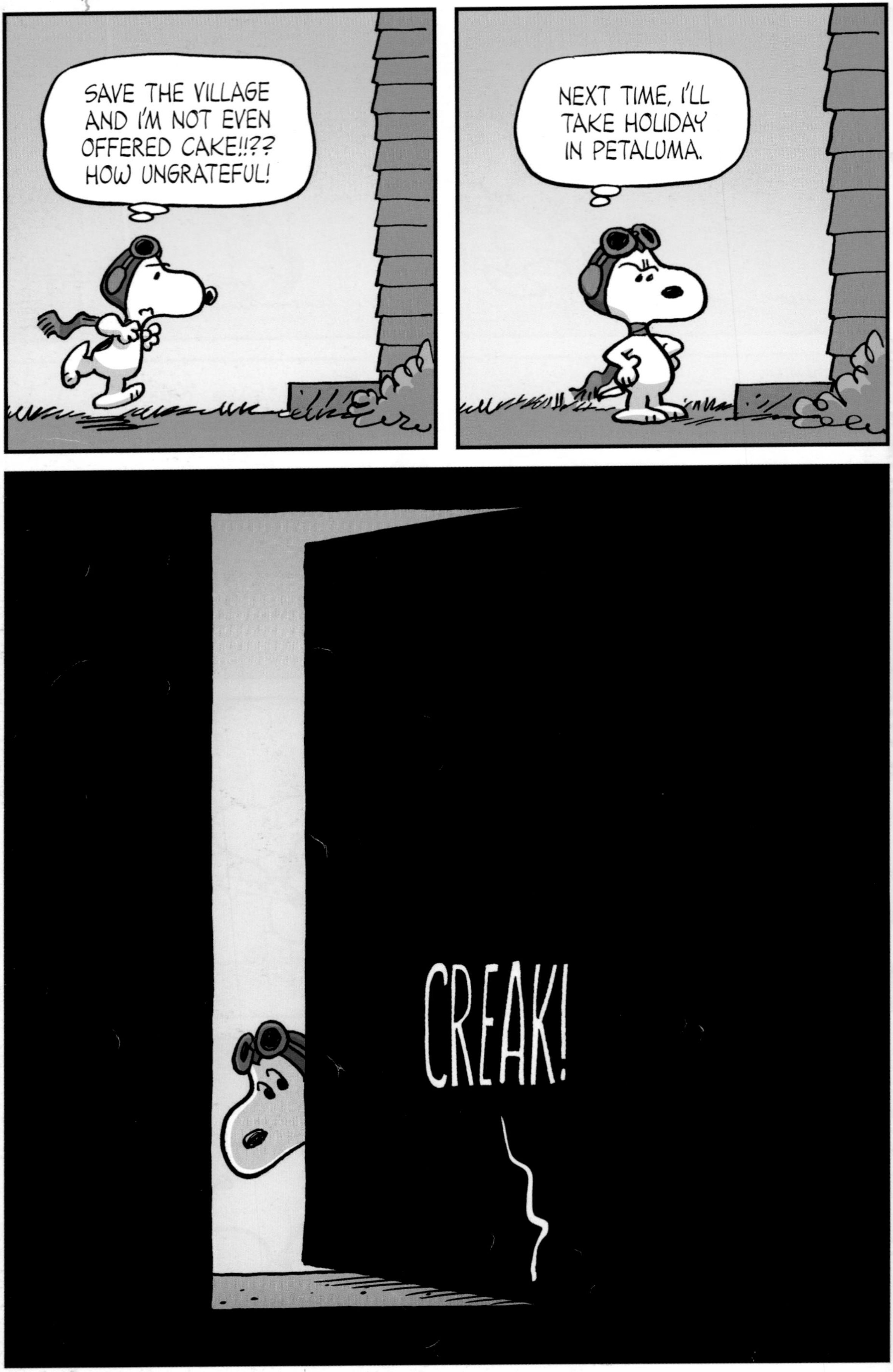
SAVE THE VILLAGE AND I'M NOT EVEN OFFERED CAKE!!?? HOW UNGRATEFUL!
NEXT TIME, I'LL TAKE HOLIDAY IN PETALUMA.
CREAK!

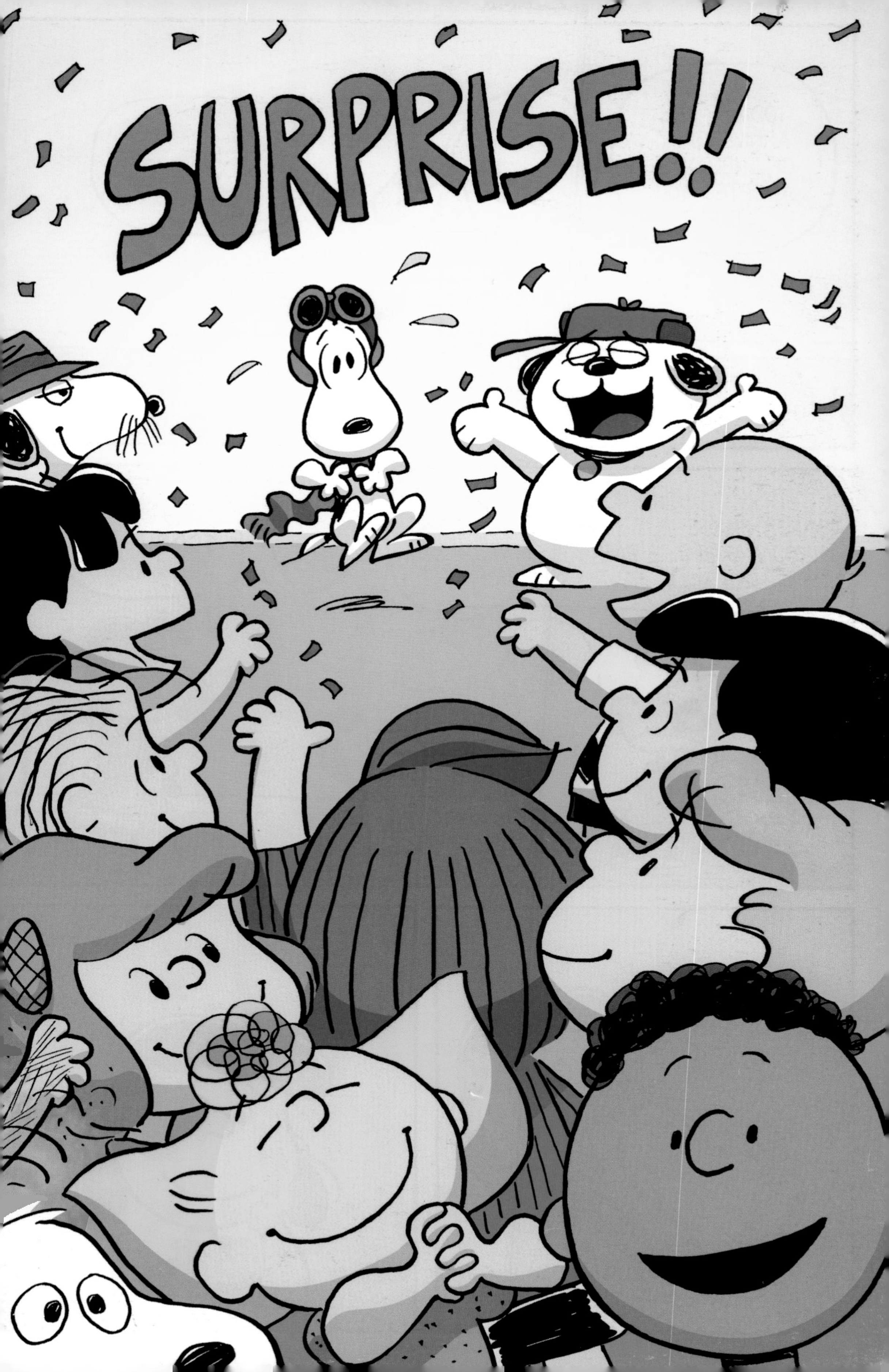
SURPRISE!!

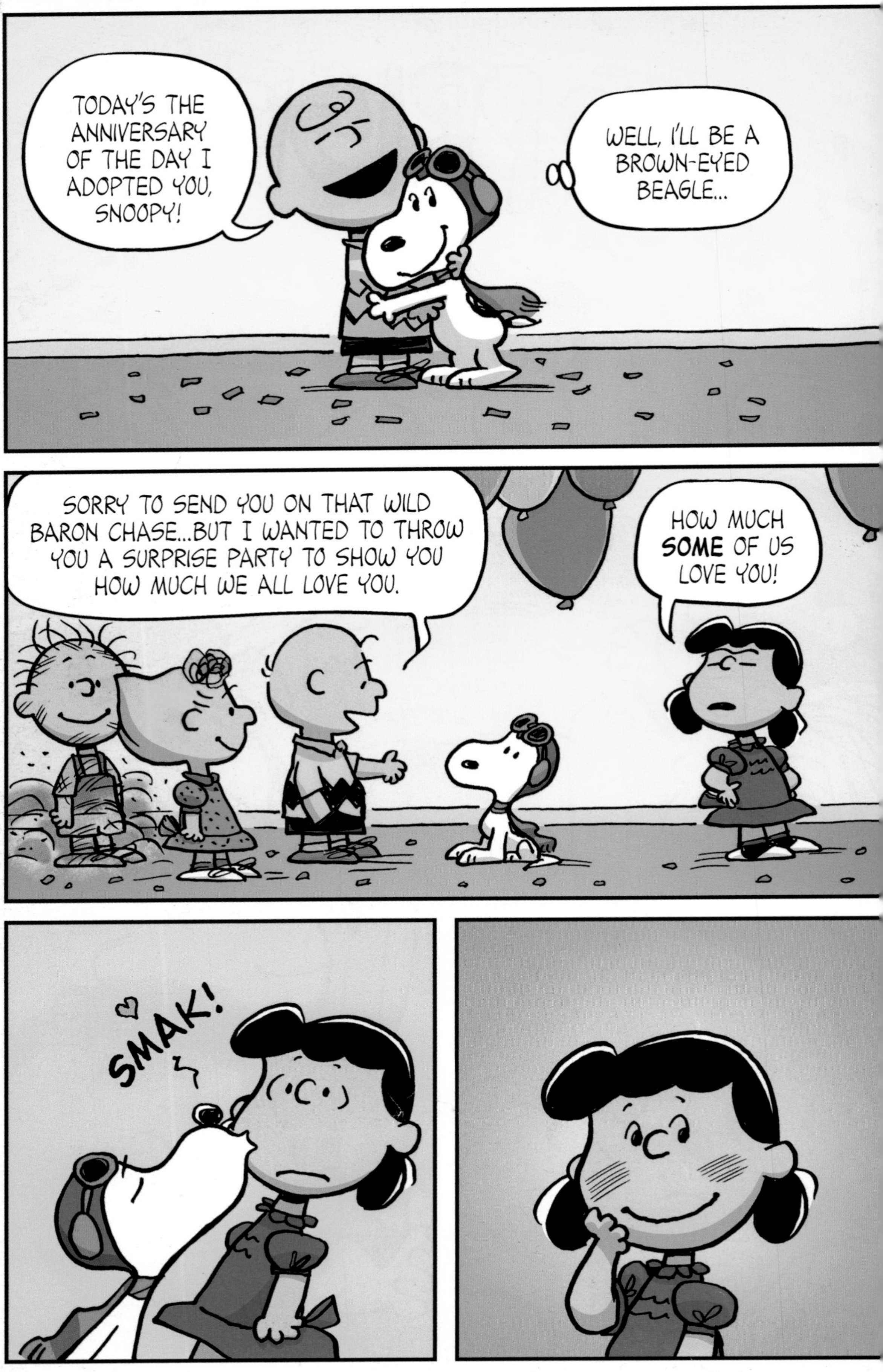
TODAY'S THE ANNIVERSARY OF THE DAY I ADOPTED YOU, SNOOPY!
WELL, I'LL BE A BROWN-EYED BEAGLE...
SORRY TO SEND YOU ON THAT WILD BARON CHASE...BUT I WANTED TO THROW YOU A SURPRISE PARTY TO SHOW YOU HOW MUCH WE ALL LOVE YOU.
HOW MUCH **SOME** OF US LOVE YOU!
SMAK!

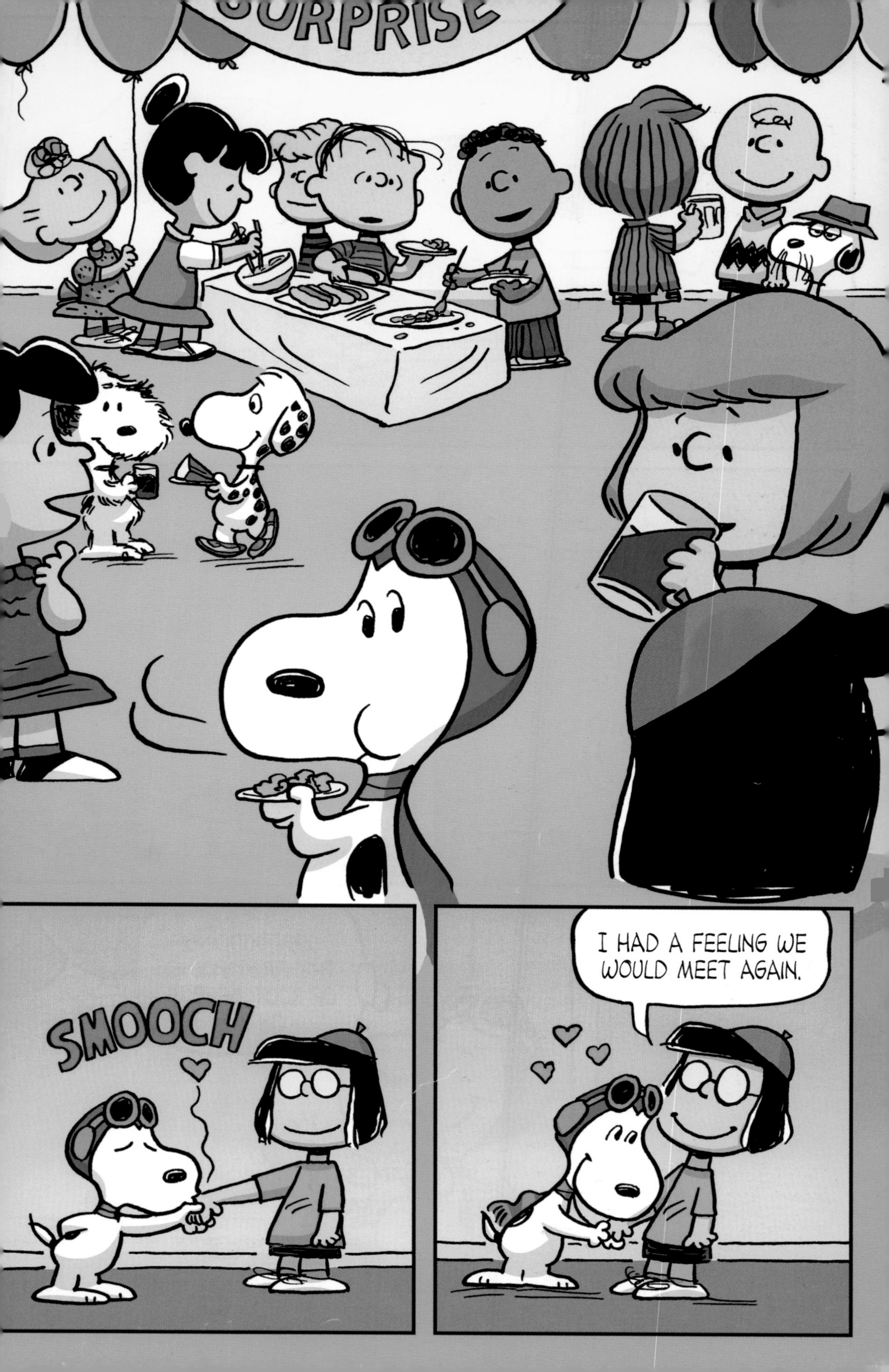
SURPRISE
SMOOCH
I HAD A FEELING WE WOULD MEET AGAIN.

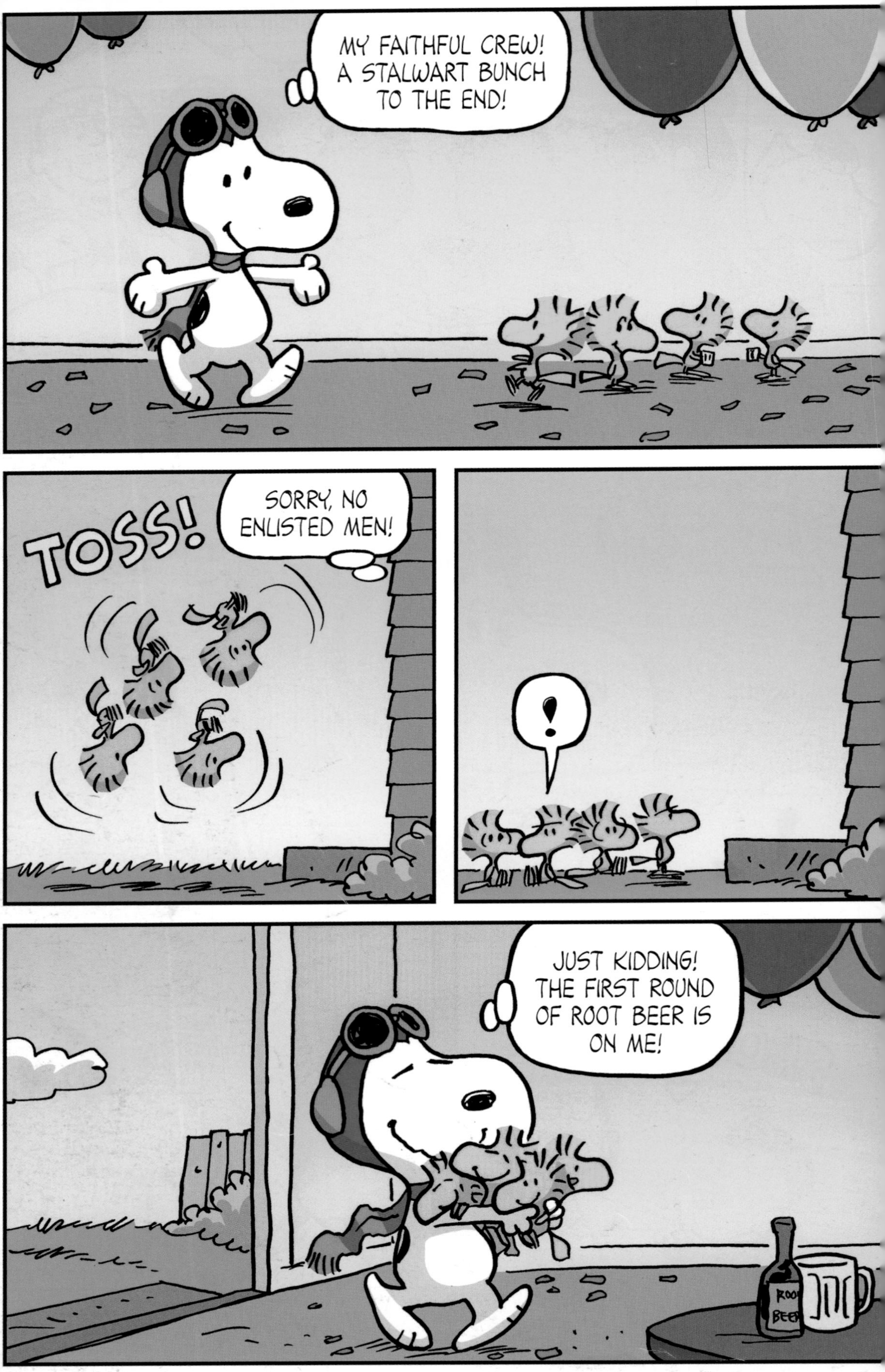
MY FAITHFUL CREW! A STALWART BUNCH TO THE END!
TOSS!
SORRY, NO ENLISTED MEN!
!
JUST KIDDING! THE FIRST ROUND OF ROOT BEER IS ON ME!
ROOT BEER

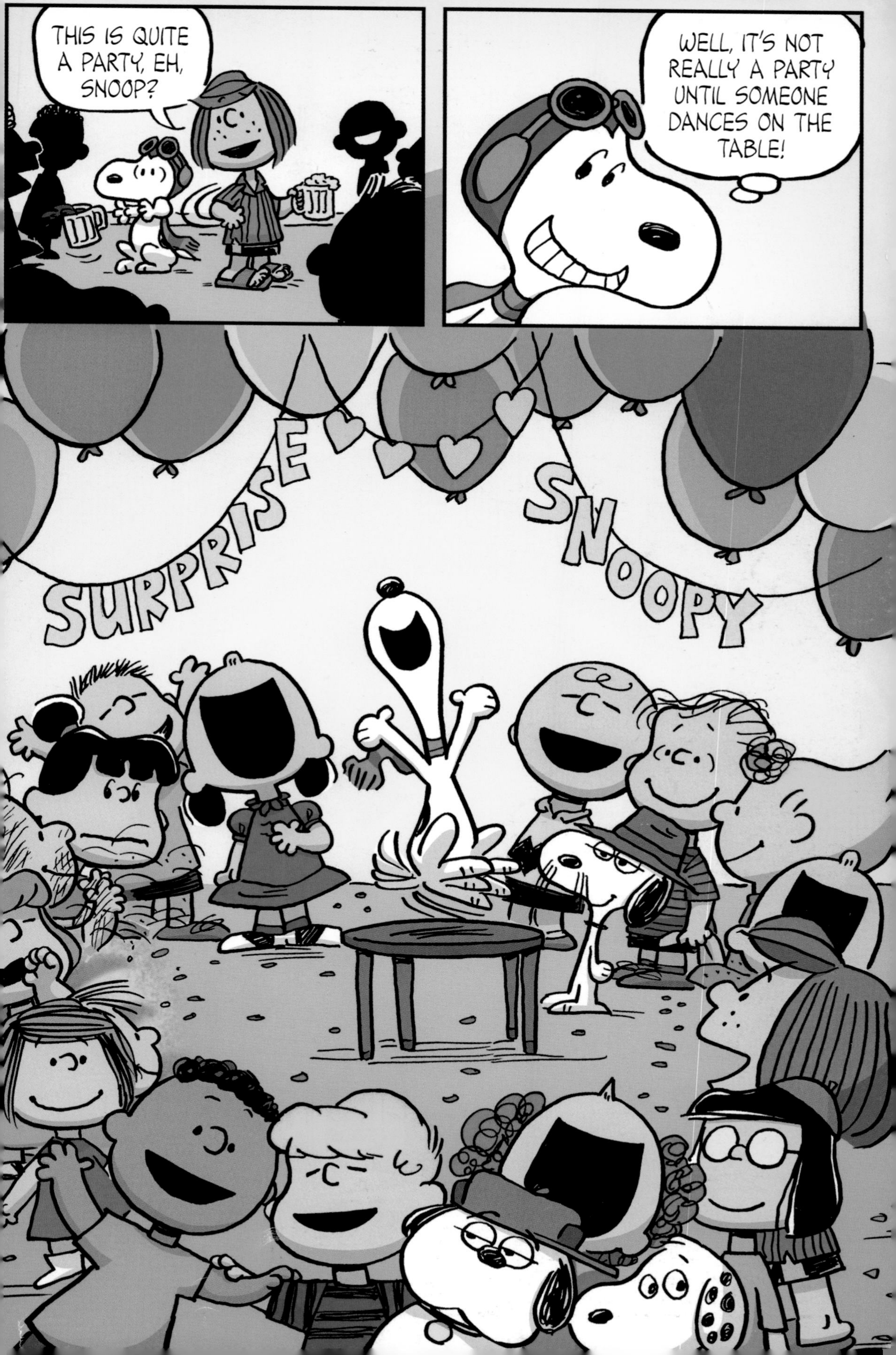
THIS IS QUITE A PARTY, EH, SNOOP?
WELL, IT'S NOT REALLY A PARTY UNTIL SOMEONE DANCES ON THE TABLE!
SURPRISE SNOOPY

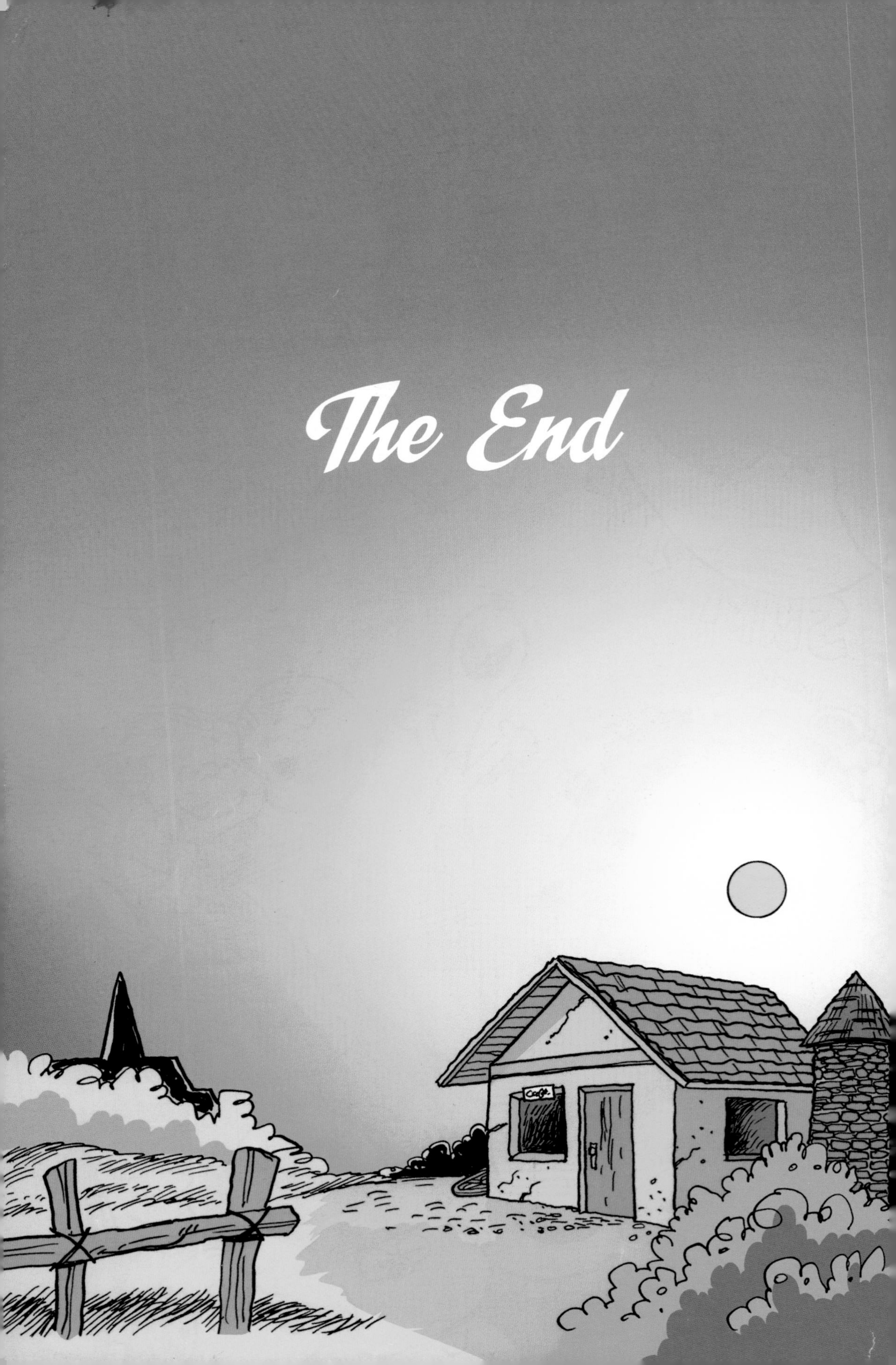
The End

Behind-the-Scenes

Where Beagles Dare!

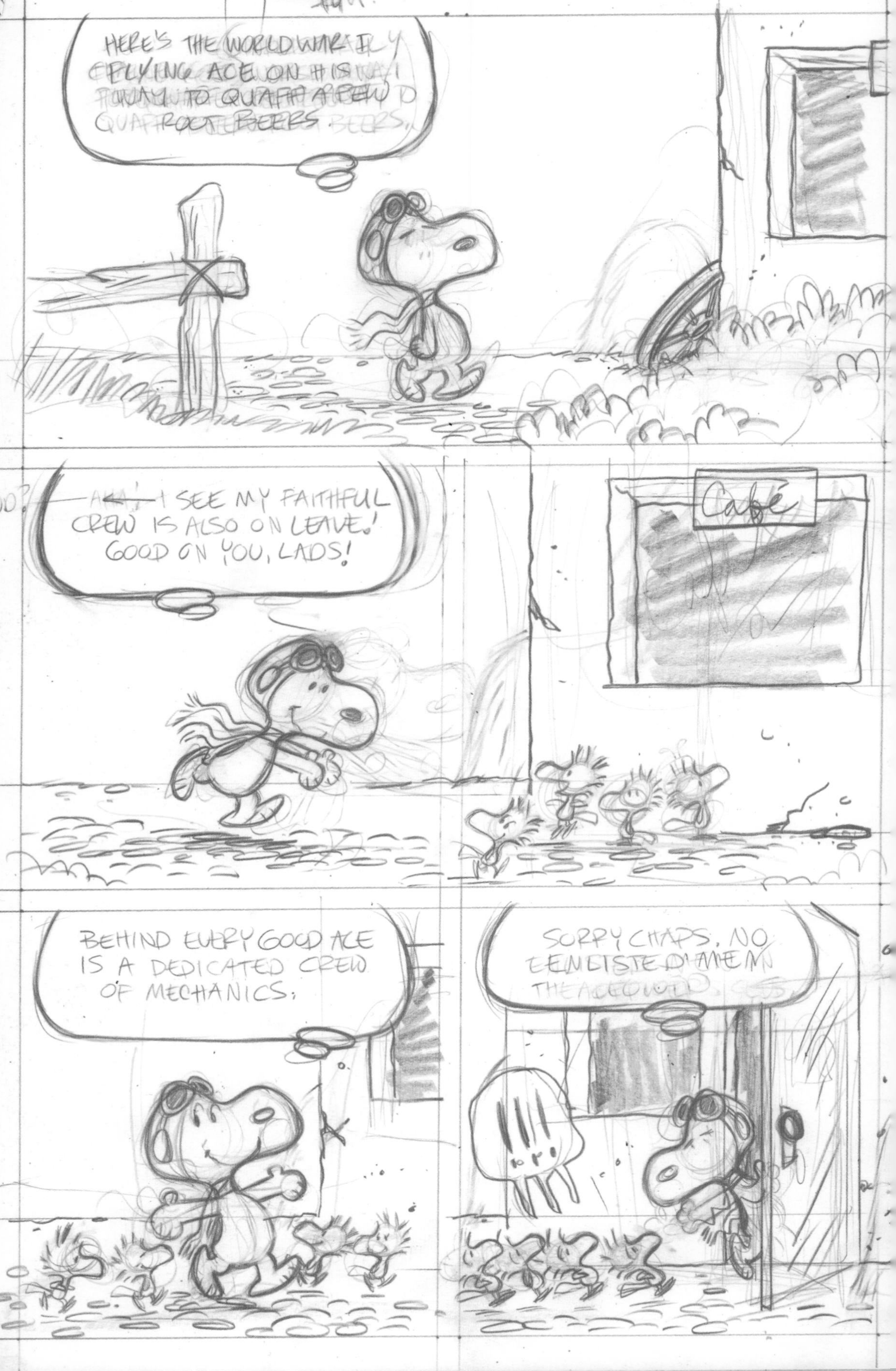
HERE'S THE WORLD WAR I FLYING ACE ON HIS WAY TO QUAFF A FEW ROOT BEERS.
AH, I SEE MY FAITHFUL CREW IS ALSO ON LEAVE! GOOD ON YOU, LADS!
Café
BEHIND EVERY GOOD ACE IS A DEDICATED CREW OF MECHANICS.
SORRY CHAPS, NO ENLISTED MEN

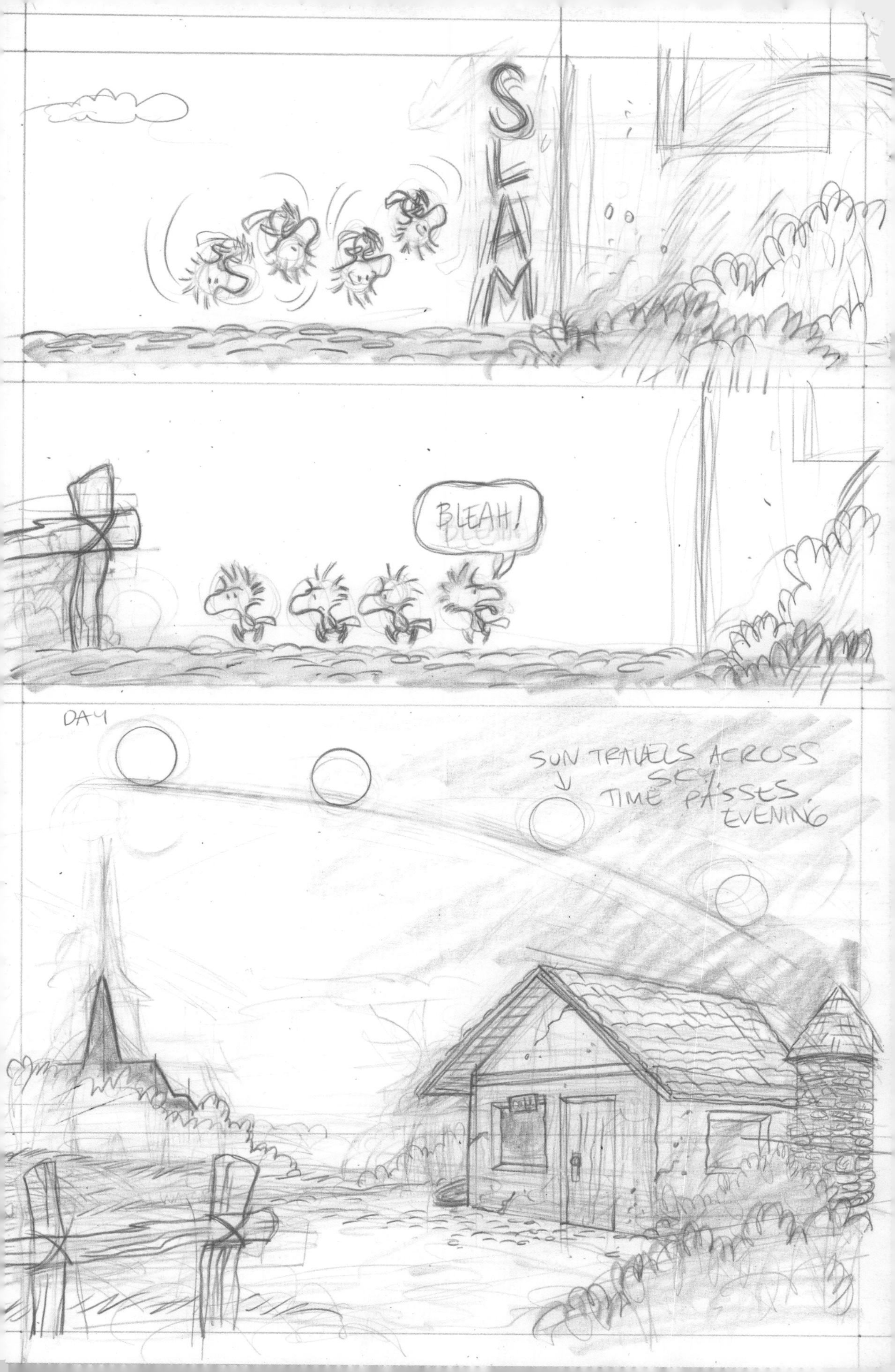
SLAM
BLEAH!
DAY
SUN TRAVELS ACROSS SKY
TIME PASSES
EVENING

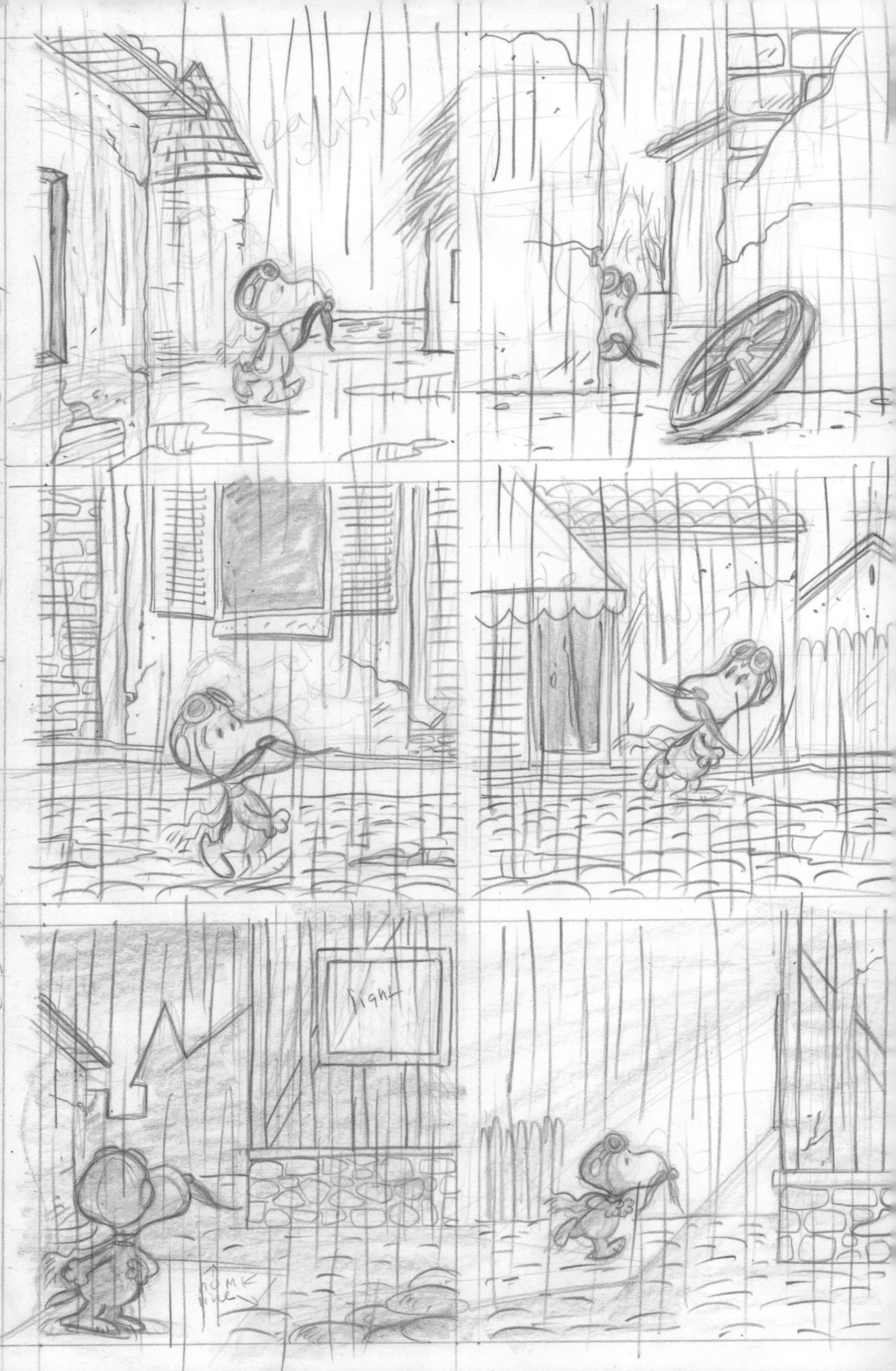

fight

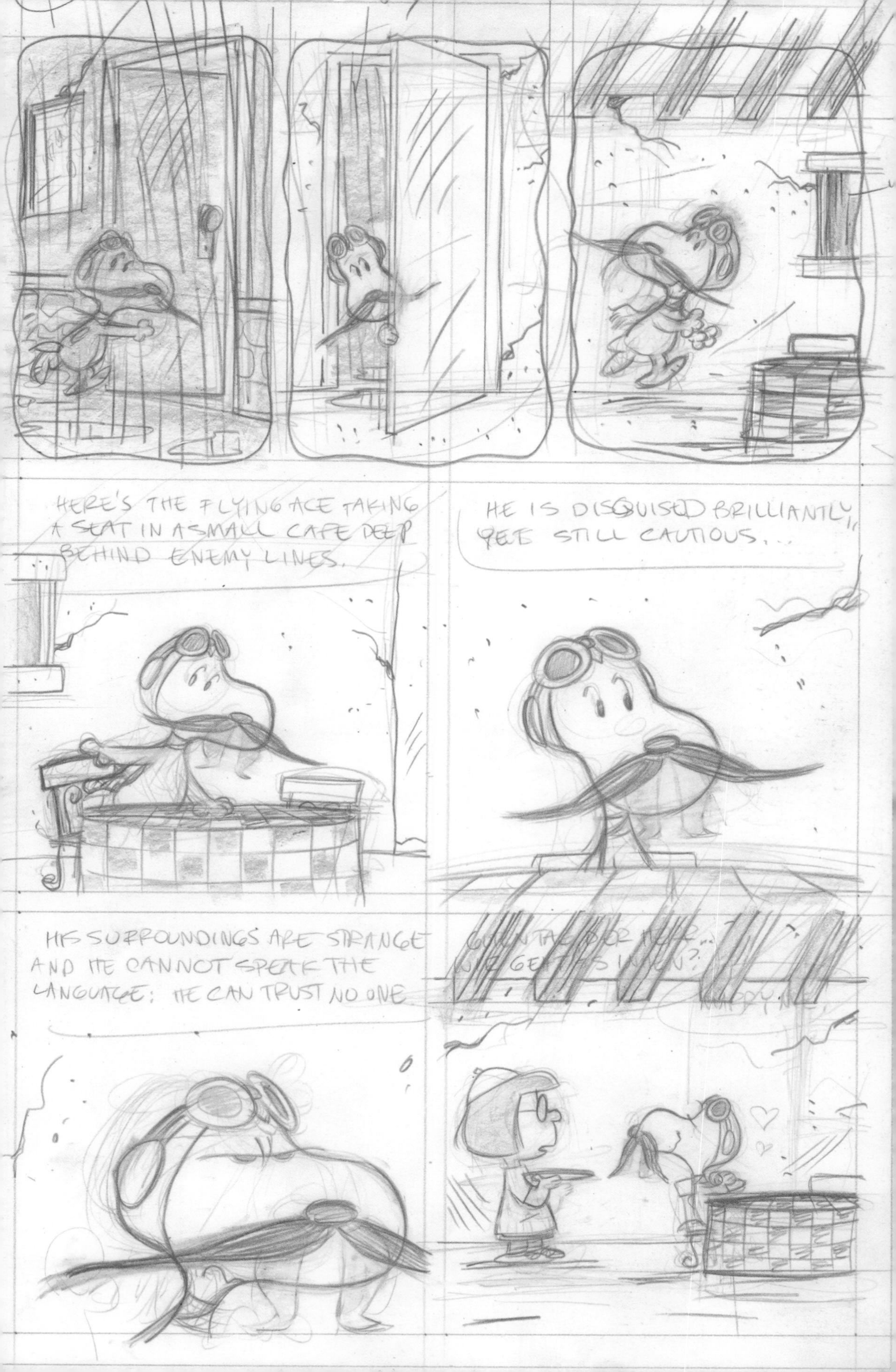
HERE'S THE FLYING ACE TAKING A SEAT IN A SMALL CAFE DEEP BEHIND ENEMY LINES.
HE IS DISGUISED BRILLIANTLY, YET STILL CAUTIOUS...
HIS SURROUNDINGS ARE STRANGE AND HE CANNOT SPEAK THE LANGUAGE: HE CAN TRUST NO ONE

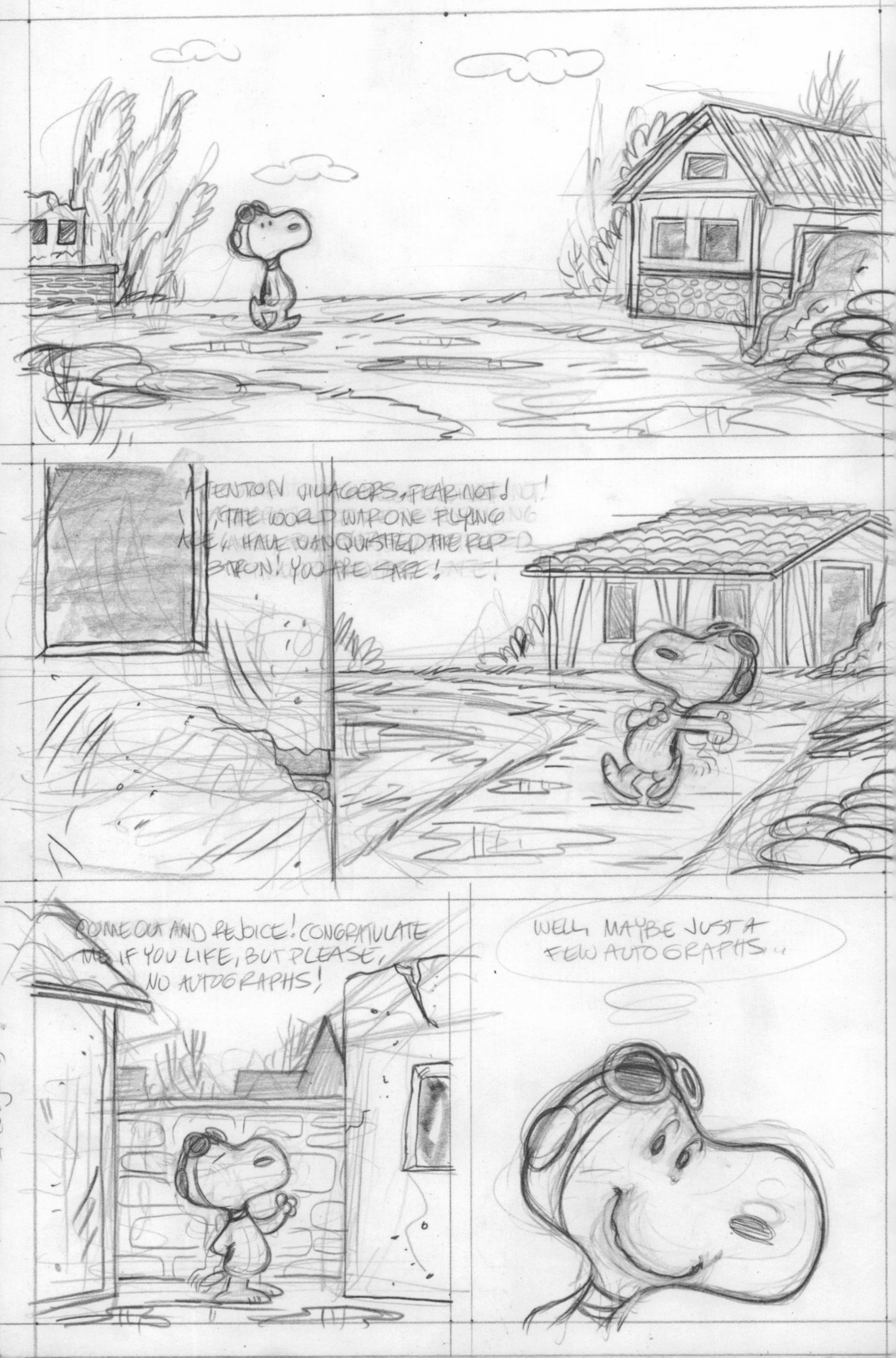
ATTENTION VILLAGERS, FEAR NOT! I, THE WORLD WAR ONE FLYING ACE, HAVE VANQUISHED THE RED BARON! YOU ARE SAFE!
COME OUT AND REJOICE! CONGRATULATE ME IF YOU LIKE, BUT PLEASE, NO AUTOGRAPHS!
WELL, MAYBE JUST A FEW AUTOGRAPHS...

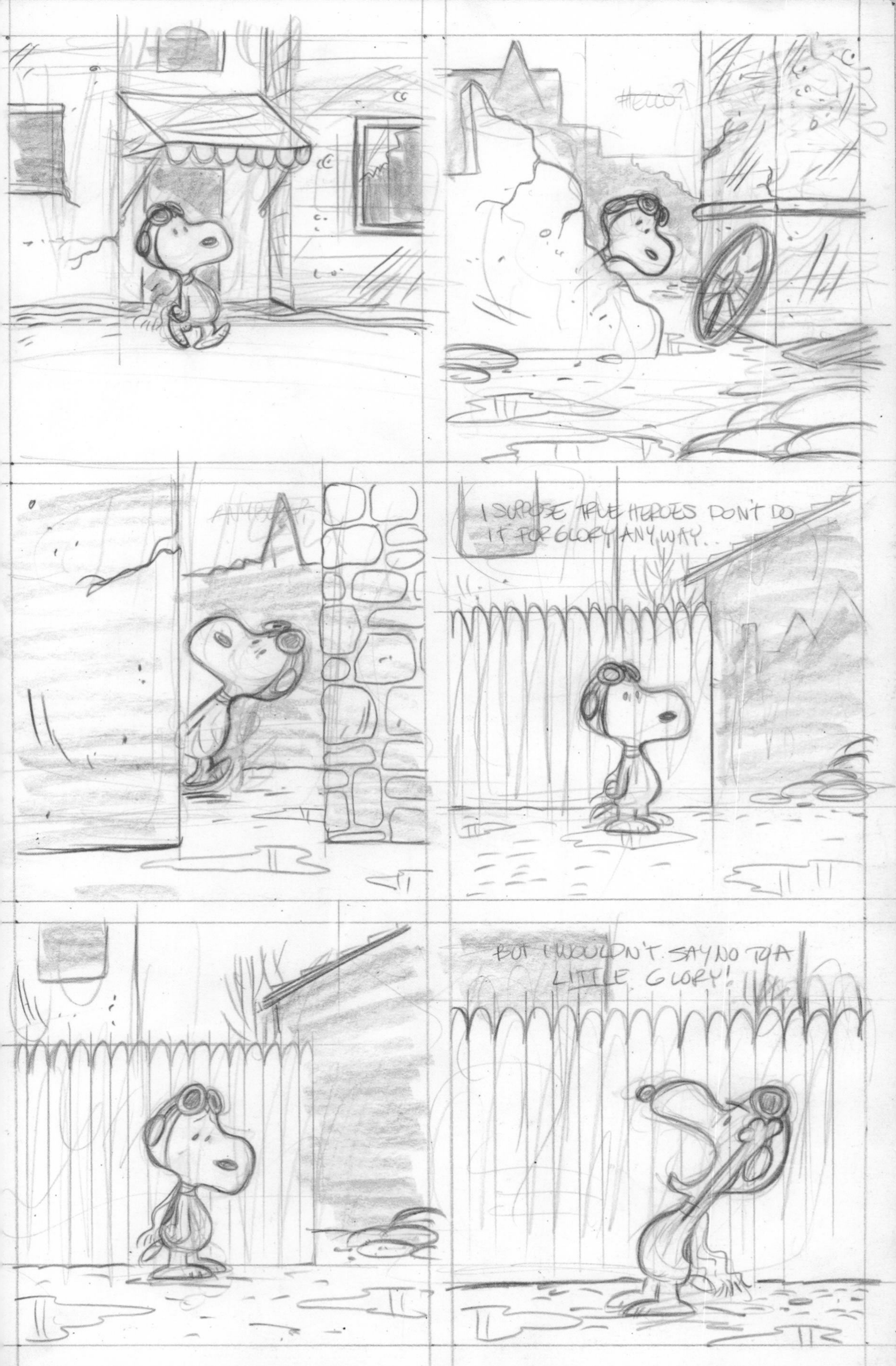
HELLO?
ANYBODY?
I SUPPOSE TRUE HEROES DON'T DO IT FOR GLORY ANYWAY...
BUT I WOULDN'T SAY NO TO A LITTLE GLORY!

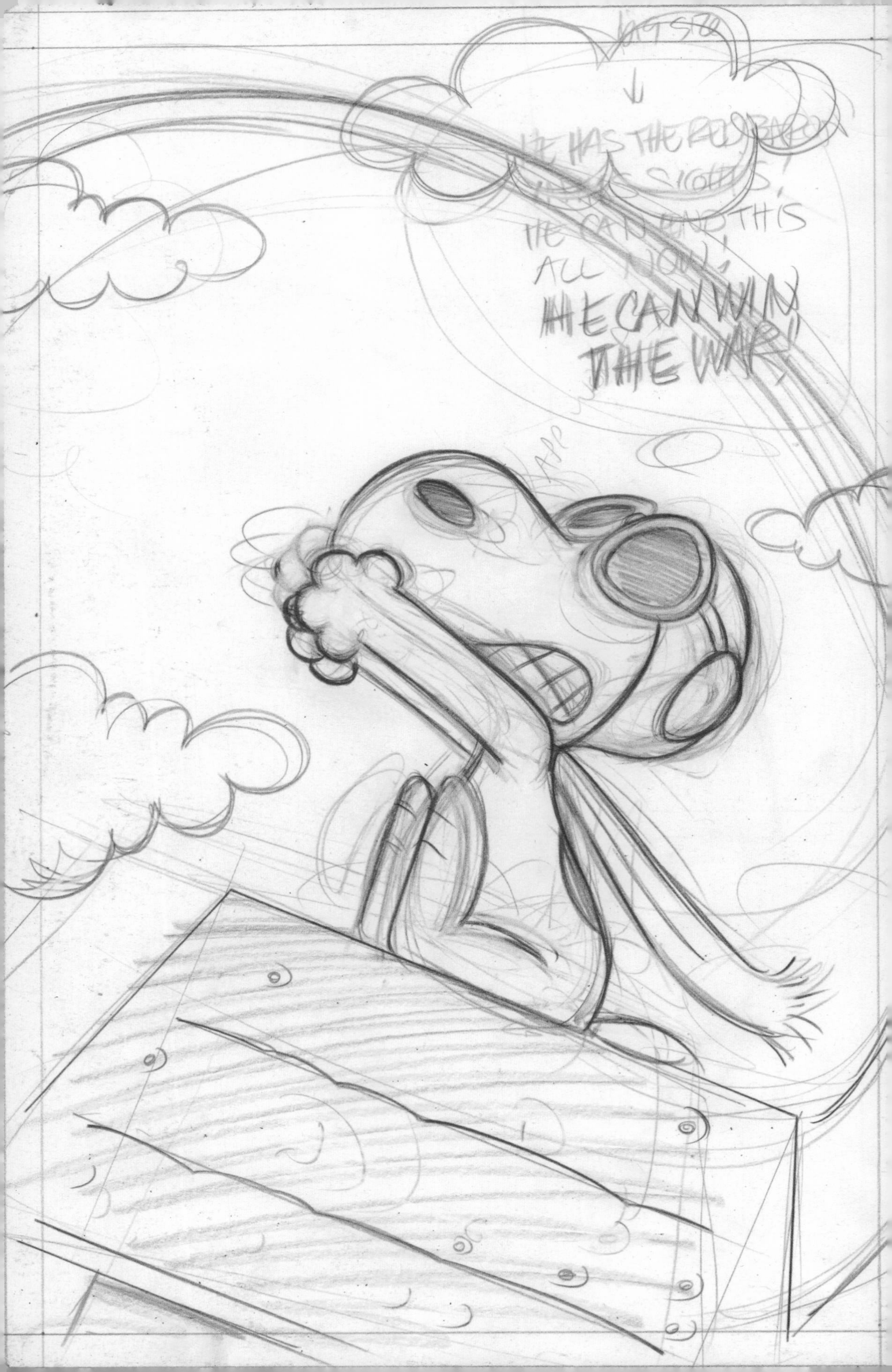
HE CAN WIN THE WAR!

About the Creator

Charles M. Schulz

Charles M. Schulz once described himself as "born to draw comic strips." Born in Minneapolis, at just two days old, an uncle nicknamed him "Sparky" after the horse Spark Plug from the *Barney Google* comic strip, and throughout his youth, he and his father shared a Sunday morning ritual reading the funnies. After serving in the Army during World War II, Schulz's first big break came in 1947 when he sold a cartoon feature called *Li'l Folks* to the St. Paul Pioneer Press. In 1950, Schulz met with United Feature Syndicate, and on October 2nd of that year, *Peanuts*, named by the syndicate, debuted in seven newspapers. Charles Schulz died in Santa Rosa, California, in February 2000—just hours before his last original strip was to appear in Sunday papers.